THE RISING DARK

By Celia Thorn

A catalogue record for this book can be obtained from the British Library.

Cover art by Claudia Caranfa
Cover design by Charlie Bramald
Sisters of Twilight logo by Alina Baranova

ISBN 978-1-7395111-3-5 (paperback)
ISBN 978-1-7395111-2-8 (ebook)

Published by Nyx Publishing 2025
United Kingdom
www.nyxpublishing.com

For all vampire lovers

We know they've never gone out of style!

Chapter One

Darkness pooled around the underground platform as Michelle stepped out of the carriage. With a hiss, the doors closed behind her, and the train shrieked as it disappeared into the wide mouth of the tunnel to continue its journey. She snuggled deeper into her coat, shouldered her bag, and followed in the footsteps of the single other passenger who had gotten off at this Tube station.

It had been a busy day—but then again, in the crowded wards of the hospital, every day was a busy day. She was glad of the silence of the night after the chaotic and loud shift she had just had. It was impressive, really, the sheer racket that a four-year-old who did not want to receive an IV could produce. The high-pitched screeches still rang in her ears.

She followed the winding way of the underground station until she was disgorged onto the dark streets of the London suburb she lived in. Only a short walk and she would be at her apartment. She couldn't wait to take off her shoes, put on her pyjamas and watch an episode of her favourite TV show, *Harrogate Homicides*, the long-running crime drama she had been a fan of for years. It was the season finale—the murderer would be revealed and justice would be restored in the sleepy English village. A perfect ending to an exhausting Thursday.

She walked past the handful of takeaways that lined the main road, their bright fluorescent lights illuminating the pavement. It wasn't completely quiet, of course. London was never truly still, its millions of inhabitants coming and going, chatting, laughing, drinking, fighting. Just a couple more streets until she was home. The glow of the brightly lit shops faded behind her.

A loud thud stopped her in her tracks. A wheeze followed, which made her think of a punctured lung. She stood only a couple of paces from the mouth to a dark alleyway, a place where the light of the street lamps could not quite reach. Another thump, this one sounding like flesh pounding into flesh. Michelle's heart started to slam against her ribcage. Her hand slid into her pocket, enclosing her phone. It wouldn't be the first time that someone was fighting in this neighbourhood. She would have a quick glance and call the police. Interfering was a fool's errand, but at the same time, she couldn't just walk away. What if someone was being robbed? What if someone was in real trouble? She couldn't just leave someone hurt, helpless. She crept closer, her comfortable sneakers quiet on the asphalt.

Another thud, and a low voice swearing. It sounded like a woman's voice. Bracing herself, Michelle peeked around the corner, staying as close to the brick wall as she could, fervently hoping that the shadows would hide her in case anyone was looking in her direction.

It took a moment for her to realise what she was seeing. In the darkness, two shapes writhed. There was something about them, something about the way they moved, that looked wrong. But before she had time to consider this more closely, the shapes detached, the metallic glint of a blade flashed between them. A shriek rent the air; a dark liquid drenched the ground.

Michelle swore under her breath. This didn't look like a drunken brawl. She had no idea what this was, but it was bad.

Really, really bad. She pulled her phone from her pocket. She had to call the police, call an ambulance. Probably both.

Before she could dial, a crash sounded, and she started. Her phone slipped from her fingers and tumbled onto the ground with a sharp crack. For a moment she was torn between picking up her phone, its screen surely shattered, and running for help. She could go into one of the shops, ask them to call the emergency number.

A low moan came from the alleyway. What the hell was going on? Heart beating in her throat, she hazarded another glance around the corner. The scene had changed substantially. There was only one person now—a woman slumped against the wall, clutching her side. The scant light that made its way into the alley glimmered on a black wetness that covered her hands. Behind her, a dark shape flitted around the corner, disappearing into the night.

"Shit," Michelle said, all caution thrown to the wind. She ran to the woman, medical training kicking in. She assessed her quickly in a single glance, noting her pale skin (possible result of blood loss), the sweat on her brow (possible shock), the dilating pupils (could be drugs, could be something else). There were no wounds visible except for the one on her side.

"Let me have a look," Michelle said, peeling the woman's hands away from her abdomen without waiting for a response. The woman's white T-shirt was soaked with what could only be blood.

"Wait—" the woman said, but Michelle lifted the T-shirt, the fabric reluctantly releasing from the wet skin. The woman's abdomen was surprisingly muscular. She quickly assessed the depth and size of the wound and lowered it again.

"You need medical attention," Michelle said. "It doesn't look like it hit anything vital, but you need to go to the hospital to be sure."

The woman laughed: a deep, throaty laugh. More details swam into focus now that Michelle had a moment to take a breath. The woman was tall—slightly taller than Michelle, but not by much. She seemed about thirty, a bit younger maybe. She was very beautiful. Her skin was smooth, her features perfectly symmetrical with high cheekbones and a full mouth. She wore her long blonde hair in a low ponytail. The chill of the clear autumn night didn't seem to bother her—she wore only a T-shirt and jeans. If she had taken some kind of drug, she might not even notice the cold. Michelle frowned and shrugged off her coat.

"You probably need stitches," she continued. "You may want to sit down or you could pass out from the blood loss."

The woman was still smiling. Michelle didn't understand what was so funny, but then again, people did weird things when they were in shock (or high). "I'll be fine," the woman said.

"Sure," Michelle answered. She balled up her coat and pressed it onto the wound. "Here, hold this, I'm going to grab my phone real quick and call an ambulance for you." The woman placed her right hand over the coat, but before Michelle could take a single step back to the opening of the alleyway, the woman's left hand gripped her arm like a vice.

"That won't be necessary," the woman said.

"Look, I get that you might feel fine now, but once the adrenaline wears off..." Michelle remonstrated. Truly, half the battle with patients was convincing them that they needed help. Then again, most of her patients usually didn't reach up much past her hip.

"I'll be fine," she repeated. The woman lifted the coat and revealed the wound on her abdomen. "See?"

Michelle glanced at the wound again, expecting to see the same gash framed with blood on the woman's stomach. She squinted in the dim lighting of the alleyway. Did it...? It looked better. She leaned closer, not quite believing her eyes. She'd been so certain that the slash had torn through several layers of skin and into the muscle underneath. It had looked pretty nasty, oozing with blood. Now much of that blood had gone and some of the flesh had knitted together. But that was impossible. Immediately, Michelle started to doubt her earlier assessment. Perhaps the lack of light and her anxiety had made her think the wound was more dangerous than it actually was. But that was nothing like her. Even when patients were in critical condition, she usually kept her head.

She glanced back at the coat that the woman still clutched. The amount of blood on her shirt was incongruous with this small scratch. Something wasn't adding up. Before she could investigate further, the woman pulled at Michelle's arm and kindly but insistently led her back towards the main street. Michelle's phone lay face-down where it had fallen. In a daze, Michelle picked it up. A spiderweb of cracks covered the screen.

"As you can see, I'm perfectly fine. There is no need to worry." The woman's voice was soothing, like she was speaking to a spooked animal. "It was very kind of you to look after me, but you can go home now. I will walk with you, just to see you home safe. Looks like there are plenty of pickpockets around here."

Pickpockets? Michelle's mind was reeling. Was that what she saw earlier, a thief? Her memories were fragmented now, moments only surviving as flashes, and none of the images that rose to her mind added up to a mugging. What was that strange shape she had seen fleeing the scene? Where was the blade that she had noticed? She tried to glance back into the alley, seeking out the gleam of a knife, but the woman whisked her onwards. The woman kept up a steady stream of chatter in her low, calm voice. *She is trying to distract me*, Michelle thought. *But distract me from what?*

"Such a shame about your phone. It looks like the screen hit the ground the wrong way. I hope you can have it repaired. What way were you going? Down this street? Great. It's a nice night, isn't it? The moon is so clear in the sky..." After several more inane remarks on the weather, Michelle's apartment building came into view. It was a rather nondescript five-storey structure made of crumbling concrete. It wasn't pretty, but it was home.

"This is where I live," Michelle said. Fear was building in the pit of her stomach now that the adrenaline was fading. Something wasn't right here. She had gotten herself caught in something bad. What was it? Was this woman a drug dealer? Had she stepped into some kind of drug war? You heard about those things on the news all the time, of people getting killed for being in the wrong place at the wrong time, didn't you? But if it was a drug thing, then why had the other shape seemed so... inhuman?

The woman finally let go of Michelle's arm, and she suddenly found herself missing the support, feeling unmoored in the night. She stared at the woman mutely, unsure of what to say.

"Oh, your coat." The woman held out the bloodied jean jacket. "Sorry about—"

A sigh sounded behind them. The woman whirled around, the coat dropping into a heap on the ground, a blade suddenly in her hand. Where had that come from? How could she have missed it before? Had she been hiding it underneath her clothes somehow? Michelle felt panic rising, with anger closely behind. Whatever the hell this was, she didn't want any part of it.

A strange silence surrounded them. The woman stood in a pose that should be ridiculous, the blade in front of her, poised to strike. But there was a strength in the lines of her body, a natural grace that made the pose seem second nature. Only now did Michelle notice the breadth of her shoulders, the woman's powerful build. It wasn't the ostentatious muscularity of a bodybuilder, but the kind of understated strength of an athlete.

The woman seemed ready for some kind of danger, but Michelle couldn't see anything. No scary people skulking behind lampposts or in the shadows around them. She started to back away from the woman, inching towards the front door of her building. It was only thirty paces away or so; if she broke into a run now, she would be inside within seconds...

"Stay behind me," the woman hissed. "Don't draw its attention."

Michelle was about to give the woman a piece of her mind, but the words fled as something rose in front of them. Her mouth dropped open, her body frozen painfully still. For a moment, her mind was unable to parse what it was seeing. This was certainly no drug dealer, no mugger.

Whatever this was, there was absolutely no way that it was human.

For one thing, it seemed to be made of smoke. Michelle could still see the outline of the houses on the other side of the street through the creature as it shambled towards them across the asphalt. It didn't have a body, exactly, although it did have the rough shape of four limbs. It had no facial features, the shape of its head just an emptiness of shadow. As it came closer, its eyes opened, two gleaming orbs of fire which were somehow even more uncanny than the lack of features had been.

Michelle's feet were rooted to the ground as the woman turned into a whirlwind of action. She dashed towards the shadow, lunging forwards, blade outstretched. The shadow dodged the strike and continued its path forward, advancing towards Michelle. The woman stepped aside and struck again. This time, the strike hit—bright flames sizzled on the surface of the blade where it passed through the shadow creature. There was a loud hiss, and Michelle couldn't tell whether it came from the creature or the blade itself.

This strike drew its attention. The creature turned onto the woman, and the two locked into a battle that moved faster than Michelle could follow. A strange black liquid oozed out of the shadow creature, splashing the ground and the woman's hands, slicking the blade. The shade slashed at the woman's head, causing her to duck and roll out of the way. Immediately, the shade surged forward towards Michelle.

It all happened so quickly, she had no time to react, to duck, to run, before it filled her vision. It reached, a tendril of its uncanny shadowy body licking against her cheek. Agony exploded across her face, and for a moment the pain was so intense she only saw a blinding white light. It was only when the searing pain subsided the tiniest amount that she was able to focus on what was happening. She was on the ground—how did she get here? Did she fall? A loud grunt nearby revealed the woman, still locked in close combat with the shade.

The shade tore at her, somehow leaving bright red scratches on the skin of her arms, as if the shadows of its body hid claws. Though the creature was fast, the woman was faster, slashing, stabbing, relentlessly pressing forwards, moving the shade away from Michelle, shielding her. Then, with one last lunge, she lanced through the shade in the middle of its body, flames combusting it from the inside out, until it disappeared in a puff of smoke.

The woman's blade dropped beside her, her shoulders rising and falling with fast breaths.

"What the actual hell was that?" Michelle said, her voice shrill, echoing down the empty street.

The woman turned around. From Michelle's position on the ground, she seemed larger than life. The light of the streetlamp fell dramatically across her face, revealing the black splatter of what Michelle assumed was the creature's blood. The woman smiled wryly, wiping her blade on her black jeans. "Hell is about right."

Chapter Two

"Seriously," Michelle said as the woman walked towards her. "That... that thing..."

The woman held out a hand to help Michelle off the ground. Michelle grabbed it, feeling the dampness of the creature's blood on the woman's skin, and was heaved back onto her feet without any apparent effort.

"Let's get you home," the woman said, clearly determined not to answer or explain anything. She picked up the blood-stained coat where she'd dropped it earlier.

Michelle let herself be led to the door of the apartment building. She mechanically took her keys from her shoulder bag, moving through the motions she had repeated hundreds of times, their familiarity now feeling fragile. The woman followed her inside. She walked behind her on the staircase and through the corridor up to her front door. Michelle's hand shook as she put the key into the lock. The familiar sight of her apartment, of all of her things, of the life she had lived contentedly over the last couple of years, no longer felt as steady a foundation as they had before. She walked in and turned on the light, not surprised when the woman followed and closed the door behind her.

Michelle dropped her bag onto the ground and turned

towards the woman, crossing her arms to hide the shake of her hands. "So?"

The woman sighed and ran a hand through her hair. Some of it had come loose from its ponytail, framing her face. "Do you have a first aid kit?"

Without a word, Michelle walked to the kitchen cupboard, her knees unsteady. "It's... it's..." Pain radiated across her face, causing her eyes to water. Black spots danced in her vision.

"Please sit down." The woman led her to a chair and slowly lowered her into it. The tap hissed for a moment as she washed her hands of the grime that covered them. Then, she was back with the first aid kit. Without any hesitation, she unwrapped some sterile gauze and started dabbing some disinfectant onto Michelle's face. In the bright light of the kitchen, Michelle got her first proper look at her.

Her long, straight hair shone golden except where the creature's blood had darkened it. Her eyes were green, her long eyelashes giving a softness to her face. She didn't wear any make-up, not even to cover the silvery scar running through one of her eyebrows, down across her temple, disappearing in her hairline. Michelle wondered what it would be like to trace that line with her fingertips. The woman was incredibly beautiful, like an Amazon from Greek myth. She looked like a woman who could face anything.

Her touch was unexpectedly gentle, her hand cupping Michelle's chin soft and warm. Despite the searing pain of the disinfectant on the wound, she found herself leaning into the touch, finding a moment of solace in the contact with another solid, human being. It didn't hurt that she was also gorgeous.

"I'm sorry it got to you," the woman murmured, carefully wiping Michelle's cheekbone. Intent on her work, the woman's face was so close. Michelle could see every individual eyelash, the dewiness of her mouth. Up close, she looked almost vulnerable, a sharp contrast to the fierce woman who had expertly wielded a knife only moments ago. Michelle closed her eyes, using the pain as an excuse. Now was not the time to swoon at the potentially dangerous woman standing in her kitchen. She blamed the lack of any romantic action in her life. It had been too long.

Closing her eyes, however, brought back images of the horrible creature. She saw it coming at her again and again, its strangely shaped limbs outstretched.

She opened her eyes. "What was that thing?" she finally asked. Her voice came out almost as a whisper. It was a question that held immense weight. What she was actually asking was not only what that creature had been, but also who this woman was and what role she played in all of it. Michelle couldn't grasp how her safe, almost boring life had turned into this: being attacked on the street in the middle of the night by... whatever that was.

She didn't expect a reply. The woman continued to clean the scratch on her cheek. Michelle was surprised when she started to speak. She almost sounded apologetic.

"You were right before. I think people, without realising, instinctively know one when they see it. It was a demon."

"A demon," Michelle repeated. She wasn't sure whether to laugh or to cry.

"Yes. A tenebris, to be more specific. Some demons are powerful enough to walk the earth without being summoned. A tenebris, however, has to be summoned."

Michelle mulled on that for a moment. "Who summoned it? And why?"

Silence followed. The woman stared at her intently. Michelle felt caught by her intense gaze. "I think," she said, "that it was coming for you."

"Me?" Michelle said incredulously. This idea was even more preposterous than the existence of demons. Even if she could accept that supernatural creatures made of nightmares stalked the streets of London, there was absolutely no reason why anyone would want to set one loose on *her*. She was a nurse, for God's sake. Though the parents of patients could sometimes get belligerent, often out of fear for their child, she couldn't imagine any of them sending a *demon* her way. Other than them, she didn't live an exciting enough life to have ever made any enemies.

This must have all been one massive mistake. It had to be some weird fever dream that she would wake up from tomorrow.

"I don't know why," the woman said. "Nor do I know who sent it. But I intend to find out." For a moment, they sat suspended, the woman still cupping Michelle's chin in her hand. Then she retreated, closing the first aid box. Michelle found herself missing her touch. At least that had felt real.

The woman continued. "I'm afraid you can't stay here tonight. While I don't think whoever summoned the demon is going to try again immediately, it's not safe here. You'll have to come with me."

"Come with you where?"

"I can take you to a place where you will be safe. There will be more people like me to protect you. I realise this is quite a shock to you, but I'm asking you to trust me. I wouldn't take you from your home if I didn't think it was necessary."

Michelle considered the tall, muscular woman standing in the middle of her kitchen, splattered with gore. She had seen how strong she was, how fast, how she had stabbed a creature and made it disappear. If she'd wanted to hurt Michelle, there would have been plenty of opportunities. She looked at her open expression, her large green eyes pleading. She thought about how gentle her hands were, and how even the memory of the demon created a pit of fear in her stomach.

She could not imagine sleeping in her bed tonight, knowing that something like that could come after her again.

"I'm not sure I trust you," Michelle said, wrapping her arms around herself. There were more questions in her mind than she thought she could handle answers to.

The woman didn't seem offended. "That's fair enough."

Michelle looked around her apartment. The second-hand furniture she had collected over the years. The laundry bag sitting beside the sofa, exactly where she had left it this morning. The pictures of friends and family on the walls, all smiles. Somehow it was all wrong. "But I also don't think I can stay here." Not while the image of the demon still lingered on her corneas.

"You will stay with us," the woman said in a definitive tone. She slipped a phone from her pocket, swiped a couple of times, and pressed it to her ear. "Hey, it's me. Could you come pick me up? We've got company." Without waiting for a reply, she ended the call and focused back on Michelle. "You may wish to pack anything you may need for the next couple of days."

"Right." She would need her toothbrush. Underwear, socks. A couple of changes of clothes. All she had to do was grab some of these everyday items. Yet somehow she couldn't make herself stand up, couldn't force herself back into action. A tremor ran through her arms, and she couldn't make it stop. Her bottom lip quivered and her eyes filled with tears.

"I don't even know your name," Michelle said, her voice straining past a sob that was trying to escape.

Immediately, the woman was by her side, gently grasping her hand between her own.

"It's Lavinia. What's your name?"

"Michelle," she sniffed.

The woman's face was blurred by Michelle's unshed tears. Still, she recognised the steel in Lavinia's eyes, an edge that would be terrifying if it had been aimed at her. The woman knelt on the ground at her feet. "Michelle. I promise you that we will protect you. *I* will protect you." It sounded like a vow.

◆◆◆

On Lavinia's steady insistence, Michelle managed to throw some basics into a rucksack within fifteen minutes. Meanwhile, the warrior woman tried to wash as much of the creature's blood off her arms and face as she could in the kitchen sink. Michelle had caught a quick look at the scratch on her own face in the bathroom mirror as she packed her toothbrush. It looked a lot like a chemical burn with some local abrasion, stretching along the curve of her right cheekbone, skin bright red and angry.

It seemed pretty superficial, and unless demons had some sort of poison or something that she didn't know about, it would probably heal within a week or two. Michelle counted herself lucky. If the creature had scratched her eye... With a shudder, she had continued packing her bag.

Lavinia escorted her downstairs again, and as they left the apartment, Michelle found that she struggled to look at the spot where the creature had appeared. She was glad that a sleek black car idled next to the building. Lavinia opened the door for her and helped her inside, and within a moment lowered herself onto the leather backseat beside her. Immediately, the car pulled away smoothly, driving down the quiet midnight streets of the London suburbs.

Michelle didn't know much about cars, never having owned one as a born and bred city-dweller, but even she knew that the soft purr of the engine and leather seats meant that this was a *very* expensive car. Hell, it even smelled expensive.

"Michelle, this is Zachary, our driver. Zachary, Michelle is going to stay with us at the mansion for now. She's had a rough night," Lavinia said.

The man was in his forties, had a broad face and an easy smile. He wore a neatly ironed white shirt without a tie. In the darkness of the car interior, his expertly cut hair shone black. He glanced at her through the rear-view mirror and smiled. "Nice to meet you, Michelle." His eyes flicked over to the side, and he frowned. "You look like hell, Vin."

Lavinia didn't seem fazed by the man's directness. "Sorry. You might have to wash some demon blood out of the seats tomorrow, I didn't have time to change."

The man sighed deeply, like this was a common occurrence in his line of work. Perhaps it was. Nothing in Michelle's world really made any sense anymore.

"So where are we going?" she asked. Out of London, that much was clear. He had turned onto one of the large roads radiating out of the city. Pools of streetlights flashed by as the car quietly glided down the road. She should probably be nervous that she was in a car with two strangers, going to some unknown location. It certainly wasn't what her mother had taught her to do, but after the night she'd had, this seemed a safe as anywhere else.

"I'm taking you to our base, where I can keep an eye on you. It's towards the north, past Nottingham." It would be at least a couple of hours, then. It was a relief to leave the city, and its demons, behind. The more distance between Michelle and the creature, the better.

Still, she should probably let someone know where she was. If she was being kidnapped in some very elaborate way, at least someone should know where to start looking.

Michelle slipped her phone out of the bag at her feet. Lines like a dense spider web traced across the glass screen. Michelle winced. That was going to be expensive to fix. She was still paying off the phone, and she couldn't afford a new one any time soon. Luckily, it sprang to life at her touch. She opened up the conversation with her friend Iris and quickly tapped out a message. She wrote that she was staying with a couple of new friends for the weekend, and shared the location on her phone.

She watched the little dot on the map steadily moving north for a moment. Iris would see the message in the morning and would almost certainly be full of questions. That was a problem for tomorrow. For now, Michelle felt a little better knowing that at least someone would know where she'd gone. Even if she didn't exactly know where she was going herself.

If the worst happened, at least Iris would have something to show the police. She smiled to herself at the thought of her short friend yelling at some tree of a detective. The movement pulled on the scratch on her cheek, and turned into a grimace.

Lavinia glanced at her, focusing on the wound. "Is it giving you trouble?"

"Not too much," Michelle lied. She didn't want to admit that the scratch throbbed with every beat of her heart. She didn't want to complain about her scratch when Lavinia was covered in them. She was about to ask Lavinia about hers, when she caught a look at Lavinia's arms. Michelle did a double take. Even in the bad lighting, it was clear that the skin of her bare arms was smooth and unblemished.

She could have sworn...

"I should have given you some painkillers," Lavinia said. "Zachary, when we get out of the city, let's stop at a gas station and get some for Michelle."

"No, that's okay—" Michelle started. She didn't want to be a bother.

"I insist," Lavinia said with a smile to soften the steel in her voice. Michelle couldn't help smiling too. It wasn't often that someone took care of her, instead of the other way around. She settled deeper into the soft leather of the seat and let herself be carried to some mysterious place in the north of England, in the care of this beautiful warrior woman.

Chapter Three

Michelle surfaced from a fitful sleep. Slowly, she regained her senses. First sound, the low rumble of an engine and soft voices, then smell, leather and a whiff of old aftershave and cigarette smoke. It took her a moment to realise where she was, but then the events of the night all streamed back with horrifying clarity.

"Are you sure this is a good idea?" a male voice asked.

"It was the only option. I can't leave her there. Not only is it too dangerous, she is the only real connection we have to whoever summoned that demon."

"Luce isn't going to like it."

"Luce doesn't like anything. It's her job."

The man chuckled. Zachary, that was his name. "True."

The leather creaked as Lavinia shifted. "Besides, I've got a strange feeling about this. She isn't one of us, so why is she a target? It seems strange, and I want to know what's going on."

"You know what they're like. There isn't always a rational reason why they do the things they do."

Lavinia sighed. "I know you're right. But something about this feels off."

"You're getting attached." There was a note of reproach in Zachary's voice.

"I know," Lavinia said softly. "But I can't stand idly by either. And neither could you, if you were in my position."

A pause, and then Zachary said, "True. Sorry. It's not my place to criticise you." He sounded embarrassed.

"I am always happy to hear your thoughts. Even the insolent ones."

Both of them laughed, the tension dissipating.

In the silence that followed, Michelle blinked the sleep from her eyes and peeled her face from the leather seat. Lavinia smiled at her, and her heart skipped a beat. Damn, she was gorgeous. In the twilight of the car interior, it was almost as if she glowed. Her pupils were pools of darkness in which it would be so easy to drown. "We'll be there soon," Lavinia said.

"I can't believe I fell asleep." Michelle started to rub her eyes, then remembered the scratch, and thought better of it.

"You've had a big shock. Plus, it's pretty late." The clock on the car dashboard read 3:30 AM. They had left the glow of the city behind, driving down a dark highway with hills rising around them. Only a few distant rear lights flared ahead, like beacons in the dark.

"That usually doesn't bother me," Michelle explained. "I'm a nurse, late hours are part of the job. When I have the evening shift, I usually don't get home until one at night anyway. After a shower and some food, it can easily be two or three in the morning."

"So you're a night owl then?"

"I guess so. Late nights have always been fine. It's the early mornings that get to me." There was nothing worse than an early shift after a string of late ones. It always took her several hours to feel even remotely human on those.

"You'll fit right in at our house then," Lavinia said, a smile tugging at the corners of her mouth.

"How come?"

"All of us are night owls too."

"They're not really big on sunshine," Zachary added. His and Lavinia's eyes met in the rear-view mirror, and they laughed. Michelle didn't understand the joke. Then again, her brain was hardly firing on all cylinders at this point.

"What do you do?" Michelle asked Lavinia. She realised she didn't know a single thing about her except her first name, and that she was apparently loaded enough to have a personal driver.

Lavinia's facial expression was inscrutable. "I work in law enforcement."

"So, like the police?"

Lavinia didn't look like any police officer Michelle had ever met. And none of them conducted their business alone at night in the city's back streets.

"A lot like that, actually."

"Was that what you were doing tonight?" Sneaking around alleyways with a knife looking for demons certainly wasn't the kind of job you'd find in any career prospectus. Part of Michelle still didn't trust her own eyes, her own ears, couldn't parse the explanation Lavinia had given her. It was as if she had decided to play along for now, but that at some point the curtain would be pulled back and it would all be one gigantic joke. Perhaps they'd all laugh about it someday.

Lavinia nodded. "Part of my job is keeping the public safe from... bad people. I was looking for one when I found a demon instead."

"What kind of bad people?" Despite the toasty interior of the car, a cold shiver ran down Michelle's spine.

"Serial killers, mostly," Lavinia said without a trace of humour.

"So not only is there a demon appearing right in front of my home, there are also serial killers hanging out in my neighbourhood?" Michelle said. There was a note of hysteria in her voice. She swallowed, trying to suppress the panic.

"Many things exist in the shadows of the world, some of them good, some of them bad. A lot of us work every day to keep the bad away, as much as we can."

A wave of nausea rose in Michelle's stomach. This was all too much, and somehow she had gotten entangled in it all. She missed the ignorance of yesterday.

"Let's talk about anything else," she said. "I've got enough nightmare fuel to last me a lifetime."

"Of course." Lavinia leaned back into her seat. She was the epitome of ease, yet there was a hint of watchfulness to her even in this relaxed state. "Tell me about your job. What is it like to be a nurse?"

Within minutes, Lavinia had drawn Michelle into telling various stories of nursing school and the latest gossip among hospital staff. Lavinia was surprisingly easy to talk to—attentive, always ready with a follow-up question or an appreciative laugh. Michelle noticed she didn't share much about herself, always turning the conversation back to Michelle, but she was an excellent listener. Despite everything, Michelle found herself longing to make her laugh and felt a stab of satisfaction whenever she succeeded.

Within half an hour, they left the motorway for an unlit country road, winding through the hills and valleys of the Peak District National Park. Soon the asphalt disappeared completely, and Zachary slowed down to accommodate the ruts in the dirt road. Trees loomed overhead, the light from the headlights swallowed up by a deep darkness. A tight turn, and the engine stilled. Zachary took the key from the ignition, the headlights extinguished, and opened the door.

"Come on," Lavinia said. A tendril of anxiety rose within Michelle. There was nothing here, no sign of habitation whatsoever, no light. Her hands were clammy as she grabbed her bag from the floor and stepped outside into the cool night air.

She closed the door of the car and the dome light snuffed out, leaving her in a suffocating darkness unlike anything she'd ever experienced.

Michelle had lived in London all her life, its diffuse blanket of light pollution always keeping true darkness at bay. This, this was the real night. This was the kind of night they used to tell stories about in the safety of the fire of the hearth, the kind of night that stole children from their cradles and made unsuspecting villagers lose their way. It was a cloudy night, so not even the beacon of the moon or the comfort of stars could provide any guidance.

"This way," Lavinia's voice sounded from a couple of paces away. Michelle couldn't make out her shape in the textured shadows that surrounded her.

"I can't see you, I—"

Lavinia's and Zachary's voices murmured, a click sounded, and Michelle's world came back to life in the beam of a torch. It was a relief to be anchored by the pool of light, to not feel the weightlessness of not being able to see anything, to not know completely for sure if this was reality.

Lavinia took Michelle's bag and guided her down a narrow path between the trees. Michelle was about to ask where they were going, to demand some sort of explanation, when they went around another bend and a house appeared. Lavinia led her up the stone steps, the brickwork stretching into the darkness outside of their narrow beam of the flashlight. The building, with its solid stone façade, was a welcome relief to Michelle, although no light leaked from the windows. If anything, the house seemed abandoned. Without a word, Zachary trod down a path leading into the darkness, his footsteps confident as he was swallowed by the dark.

Before Michelle could ask where he'd gone, Lavinia knocked on the door, three short taps on the varnished wood. The knocks echoed, and Michelle half expected no one to show up.

With a soft click, however, the door opened, and an abundance of light and sound burst out into the night. A tall, muscular woman in sweatpants and a sports bra stood framed in the doorway. Curly black hair framed her face, forming a dark halo around her head. Intricate tattoos whirled around her biceps and one side of her stomach.

She showed no surprise at two people standing on her doorstep in the early hours of the morning. "There you are. You had both better come inside."

Lavinia gestured for Michelle to go first, and Michelle stepped over the threshold, feeling like Alice tumbling down the rabbit hole.

"I'm Proserpina, by the way," the tattooed woman said to Michelle. Lavinia closed the door behind them, several locks clicking shut in rapid succession. They stood in a small foyer, the marble stone floor covered with an intricately designed carpet. Several doors branched off from the hallway, but what drew Michelle's eyes in particular was the huge curving staircase leading up to the next floor. The woodwork of the balustrade looked hand-carved into fantastical designs, nymphs wrapped around the banister, fawns traipsing up the steps. Wherever Michelle looked, there was the quiet opulence of an old country home, where generations of wealth had been left behind like layers of sediment. She must have been staring because Lavinia leant close and said in a low voice in her ear, "It's a bit much."

"Lavinia likes her surroundings more Spartan. You should see her room, barely anything in it," Proserpina said.

"It's beautiful," Michelle said, unsure of how to respond to the onslaught of luxury. She thought of her one-bedroom apartment in London that she had left only a couple of hours ago. She thought of the bedroom which only just had enough space for a bed and a wardrobe, the thin walls that separated her from her neighbours, the tiny kitchen that didn't even have enough room on the counter for a coffee machine. That apartment had felt like her palace only a day ago; her walls might have been unpainted per her landlord's rules, the bathroom faucet might have a drip, and the bedroom window never shut completely, but it had felt like exquisite luxury to have space to herself in the city. First the driver, now the big mansion—Lavinia clearly lived in a completely different world. And that was not even including all of the demon stuff.

Michelle's eyes didn't know where to look as they walked into a massive kitchen with cooking facilities that could easily serve a small hotel.

"Are you hungry? I could get the housekeeper to make you something," Lavinia said.

Of course there was a housekeeper. Michelle imagined there was a butler hiding in the pantry as well. "No thank you." Eating was the last thing on her mind right now.

A small woman with a brow so furrowed it almost radiated off her face marched into the room. She looked to be in her late sixties, her skin weathered by age and experience. Despite her thunderous expression, she wore an incongruously cheerful summer dress sporting bright yellow sunflowers.

"Mrs. Frost, there you are. Is Michelle's room ready?"

"Of course it is," she snapped rudely. If anything, her frown turned even more threatening. Michelle stayed very quiet, hoping not to draw any attention from the angry little woman.

"Thank you, Mrs. Frost," Lavinia said easily, clearly brave enough to weather the woman's temper. "The blue room?"

The housekeeper grunted something that might be assent before turning and stalking off through a doorway on the far side of the kitchen.

"Come, I'll show you," Lavinia said. Leaving Proserpina, they retraced their steps back to the entrance and climbed the grand staircase. Their footsteps were muffled by the thick carpet beneath their feet, and Michelle enjoyed the simple pleasure of the smooth wooden banister under her fingertips. "I'll give you the grand tour tomorrow, but it might be helpful to know that the building is shaped like a U. We are currently at the bottom of the U, and two wings branch off, east and west. Your room will be in the east wing, where the guestrooms are. My Sisters and I have rooms in the west wing, and the staff have their rooms on the second floor. Although some, like Zachary, live in their own cottage on the grounds as well."

They reached the first floor, the corridor branching off to the left and right. They turned right and passed several closed doors until Lavinia reached one that had been left ajar. She opened it wider for Michelle to pass through. "The bathroom is through the door over there. Feel free to use anything that Mrs. Frost left in there for you." At Michelle's sceptical look, Lavinia laughed. "Don't worry, you'll get used to her. She is actually a sweetheart."

"I'll believe it when I see it," Michelle said, still not convinced.

Lavinia placed Michelle's bag on a wooden rack beside the door. "There's a phone next to the bed, for outside calls press zero first, but if you just need some help, just pick it up and it will ring automatically. Someone should be around all night. Of course, you're also welcome to come back down."

Eyeing the massive bed at the centre of the room, Michelle said, "I think I'll try to sleep. It's been a long day."

Lavinia nodded, looking as if she wanted to say something else. Michelle waited, but nothing followed.

Filling the awkward silence, she said, "You may wish to change your shirt, by the way."

Lavinia glanced down at her splattered white T-shirt and the blood that had dried to dark brown plaque, raising the hem to get a better look.

"You're right," Lavinia said dryly. "That may explain Mrs. Frost's temper. Demon blood doesn't come out in the wash easily." Michelle couldn't help but smile at the muscular, self-possessed woman peeling a blood-covered shirt from her stomach as if it were nothing.

Then she turned serious again. "Thank you. For doing all of this for me, I mean." Michelle gestured at the room, the mansion, everything.

"No problem," Lavinia said with a smile, enigmatic as always. She left, closing the door softly behind her.

Michelle took a deep breath through her nose, exhaling through her mouth and willing her heart to beat more slowly. She looked around at the pale blue wallpaper and hardwood floors, the massive bed that looked like an antique, the tasteful paintings of mountainous landscapes neatly framed. Real oil paintings, not just the cheap reproductions on canvas that you could get at any furniture store. She peeked through the door to the bathroom and gasped slightly at the spacious walk-in rain shower and separate claw-foot bathtub. Fluffy white towels had been laid out for her, small colourful bottles of toiletries neatly arranged, ready for her use. She couldn't quite believe that sour woman from downstairs had done all this, possibly within the last couple of hours.

Remembering Lavinia's insistence to make use of what was left for her, Michelle rummaged through her backpack, its faded grey canvas looking incredibly cheap next to the luxurious materials in this house. She took out a clean change of clothes and stepped into the bathroom.

She set the shower's water temperature as high as she could bear, letting it wash away the horrors of the evening. The droplets stung her face but she welcomed the pain, letting it ground her. Unbidden, her mind roamed back to Lavinia, standing in the doorway, silent, smiling. Over and over, her mind kept coming back to this image. Then, as she was lathering her shoulders with the shower gel, which smelled enticingly of coconut, a shock ran through her. That was what had been bothering her—that when Lavinia had peeled the shirt away from her stomach, all that had been underneath was smooth skin, covered in dried flakes of blood. There had been no wound, no scratch whatsoever. It had been gone completely.

Right now, she was going to enjoy this damn shower. She deserved to feel clean. Tonight, she would rest. And tomorrow, she would find out what the hell was going on here.

Chapter Four

Lavinia walked down the hallway of the east wing, the smell of Michelle still lingering in the air, floral with a hint of cinnamon. It was tinged with a suggestion of blood, just the tiniest aroma of iron and plasma. It was enough to awaken a tendril of hunger.

She ducked behind an elaborate tapestry halfway down the hallway and descended the hidden staircase that wound itself deep below the earth. As large as the section of Thornblood that stood aboveground seemed, the majority of the building was hewn into the rock beneath. Not meant for the public eye, these stairs were a simple white-washed concrete affair, lit by the red glow of sparse lights dotted along the walls. Even Lavinia's eyes needed a modicum of light. The absolute darkness of being underground was as impenetrable to her as it would be to anyone else. The remnant of Michelle's scent on Lavinia's clothes became overpowered by the smells of stale air, cement, and the stench of the demon's blood caked on her shirt. She found herself missing it.

No matter. She had more important things to worry about. On a landing that looked identical to various others she had already passed, she pushed through the reinforced iron door, strode through another nondescript corridor. Her feet had tracked this path so many times that they took her to her destination without further interference from her brain, giving her a precious moment to centre herself. The red door to the command room rose before her. She took a deep breath and stepped inside.

Lucretia was already there, of course, seated at the head of the table that dominated the otherwise plain room, her expression predicting nothing good. Proserpina had already made her way down here as well after having welcomed Michelle and Lavinia at the front door. She was leaning back on her chair staring at the ceiling as if the plain concrete would reveal its secrets if only she looked hard enough. Quintia sat at Lucretia's right-hand side, scowling. Then again, that was neither good nor bad—Quintia always scowled. Lavinia sometimes wondered whether she had been born with a scowl across her tiny infant features. Vesta, on Luce's left side, was as serene and poised as always.

Lavinia always thought of Quintia and Vesta as Luce's angel and devil, each whispering advice into her ear. They certainly looked the part: Quintia wore her dark brown hair shaved at the sides, leaving it longer along the top. Her pierced ears glinted in the overhead light. Quintia preferred torn jeans and black T-shirts, while Vesta wore long, flowing garments in whites and pastels, fashionable in high society. Strands of golden thread were braided into her long blonde hair. Yet, looks were deceiving. Both were blood-sworn Sisters of the Sword, at the pinnacle of their physical strength, and skilled in hand-to-hand combat. While Quintia's intimidating demeanour certainly had its uses and Luce hardly ever appeared in public without her by her side, it was Vesta who more often steered her decisions.

"Welcome home, Sister," Vesta said, smiling warmly.

"Sisters," Lavinia answered. Proserpina's gaze lazily drifted towards Lavinia, almost as if surprised to find her there. Quintia scowled. Lucretia folded her hands onto the table in front of her. The skin was a mottled red of scar tissue, the result of a serious burn. Lavinia had never asked about the source of the scars. As Sisters of Twilight, they all bore more scars than they could count. It was better to leave the past in the past than drag it kicking and screaming into the present.

Lavinia waited for what was coming.

"What the fuck were you thinking?"

There it was. Lucretia radiated frustration, her black eyes spitting fire. Her shoulder-length hair grazed the top of the collar of her white shirt as she leaned forward. Behind Lavinia, the door opened softly, and Brigh slipped into the room. The youngest member of the Sisterhood quietly sat down on a chair beside Quintia, the bright copper of her pixie cut one of the only pops of colour in the room.

"What our dearest Sister means to say is, why did you bring the human here?" Vesta said, unperturbed by the glare thrown in her direction across the table by Quintia.

"As you all know, I have been searching for the rogue who has killed several humans over the last two months. There is some geographical variance in their victims, but they mainly concentrate around London—"

"Get to the point, Vin," Lucretia interrupted.

Lavinia took a deep breath. "As I was looking for any clues that might help our search for the rogue, I encountered a tenebris. I initially fended it off, wounded it sufficiently that it retreated. Michelle thought I was hurt—I thought it would be best to make sure she got home safely." Lavinia looked at her Sisters, their faces unreadable. "The demon reappeared. Despite my attacks, it was focused on Michelle, trying to get to her.

"I think Michelle was targeted by some kind of summoner. She has no idea about the supernatural world. The surprise she showed at the demon's appearance couldn't have been faked. The appearance of the demon around the same area that the rogue has been active in feels like a strange coincidence. In my opinion, keeping Michelle here is our best chance of keeping her safe."

"We could have surveilled the human," Proserpina said reasonably. "Kept an eye on her to see whether the warlock tried to send a demon to her again."

"The risk to the human was too great. Even under surveillance, we might not be able to interfere in time."

Lucretia sighed, massaging her forehead with her fingers. "You're such a bleeding heart for humans, Vin."

Lavinia didn't reply. There was no use in denying it. While some others would consider the loss of a human life or two a regrettable but tolerable outcome, she had never been able to accept this. It was her job to keep everyone safe, and she took her oath seriously.

"Besides, we used to have human guests." It wasn't a strong argument, and Lavinia knew it even as she said it. Sure, Thornblood had been built with a dual purpose. It was both a stronghold, with visible and invisible defences, but it had equally been built as a space in which the Sisterhood could entertain and welcome humans. A place where they could present a front of respectability to their neighbours whenever necessary. In the eighteenth and nineteenth centuries, they had thrown lavish parties, inviting the humans from surrounding areas. Even in the Peak District, with its rugged landscape, humans had a tendency to spread into every nook and cranny of the world. But the compound hadn't seen any human guests for decades.

"This is different, and you know it," Quintia said. Her voice was low, almost a growl. Like many vampires, Quintia considered it too dangerous to let humans get too close. Before the advent of smartphones and mass media, being unveiled to the human population at large had been a manageable risk. Nowadays, many vampires agreed it was too dangerous. Once information leaked into the public consciousness, there would be no way to go back to how things were before.

Lavinia didn't respond, but looked at the others. There was a possibility that they would expel Michelle, force Lavinia to retract the protection she had offered her. If Luce ordered it, Michelle would be on her way back to her small apartment in London within fifteen minutes. And Lavinia would allow it to happen. She knew how to bend the rules to her own purpose—but she had no interest whatsoever in challenging Lucretia's leadership.

Lucretia leaned back, considering the issue. "What do you think, Proserpina?"

Pina waved one hand in the air as if the whole discussion was moot. "She's here now. We have little to fear from a single human. She seems harmless enough. I consider the risk to our safety low, and the potential benefits in finding the warlock possibly substantial." A sliver of hope blossomed in Lavinia's chest. If Pina was on her side, the others would follow. Security was Pina's remit—the others would take her recommendation seriously.

"I agree with our Sister," Vesta said. Quintia grunted, an eloquent sound that expressed begrudging approval as well as her displeasure at being manoeuvred into an approval in the first place. Brigh nodded her assent.

Lucretia stood. Lavinia held her breath awaiting her judgement.

"She can stay. But *you* will not rest until whoever is killing humans in London is caught. I expect you back out in the field tomorrow. And if no progress is made within the next week, the human will be released. We will not unduly raise suspicion, even if a life is on the line."

Lavinia inclined her head, accepting the orders. "Of course, Sister." It was as good a result as she could have hoped for. Michelle would be safe here, under the watchful gaze of her Sisters and their loyal staff. She would have preferred to look after her herself, but there was a serial killer to be caught, and the sooner they were, the sooner Michelle would be able to go back to her life. And that was the goal, wasn't it? Yet, a note of dissatisfaction tinged her thoughts when the others rose and filed past her to their own tasks. Only Pina lingered after the others had left.

"You like her," Pina said, leaning against the table.

"What?" With some difficulty Lavinia extricated herself from her own musings.

"The woman."

Lavinia shrugged. "Like Luce said, I have a soft spot for them."

Pina narrowed her eyes. "Don't play the fool with me, Vin. I know you, and I know what you're like. This is different. It's not like you to make a decision like this in the field without checking with the rest of us."

"It was an impulse," Lavinia agreed, but otherwise stayed silent. The less said, the better. Pina did know her—even before they had become Sword Sisters, they had grown up together, their families closely connected through marriages and alliances. Vesta might be the Sister with the best social insight, but it was Pina who *truly* knew Lavinia.

"Be careful," Pina said after a moment, resting her hand on Vin's shoulder. "I do not wish to see your loyal heart hurt."

Lavinia's hand covered Pina's and squeezed it briefly. "I will. Don't worry."

Proserpina smiled, but the smile did not reach her eyes. Together, they walked back up one of the staircases to reappear through a reinforced doorway near the foyer. "Are you hungry?" Pina asked.

"Starving."

"Let's eat." They sat down for their meal at the high counter of the kitchen, tearing into a stack of burritos that had been left in the refrigerator by Mrs. Frost. The remainder of the night passed pleasantly, normally. Pina updated Lavinia on some of the repair work to the digital security system protecting the grounds, which had become necessary since some animals had chewed through a couple of cables. Lavinia finally changed out of her ruined shirt, sighing over the wastefulness of having to discard it after only a handful of wears, but knowing that if she tried to mend the large tear in it, her Sisters would laugh at her for her frugality.

As much as they all loved each other, they didn't quite understand Lavinia's strong desire for a simple life. She found comfort in the white of her walls, the bare room, with only a simple wooden bed and a plain desk and chair among the few belongings she allowed herself, in a way that she couldn't quite explain. What she had, as little as it might seem within the confines of the opulence and abundance of the mansion's resources, was truly hers. It was within her control. And that feeling was precious.

There was just one niggle in the back of her mind: the human. Even the routine pleasure of cleaning her knife in the armoury was disrupted by her. Lavinia's hands went through the mechanical motions of removing the demon's blood from the smooth silver surface while some of her Sisters sparred, their practice blades clashing against each other. Lavinia's thoughts kept going back to Michelle, sleeping several floors above them. *That* was not simple.

For the first time in over a century, she had acted on impulse, allowing herself to become part of a human's life. While the demon had broken through Michelle's ignorance of the supernatural, Lavinia had done nothing to try to rebuild that ignorance. Sometimes humans could be convinced that their memories had been mistaken, that it had all merely been a trick of the light, figments of imagination resulting from trauma.

Lavinia had *wanted* to tell Michelle everything. Had taken one look at the nurse, her sweet concern for the scratch on Lavinia's stomach. She had been softened by Michelle's courage and had wanted to reveal herself, show herself for who she really was, despite the differences between them.

She had lost control. And she found that she had liked it. In the background, Pina whooped, having floored Quintia. Lavinia didn't join them, instead choosing the solitude of her confused thoughts.

Chapter Five

Michelle awoke in a haze of fleeting dreams—nightmares, really. Long strings of images and impressions of being chased, of being hunted. Of shadows made of smoke reaching towards her, grasping her. When she opened her eyes, though, soft light streamed into the room from behind the curtains. She blinked for a couple of moments to reorient herself, taking in the thick, downy duvet and wood panelling on the walls. Memories of last night flooded in, and she got up with a renewed determination to no longer be a passive leaf blown about by the wind of circumstance.

Her phone, screen cracked and battery almost completely drained (she hadn't bothered looking for a plug socket before crawling into bed last night), told her it was almost ten in the morning. Barefoot, she trod to the curtains and pulled them open, expecting to see some vista of forest and hills. She started back in surprise and dawning horror. There was glass, certainly, but behind it lay a sheet of dull steel, completely sealing the outside world from the room. Not even a hint of light penetrated through the minutest of seams. It was like looking into the darkness of a cave. The light that she had assumed was the morning sunlight was in fact created by a row of lights recessed within the wall, the bulbs providing a soft, even glow.

Well, that was concerning, wasn't it? Suddenly, the opulence around her felt cloying, suffocating. What if she had made a tremendous mistake? What if all of this was just one really fancy prison cell?

She grabbed her favourite pair of jeans from her overnight bag, pulled the jumper that Iris had knitted for her last Christmas over her head, splashed some water in her face (the scratch was still looking angry and certainly made itself known), and tried the door of her room. The handle turned easily, the door opening without a sound, providing at least a minor sense of relief. She marched down the corridor, past several closed doors, and descended the magnificent staircase. The house was quiet, no sounds or voices carrying into the foyer. Faced with various doors again, she walked into the one she knew led to the kitchen, choosing familiarity over the unknown.

It was empty. Of people, at least—a breakfast that could easily feed a dozen was laid out on the counter. A quick glance revealed sliced fruits in glass bowls, various kinds of muffins placed in a pleasing pyramid shape, different types of cereals, fresh milk in old-fashioned glass bottles, and what smelled like freshly baked bread covered with a cheerily striped tea towel.

Michelle's stomach growled, uncomfortably reminding her that she hadn't eaten in a while. Feeling somewhat like a naughty schoolchild, Michelle took one of the muffins. She bit into it, briefly enjoying the zingy burst of lemon and the sweetness of honey, before she continued her quest.

She walked through an archway to an equally empty dining room, which featured a huge dark wooden table surrounded by twelve chairs. How many people actually lived here? Lavinia had mentioned sisters—there had been the woman who opened the door, and voices had carried out into the hallway. Was everyone else still sleeping? Emboldened, she explored further, stepping through an empty living room furnished with several large comfortable-looking sofas and, to Michelle's relief, a large window overlooking what Michelle assumed was the back of the house. From the corners, the two wings protruded forwards, and a well-kept garden sheltered in the middle. The house wasn't completely shut up, then, and being able to see the clouded sky made Michelle breathe a little more easily. She chewed on the last bit of the muffin and opened another door at random, stepping into a small study.

She flinched backwards as the desk chair swivelled around and revealed a tall, statuesque woman. She wore part of her shoulder-length dark brown hair in a topknot, her face all angles and planes. She had a masculine energy, and only her mouth brought a touch of softness to her features. Her penetrating black eyes assessed Michelle with intensity.

"Oh, I'm sorry, I didn't know someone was in here," Michelle said, stepping backwards. "Sorry to disturb you."

"Michelle," the woman said. She had a rich voice, tinged with a slight accent that Michelle couldn't place. "Please have a seat." She gestured to the seat in front of the massive mahogany desk. Truly, every single room seemed as if it had been furnished by raiding an antique store. Michelle couldn't help but look at the various oil portraits of stern-faced women in elaborate gowns that covered the walls. Michelle lowered herself into the seat, somehow feeling like a child called into the principal's office. She still held the little paper wrapper that had encased the muffin. She resisted the urge to fidget.

The woman spoke first. "I am Lucretia." Lucretia—was this the Luce that Lavinia and Zachary had mentioned yesterday? The person they thought would be displeased with Michelle's presence? Michelle braced herself for whatever was coming next.

"I understand you were attacked by a demon last night.

Lavinia was somewhat... hasty in her decision to bring you here, but I hope you will find our house comfortable. You are free to use the rooms on the ground floor, and of course your bedroom." There was the echo of a warning in her voice. *Don't stray beyond where you're allowed.*

"When can I leave?" Michelle asked. Yesterday had been such a whirlwind. In the clear light of day, practical considerations started creeping in. What about work? When would she be able to go home?

"Hopefully, your visit will be brief. You are, of course, free to leave at any time, but Lavinia has made the argument that it would not be in your best interest to do so at the moment."

Michelle narrowed her eyes at the verbal gymnastics. If she wasn't welcome here, she'd rather know outright. "And what do you think?"

Lucretia sighed and leaned back, exuding an exhaustion that usually spoke of age, but she couldn't be older than late thirties. There was only the faintest hint of crow's feet around her eyes. "I trust my Sister's judgement, even if it does not align with my own."

Lavinia. Michelle's throat constricted slightly at the memory of her. She ignored the feeling, focusing back on Lucretia. "Lavinia mentioned sisters. Are you... her sister?" she asked with hesitation. Besides the fact that Lavinia, Lucretia, and the woman who had led them inside last night were all built like professional athletes, their features shared no resemblance. Lucretia had a strong jaw, and somehow the light made her eyes seem completely black, as if the pupil had swallowed the iris. They were nothing like Lavinia's green eyes, her high cheekbones. It seemed unlikely all three of the women she had met so far had somehow come from the same parents.

"We are Sword Sisters." The finality of the statement gave the impression that this explained everything.

For Michelle, it explained exactly nothing. "What does that mean?"

Lucretia tapped short fingernails on the wood of the tabletop. A sign of impatience? "We are sworn by oaths and by blood to protect our kind, to stand with our Sisters, and to give our life if necessary. There are nine of us." Michelle felt the urge to laugh because it sounded ridiculous, but under the calculating gaze of Lucretia, she found herself believing it. Besides, she had seen what Lavinia could do with a knife. Apparently, she was not the only one.

"I understand you may have a lot of questions. I am not able to answer all of them right now, but I do open my house to you. Please avoid any locked doors." Her tone implied dismissal. Michelle thanked her and escaped back into the living room.

Nine "Sisters". Sworn by blood to... what had Lucretia said? Protect their kind. Surely she meant people—humans—right? But there was something about the way she'd said it that made Michelle think that that *wasn't* what she had meant. There was a truth here, underneath it all, if she could just grasp it...

She was mulling over the conversation, looking out the window with unseeing eyes, when someone called her name. The word was edged with warmth. Before turning, she recognised Lavinia's voice and found herself smiling.

Lavinia joined her at the window to contemplate the courtyard, the hills in the distance framing the scene. She had finally changed out of the bloody clothing from yesterday, and Michelle's heart skipped a beat at how beautiful she was. Her long blonde hair was pulled back into a neat ponytail, and she looked casual in a fitted white shirt and jeans. Her face was bare of make-up, and her skin appeared like it would be wonderfully soft to the touch.

It was almost ridiculous how good she looked, and Michelle caught herself staring. Keen to think about anything except how attractive Lavinia was in the bright light of day, she turned back towards the window. She forced herself to take a calming breath, her heartbeat surprisingly fast in her chest.

She had more important things to worry about than how stunning Lavinia was, as much as her heart wished otherwise. "Why are there shutters in front of my window? In the bedroom upstairs, I mean." It was a minor mystery compared to the existence of demons and a secret group of women warriors stabbing them willy-nilly. Still, she needed to know, even if it was just a small piece of the puzzle.

"Ah. They serve a dual purpose. They keep out the light and protect the windows, just in case."

"For storms and things?" Michelle could easily imagine that the weather could be quite severe in such a rural place. She had heard several stories of the Peak District becoming inaccessible because of snowstorms or flooding in the valleys.

Lavinia smiled. "Things like that. If you prefer them to stay open, there is a button beside the window sill." Her smile faded again. "I came looking for you because I'm afraid I will have to leave you for the day. I won't be able to show you around like I promised last night."

"Where are you going?"

"I would like to have another look at the alleyway and perhaps the street where you were attacked. There might still be some evidence that can lead us to the warlock."

"Warlock? You mean the person who sent that demon thing after me?" Warlock? It made some kind of sense, as a term for someone who sent demons after people. Still, it all felt a little bit too fantasy novel for her to roll with it.

"That's right."

They stood in silence for a moment as they watched the clouds pass. "Lavinia, no offense, but none of this makes any sense. Demons aren't real."

Lavinia turned towards her. She was standing so close, Michelle had to tilt her head up to be able to look her in the eyes. Her expression was serious, the corner of her mouth conveying a grimness. "Unfortunately, they are real. But when this is over, I promise, you can go back to your life. You can forget any of this ever happened."

Michelle tried to smile, to acknowledge the kindness in Lavinia's words. Instead, she drowned in the finality of them. Lavinia, this house, Lucretia in the study behind them... This was all real. It wasn't a nightmare she would wake up from tomorrow, the memory of fear already fading with the light of a new day. Tears stung her eyes. Someone *had* tried to kill her. And demons existed. She was unable to form any words. Everything had been real. A flesh-and-blood woman stood in front of her, in broad daylight, who had killed a demon with a knife.

Nothing would ever be the same again.

"I don't think I will be able to do that," she finally said, forcing the words around the lump in her throat.

Lavinia laid a reassuring hand on her shoulder. "You can and you will. Most people do. People are resilient."

Michelle didn't answer. Part of her was having an existential crisis, suddenly questioning everything that she thought was true about her place in the world. Another part of her, a quiet and small part, was enjoying the warmth of Lavinia's hand seeping through the fabric of her jumper. She looked at Lavinia, tracing the shape of her features, following the line of the thin scar that ran through her eyebrow and into her hairline. If anything, even if Michelle would be able to stuff the idea that demons were real into some box in the back of her mind, even if she would be able to forget that, she didn't think she would be able to forget Lavinia. The thought surprised her, but then again, you don't get rescued by a gorgeous woman with a blade every day.

Lavinia made sure that Michelle had everything she needed

and then disappeared through the front door with Zachary, who appeared from somewhere in the house in a fresh suit. Michelle watched them go from the window in a front room and felt an unexpected pang. The house suddenly felt impossibly large and empty without Lavinia's presence in it.

Chapter Six

Not knowing what to do with herself, unable to relax in the unfamiliar environment with thoughts swirling in her mind, Michelle wandered back to the bedroom. She sat down on the bed, which someone (perhaps Mrs. Frost?) had made in her absence. Going over what she had found out so far, which felt incredibly limited, she decided that at the very least she would have to call in sick to work. Her fear of the demon returning was strong enough to keep her right here for now, as mysterious as the inhabitants of this mansion were.

She rang her line manager. The call was brief as Michelle explained she had sprained her ankle on the way home and wouldn't be able to come into work for the next couple of days. The lie rolled off her tongue with ease—a surprise, as she had never called in sick with a falsehood before. The hospital was always so short-staffed, and the thought of slacking off work was diametrically opposed to her sense of duty towards both her colleagues and patients. After the night she'd just had, though, those concerns seemed increasingly remote. She was no use to her patients dead. And it wasn't like she could tell her manager that a demon had attacked her.

Michelle knew exactly what that would sound like. No, she

would keep the truth to herself. Her manager wished her a speedy recovery and hung up.

She sent some texts to her mum, sent a quick message to Iris to let her know she was still alive, and scrolled through a couple of social media apps. The pictures of happy couples and food-smeared toddlers did nothing to relieve the feeling of estrangement. Frustrated, she stuffed her phone in her back pocket and padded downstairs again. Mrs. Frost was in the kitchen, slicing a mountain of vegetables. At the sight of her grey hair and bright green sundress, Michelle almost turned around to flee. Then she thought the better of it.

"Can I help you with anything?" Michelle asked. Giving her hands something to do sounded very appealing right about now.

"No." Mrs. Frost continued her assault on a massive cabbage without looking up.

Michelle was not above begging. "Please?" Even the intimidating woman seemed less of a challenge than the abyss of her own thoughts. She could deal with difficult patients and even more difficult parents—she could deal with one old housekeeper with a temper.

"No, thank you. I have a system." Although Mrs. Frost continued as she had been, Michelle thought she noticed a small, almost imperceptible softening in the woman.

"All right, I'll leave you to it. Did you prepare my room upstairs?"

That earned her a short glance before Mrs. Frost turned back to her chopping. The cabbage was being decimated into tiny shreds at a terrifying speed. "I did."

"It was perfect. Thank you."

For a moment, Michelle thought she saw a smile tug at the corners of Mrs. Frost's mouth. She must have imagined it: when she blinked, the woman's features were as stoic as they had been before.

A woman dressed all in black strode into the kitchen. She had an olive skin tone and wore her hair shaved at the sides, the longer strands from the crown of her head grazing her angular face. This woman must be yet another Sister. She had the same quiet strength, the same edge of predator that the others had possessed as well. But where Lavinia exuded a calmness, this woman gave off an air of barely contained aggression. She was the kind of person Michelle would mentally label as a troublemaker.

The woman walked up to Mrs. Frost and snatched a piece of carrot.

"Those are for later, you heathen," Mrs. Frost complained, and waved her large kitchen knife threateningly at the latest Sister. Michelle flinched at the blade flashing so close to the Sister's bare arms.

"Just having a taste," the woman answered, easily dodging the knife and pinching another two pieces of carrot.

"Both of you are bothering me. Go do something else, Quintia, and take Michelle with you."

Quintia sighed, looking eerily like a castigated teenager for a second, before she turned to Michelle.

"Fine. Come on." Quintia marched out of the kitchen without looking to see whether Michelle was following. Despite her misgivings, she found herself doing so, walking through a hallway that led to a narrow staircase. This house felt like a maze, every door hiding yet another revelation.

As they descended, she asked tentatively, "Where are we going?" The stairs were notably less fancy than the upstairs had been—no oil paintings or expensive wallpaper, instead presenting swathes of exposed concrete. Why were they going into the basement?

"I'm not sitting around babysitting you. Might as well do something useful."

"I'd be happy to do something useful." Anything was better than staying in her room, waiting for Lavinia to find whoever wanted to kill her. She chose not to be offended at the insinuation that she was a child.

Quintia ducked into a room, Michelle close behind, still unsure what a person like Quintia would consider "useful". The hallway opened up into a modern and well-lit gym, with various gleaming black exercise machines dotted across the room. The middle of the room was kept free, however, and was covered with fall protection mats, the kind used in martial arts.

"Let's see what you've got," Quintia said, grabbing a wooden stick from a rack against the wall.

"Uh, I'm afraid I haven't got anything at all. I don't know how to fight." Besides some very basic grips to ensure a child wouldn't hurt themselves while she was giving an injection or to deal with a temper tantrum or two, Michelle didn't even know any real self-defence. It had never before seemed particularly necessary.

"Doesn't matter. Come on." Quintia kicked off her black trainers and positioned herself on the middle of the mat. She gestured to the empty space before her.

It didn't seem she had much of a choice. Quintia looked at her with an impatient scowl, her brown eyes hard in the bright overhead lights.

"Right." Michelle took off her sneakers, setting them beside Quintia's. She also removed her jumper, which would surely be too bulky and warm for any kind of exercise. Luckily, she'd worn an old tank top underneath. She walked onto the mat, testing its firmness underneath her feet. It was less squishy than she thought. When she reached Quintia, the woman tossed her the stick. It was smooth wood, with only some tape to improve the grip on one end. Both ends were blunted, fortunately. Michelle didn't feel particularly confident in waving around large sharp objects.

"Hit me," Quintia said, gesturing for Michelle to come forward.

"But you don't have a stick."

"I don't need one."

"Oh." Michelle looked down at the weapon in her right hand, trying to get somewhat of a feel for it. She adjusted her grip, looked back at Quintia, and hit her.

Or at least, she tried to hit Quintia. With offensive ease, the other woman stepped aside and the stick swung into air, dragging Michelle off balance.

"Again."

Stepping forward, faster now, Michelle struck, this time thrusting straight ahead instead of using an overhead swing, aiming at the middle of Quintia's stomach. Again, she dodged, as naturally as if she knew exactly what Michelle intended to do before she did it. Again and again, Michelle advanced, hacked, slashed, and once even followed up with a punch of her left hand. Quintia deflected the blow with one hand as if it was nothing.

"Better," Quintia said to that, and Michelle tried to be more creative, seeking out ways in which to surprise Quintia. She wasn't nearly as fast as her, and nowhere near as strong, but she found she enjoyed the challenge. It felt good to move, to feel her muscles protest under the strain of this unexpected usage. Michelle had never been tempted to join a gym or play any sport, but this... This was fun.

"Let's pause," Quintia said after a particularly unsuccessful swing of the stick. Michelle's top was sticky with sweat, and her breaths came fast and shallow. Quintia looked just as cool as she had before they'd started. It was incredibly unfair. "Have some water." She handed over a large refillable bottle taken from a small fridge beside a treadmill. Gratefully, Michelle drank several large gulps, relishing the cool water on her tongue.

"You're so good at this," Michelle said once she had found her breath again. Somehow, Quintia had become less intimidating, the harshness of her personality somewhat mellowing as they had sparred. There was a certain wildness inside of her, but clearly she also had excellent control of herself.

Quintia shrugged. "I've had a lot of experience."

"I think I could train for years and not be as fast as you." Michelle took another sip of water.

"Well, that's just because I'm a vampire. Our reflexes are much faster than a human's."

The sip of water didn't quite make it to its destination, and Michelle coughed, for a moment unsure whether she'd heard Quintia right. "Wait, what?"

Quintia raised one eyebrow. "We're all vampires here. I thought Lavinia had told you."

"Vampires," Michelle repeated.

"Yes."

"The blood-sucking kind?"

"That's right."

"The have-to-be-invited-in-and-hates-garlic kind?"

Quintia leaned casually against a rack of weights, her arms folded. "Well, having an invitation before you enter someone's house is just polite, and I do love a good garlic naan. But still vampires."

Michelle's thoughts whirled at this new revelation. She thought back to Lavinia last night. How quickly the wound on Lavinia's stomach had healed. Her eyes hadn't betrayed her, but she hadn't understood what had actually happened. Quintia was a vampire. So was Lavinia. And Lucretia, and the woman who had opened the door last night, Proserpina. She was surrounded by vampires in this mansion.

She was completely out of her depth.

"But I've seen Lavinia go outside while the sun is up. I thought vampires could only go outside at night," Michelle said, her brain struggling to keep up with the new information thrown at it.

"Oh, we can go outside, sunlight just hurts like fuck. Burns. The sun is less of a problem for us than you might imagine. It's England. It's cloudy all the goddamn time anyway."

"Right." Michelle thought for a moment. "Are there any other revelations you want to get out of the way? A troll lives under the bridge, the tooth fairy's real, or anything else like that?"

"No, that's all. Although don't go wandering in the forest around the full moon. Our neighbours are werewolves."

Michelle couldn't tell whether Quintia was joking or not. It felt like she should laugh right now, but Quintia's expression was dour.

"What will you do, now you know?"

"What do you mean?"

Quintia pushed away from the weight rack, uncrossing her arms. She stepped forward and pinned Michelle with her stare. It made her feel small, insignificant, like a bug that Quintia could squash without any effort. She probably could.

"Will you betray us to your human friends? Tell them our secrets, lead them here?"

Michelle frowned and held her ground. It took everything not to step back and show her very real fear. "No, I wouldn't. I haven't told anyone about the demon either." And she wasn't going to. Her friends and family would only think she was suffering from a nervous breakdown.

Quintia stood painfully close, invading Michelle's space. Assessed her, measured her up, before she stepped back with a huff. "Keep it that way, human." She walked back to the middle of the mat. "Let me show you some basic stances," she said breezily, as if she hadn't just threatened Michelle.

Michelle took a shaky breath, her shoulders unclenching, and stepped back onto the mat. Quintia showed Michelle how to place her feet to improve her balance, how to jab without losing her footing, and some basic strikes. Throwing herself into the training, Michelle could almost forget what Quintia had just told her. She let the movement banish any thoughts or questions from her mind. All that mattered right at this moment was hitting the target Quintia held up for her, punching again and again, until all that existed in the world was her burning muscles and Quintia's sparse encouragements. Despite Quintia's intimidating demeanour, she was a good teacher.

After an hour, Michelle could barely lift her arms. She felt her weariness in her bones, and apologised to Quintia that she couldn't continue. "Lasted longer than I'd thought," Quintia responded, the corner of her mouth twitching upward. "Not bad, for a human."

Michelle couldn't help grinning. She left Quintia in the gym to practice in earnest, and dragged herself back up into the inhabited part of the house, up the grand staircase and into her room for another shower.

The thoughts that she had so carefully avoided for the last hour or so came crowding back immediately as the shower's hot water soothed the stiffness from her muscles. Vampires. They were all vampires—Quintia, Lavinia, Lucretia, Proserpina... Even Mrs. Frost? What about Zachary? She wondered where Lavinia was right now, what she was doing. Whether she was safe. Would she have to fight more demons or other, even worse monsters?

Come to think of it, were vampires immortal, like in the stories? How old was Lavinia? Michelle had thought she was in her late twenties, like herself. But maybe her youthful features were an illusion, and she was actually centuries old. She wondered what that would be like, to live for so long. Wondered whether she seemed terribly young to Lavinia.

Also, did they really drink blood? How did that work? She imagined a classic scene from a gothic romance, herself in a decadent gown stretched out on a fainting couch, Lavinia kneeling before her in a velvet suit, drinking from her wrist. Michelle shuddered. She wasn't entirely sure whether it was in horror or something else.

Chapter Seven

It was a quiet drive back to London. Lavinia watched the cars pass on the motorway as Zachary expertly manoeuvred the vehicle through the busy lanes. A bright noon sun shone overhead. Its rays didn't penetrate into the back of the car, the tinted windows protecting Lavinia's skin from their sting.

She wondered how Michelle was doing. The Sisterhood hadn't had a human stranger stay with them in decades, and she fretted over how her Sisters might behave. For some reason, Lavinia thought Michelle would not be the kind of person to sit still. She only hoped she wouldn't run into Quintia. Out of all of her Sisters, Quintia was the least... civilised. "Quintia has the subtlety of a battering ram," Pina had once said after Quintia had gotten them into hot water at some high society function, and Lavinia had to agree with her. She adored her Sister, appreciated her intense loyalty and relentless drive for their work, but she could only imagine what kind of first impression she would make on a human.

With surprising difficulty, she tore her thoughts away from Michelle. She forced herself to consider the matter at hand. She was meeting Octavia at the alleyway where the demon had appeared last night. Octavia had been off duty yesterday, and

Lavinia would appreciate her Sister's fresh eyes today. It was easy to miss things in the heat of the moment, and it was possible there would be clues to help them find out who had sent a demon after Michelle. Immediately, her thoughts drifted back to the human, her soft brown eyes, lined perfectly with dark eyelashes. The way she smiled, even in the face of what must be overwhelming circumstances. She had smelled so good this morning, coconut and that hint of cinnamon Lavinia had noticed yesterday.

"We're here."

It took Lavinia a moment to tear herself from her reverie. Zachary wore a questioning expression. The car idled in a quiet side street, away from the main thoroughfare.

"Right," she said, ignoring the question on Zachary's face, and got out of the car. Zachary drove off, seeking to park somewhere he could comfortably wait for a few hours. Lavinia felt a rush of appreciation for the familiar—he was dependable, but not overly deferential. He was always ready to help, acting as the Sisterhood's driver, messenger, or whatever role was required of him in that moment. Additionally, he was discreet, never showing any interest in gossip. It was difficult to find the right familiar, but Zachary was the best. Just like his father had been.

Octavia was already here. Lavinia could smell her Sister's scent of leather and rose on the cool breeze. The sun had hidden itself behind the cover of clouds again, cloaking the urban landscape in grey. The daylight caused a slight prickly sensation on the exposed skin of Lavinia's face and hands, which she ignored as she followed her Sister's scent-trail. She couldn't see Octavia initially. She wasn't in the alley where Lavinia had fought the demon and had first met Michelle, but instead had penetrated further into the warren of backstreets behind the row of shops.

"Look at this," Octavia said. Her Sister was crouching behind a haphazard stack of garbage bags, only the top of her bright blue hair flaring above the pile. Octavia had embraced the modern invention of neon hair dyes, and changed her colour every season. The blue brought out the cooler tones of her dark skin. Lavinia walked up to her, considering the pile of garbage. The contents of the bags were several days old, judging by the smell of them. Rats had eaten through the corners of some, the trash spilling out onto the ground.

Lavinia looked closer to where Octavia pointed, and saw the dark stains splashed against the brick wall. Blood. Her nostrils flared, and there it was—the scent of the blood, hidden behind the rankness of the garbage. It smelled sour with fear, with notes of alcohol overlaid with some kind of cheap cologne. It could only be a day old, the metallic undertones still strong in the air.

"Your girl's?" Octavia asked. Lavinia had updated Octavia on the phone this morning, explaining how she had taken Michelle to Thornblood. Octavia had listened without comment, but Lavinia was sure the eldest of the Sisters had some reservations about Lavinia's impulsive decision.

"No. She didn't come this way—she came from the other direction."

"Any idea whose it might be?"

Lavinia studied the splatter pattern. Several of the shops had doors opening into this alley, and one of the kitchen staff could have cut themselves on a piece of glass in the trash. There was quite a lot of blood here though, certainly more than an accidental cut. Of course, not all blood was the sign of violence, but it looked like there was too much of it to be a coincidence.

She thought back to last night. She'd come from the other direction, had heard voices echoing down the streets. There had been people talking and laughing along the main road. She had passed a man leaning against a wall smoking a cigarette, the door to the kitchen propped open with a brick. The city at night was full of sounds and smells, the stench of gasoline and concrete mingling with the traces of millions of people, a cornucopia of sensations that even an adept tracker with vampiric senses would have a hard time distinguishing.

"No," Lavinia said thoughtfully.

"Let's see if we can find any more." Octavia straightened, wiping her hands on her black jeans, and investigated further down the alley. Lavinia didn't blame her—the stench here was truly despicable, rot and rancid oil, the cloying sweetness of decay. She couldn't wait to be free from it herself. Rather than getting used to it, every breath was a fresh assault.

Bracing herself for a moment, lamenting the events that led up to this, Lavinia started removing the garbage bags one by one. The splatter pattern suggested that someone had leant against the wall here only yesterday. The ripeness of the bags would have been just as apparent then—it was hardly a place anyone would choose to rest. Unless, of course, the bags hadn't been in this spot yesterday. She heaved up one after another, disturbing a rat that skittered away carrying its lunch between its jaws. Then, she found what she hoped she wouldn't. An arm lay cradled between the grey plastic of two bags, the skin a white pallor that could only mean death.

"Found him," she called over to Octavia.

She removed two further bags, and his torso was revealed. Another unveiled his face. He was in his forties, his black hair thinning along his crown. His brown eyes stared into space, bloodshot. A gash had been torn along the side of his neck, blood clotted on the ragged flesh. A streak of blood had soaked through his jumper in a large vertical stripe, suggesting that he'd been upright when he was wounded. But if he had been killed here...

"There's not enough blood."

"No," Octavia agreed. "Not by a long shot."

Very little blood had pooled underneath the body. The body had been drained.

"Do you think it's the same guy?" Octavia asked.

Lavinia assessed the way the body was positioned. He'd abandoned the man close to where he'd killed him, had only made a token attempt at hiding it. Hadn't cared who found him. Lavinia leaned closer to the body and sniffed, but the scents didn't provide any additional information. She only smelled death and decay, with the sharpness of cologne that still wafted from the man's skin.

"Yeah," she finally said. "Unless we find any evidence to the contrary, I think we should assume it's him."

"How many does that make now?"

"Six." Six dead humans, their bodies haphazardly dumped. The first had simply been left where she'd fallen. An older woman in her sixties, still clutching her purse, her neck and wrists ravaged by teeth over and over. Witnesses mentioned a man fleeing the scene, but no usable description was given beyond that. The second, a teenage boy—he'd been living on the streets for a couple of months and was found stuffed behind some bushes close to the doorway he'd been sleeping in. The third, a young woman found floating in the Thames. Although the body had been bloated by the water, the injuries to her neck were unmistakable. Two others followed, their bodies dumped unceremoniously in places much like this one. And now another dead body, another victim. Although not all bodies had been found immediately, a pattern was emerging. The time between deaths was decreasing, the killing seemingly indiscriminate. There might be more victims, waiting for someone to find them, to acknowledge them.

Except for the young woman who had drifted several miles among the currents of the Thames, he hunted within roughly a ten-mile radius. Lavinia had been so close to him yesterday. It had only been luck, and the interference of the demon, that had prevented her from coming across this body—or his killer— sooner.

Lavinia felt her anger rising. She was used to the cycles of human death—had to be. Vampires lived much longer lives, and Lavinia had seen generations of humans thrive and wither. Humans, like all creatures, were capable of great cruelty. They sometimes seemed hell-bent on killing each other in droves, or murdered each other in moments of passion. But this was the work of a vampire—a vampire who had abandoned all control. Someone who was indulging in bloodlust, slaying people without any regards for their humanity, only to slake his own thirst. It was the lowest kind of vampire; one who had forsaken the honour of his family and his race, and who was ruled only by desire. If she found him, she would wring his neck herself, and would enjoy doing so.

"This can't be a coincidence, right? That he was killed so close to where the demon appeared," Octavia said.

Lavinia leaned back. She was glad her Sister was here. Octavia's presence always grounded her. Octavia was the eldest of her Sisters, although she hadn't been in the Sisterhood the longest, having come to the role later in life than usual. She carried her experience lightly, and Lavinia always found herself appreciating her insights. "No. At least, I don't think so. I'm not sure Luce is as convinced."

"Fair enough. It's her job to be sceptical. She can't go around making allegations that we've got a rogue vampire and a warlock working together."

Octavia spoke the uneasy realisation that had been growing among them. A drained body, only streets away from a demon appearance. Demons meant warlocks—witches who dabbled with demonic forces. Vampires couldn't manipulate magic. Even at the best of times, vampires and witches could hardly stand each other. And if the vampire had turned rogue, a collaboration seemed even less likely. Why would a vampire and a warlock work together? And to what end? The body of the man only raised more questions. How was he connected to Michelle?

"We should find out who he is, see if Michelle recognises him. Or any of the other victims."

"It's as good a place to start as any," Octavia agreed. "Let's have another look at where the demon emerged."

Lavinia led her back to the alleyway. They worked their way backwards, first studying the ground where Lavinia and the demon had fought, moving back to where Lavinia had first seen it. Not many traces were left. Some splashes of demon blood had eaten away the corner of a dumpster, the corrosive liquid dissolving the plastic rim. Otherwise, they didn't see anything out of place. They walked to the street of Michelle's apartment, but their search there was equally fruitless. Lavinia sent a quick message to Zachary to pick them up again. Octavia stood with her arms crossed, a pensive expression forming on her face.

"Has Vesta heard back from the other families?" she asked.

"Most of them have been in touch. So far everyone is accounted for, and no one has any specific concerns about any offshoots of their lineage. But you know how these things go, no one wants to report their weird second cousin to the Sisterhood. What if they're wrong—or worse, what if they're right, and the family has to bear the shame of having produced a rogue." Lavinia rubbed her face with her hands. "But you're right. The search for the rogue isn't going well. He has been getting more careful, successfully hiding his scent from us. He doesn't seem to be in touch with anyone else, or at least not with anyone who's talking. It seems like we're dealing with an unknown."

"Maybe someone from abroad? Someone not embedded in our society?"

"Could be. It's not a possibility I'm willing to exclude."

"I'll ask Vesta to expand her search and get in touch with the families on the continent. See if they've heard anything."

"Thanks." Lavinia suppressed the urge to sigh. It would not do to sulk. Still, it was frustrating that they had made so little progress. That *she* had made so little progress. Of course, it wasn't her fault that the rogue was attacking people, and it wasn't her fault that humans died by his hand. The blame lay squarely on his shoulders. Regardless, it was difficult to deal with the anger and frustration at yet another life snuffed out before its time. The humans couldn't be relied on to catch the rogue—that was the vampires' responsibility. *Her* responsibility.

"I think we need to talk to Arran. If the rogue is somehow connected to a warlock, we should widen our search," Octavia said.

There was no way around it. If a warlock was involved, the Witch Council should be consulted. But damn it, they certainly didn't make it easy to work with them. "You're right. But I don't like it."

"Me neither," Octavia agreed. "But I don't think we have a choice in the matter. I'll call him."

Chapter Eight

Arran, the vampire liaison for the Witch Council of the British Isles, sent Octavia some coordinates. They led to a dirt track in a rural area in the Surrey Hills, an hour's drive south of London. While Octavia had set up the meeting, Lavinia had called in an anonymous tip to the London Metropolitan Police, letting them know the location of the dead man. They would contact his next of kin and would use their own networks to try to find the killer. If they made any headway, the Sisterhood would hear soon enough. They had informants in most places, including in the police. Money could make even the most reticent human talk, if necessary.

"We're getting close," Zachary said. They drove through open countryside, surrounded by startlingly green fields lined with clusters of trees and shrubbery. The GPS indicated that they were almost at the specified location. No buildings or other cars were in sight.

"Why can't they just meet in a café like normal people?" Octavia said wistfully. "I could go for a coffee. Maybe a piece of cake…"

"We just had lunch," Lavinia said.

"Don't tell me you would rather meet in the middle of a

muddy field with a bunch of witches that speak in riddles, instead of having a triple espresso and some chocolate cake."

Despite the quick lunch of store-bought wraps they had eaten standing beside the car, Lavinia's stomach growled. "Stop it."

Octavia flashed a quick smile, but turned serious again when Zachary stopped the car. "This is it," he said. The view had hardly changed. The car had come to a standstill on a road that ran alongside a field. A lone tree stood along the tall grass, swaying slightly in the breeze.

"No one's here yet," Lavinia said. She looked at the time. Four o'clock. Exactly as in Arran's message.

"They'll be here," Octavia answered.

"I'll wait for you," Zachary said as the Sisters got out. For a moment, Lavinia surveyed the surroundings. Hills rose around them, the road lying in a valley of sorts. The sky was cloudy, hiding the sun. Still, being so out in the open was draining, and neither she nor Octavia would be able to rely much on their strength. Then again, strength was often useless against the tricks of witchcraft, so perhaps it didn't matter much. She tasted the air and could tell that Octavia was doing the same beside her. Traces of various animals, the sharp but faded scent of a car running on diesel that had passed down here a couple of hours ago. The grass, of course, and the ever-present sting of pollution edging every other scent. No humans nearby—no people whatsoever.

"What do we do? Just wait here?" Octavia asked. Lavinia weighed their options, assessing the land around them.

"The tree," she said finally. It looked exactly like the kind of thing witches liked—old, gnarly, its branches jutting into the sky like arms.

Octavia fell into step behind her, her movements just a tad too sharp to seem relaxed. Lavinia shared the feeling. It was always unnerving to meet witches, even if they were ostensibly their allies.

They climbed the hill, the raised position revealing more of the surrounding countryside. It was quite beautiful, in a way, but this was not the time to enjoy it. Before they could reach the top crowned by the old tree, something *shifted*.

One moment, there had been nothing. Just the rustle of the wind among the tree's leaves and the song of a lonely bird twittering in a high branch, and the next, they were there. Three figures, cloaked in shadows despite the late afternoon light, appeared without a sound. Not a single branch stirred. It was as if they had risen from the ground, spat out by the earth among the roots of the ancient oak. *Witchcraft*. The small hairs on the back of Lavinia's neck rose. They were showing off, flaunting their powers.

She kept her facial features immobile, not allowing herself to show surprise. Whatever happened, they would not reveal any weakness. The witches would exploit it, experts as they were in psychological warfare, leveraging the pressure until the person cracked. They could populate dreams with your worst nightmares, forcing you to relive them again and again. Lavinia had seen the results of a witch's retribution a century ago. She had resolved there and then to never anger a witch.

The person in the middle spoke, the shadows slowly dissolving into the air as wisps of smoke. They revealed Arran, all six feet of him, broad-shouldered and bearded. He was only in his early twenties. Arran was very young to be on the Council which usually valued experience over ambition, which was probably why he got stuck with the unappealing role of vampire liaison.

"Sword Sister Lavinia of Coriovallum, fourth of her name, and Sword Sister Octavia of Lugdunum, seventh of her name."

"Arran," Lavinia nodded. She didn't know his last name or family designation. Witches seemed to purposefully cultivate an air of mystery.

He did not introduce the two others. The one on the right, a middle-aged woman with black hair streaked with grey, looked familiar. The other, an older man with weathered skin, she had never seen before. Like all witches, they reeked of magic. Not just of the ingredients and tools they used for their craft, but magic itself: the smell of raw power, that indefinable potential that the witches somehow managed to manipulate and harness. Lavinia always thought it smelled a little bit like a warm spice, like cinnamon or maybe cardamom, but she'd never shared that thought with anyone—least of all the witches themselves.

"The Sisterhood appreciates you meeting us at such short notice," Lavinia started. Internally, she lamented that Vesta was hours away. This kind of thing was her Sister's strength. Lavinia was a soldier, not a diplomat. "We have reason to believe a rogue vampire and a warlock are killing humans in close proximity. It's possible they're working together."

The woman scoffed. In her loose-fitting black clothing, she reminded Lavinia of a crow. Arran tried to manage his expression, but wasn't entirely able to suppress his scepticism either. The man on his other side didn't make such an attempt at all. He stared at the vampires in barely concealed contempt.

"What evidence do you have of this?" Arran said.

Lavinia quickly outlined the events of last night, minimising Michelle's role as much as she could, and added the insights from today's discovery to hopefully divert their attention. She wished she could keep Michelle out of the conversation entirely. For some reason, she felt rather protective of her.

Arran, though, immediately latched onto the lack of detail. "And the demon's quarry? Where is she?"

"Safe," Lavinia said through clenched teeth.

"Under your protection, then." He exchanged a wordless glance with the woman at his side. "We will need to examine her."

"No," Lavinia growled.

Arran raised an eyebrow. "There is no need to get territorial."

Lavinia swallowed, suppressing the sudden urge to bare her fangs. "Apologies. Still no."

"Then I should perhaps remind you that the terms of our treaty clearly state that neither side will restrict access to a member of their own party, regardless of circumstances."

Lavinia frowned and said, "But she's not a witch."

"And how sure are you of that?"

"Very." It was impossible that Michelle was a witch. Her shock at the demon's appearance was genuine. Lavinia had been able to smell her fear. She hadn't known what a demon was, and had shown genuine surprise and confusion. There was no way Lavinia could have been fooled.

"What do you want with her anyway?" Octavia said.

A quiet struggle reigned among the witches. Eventually Arran won out, apparently having wrestled permission to share information from the others. "We too have a dissenter among ourselves," he admitted. *Dissenter* was a polite word for what he meant. *Warlock.*

"How long have you known?" Lavinia asked.

"Two months."

"Were you going to share this information with us at some point?"

"No," he said, straightforwardly. "We police our own, as do you."

"Would have been nice to know a witch had broken free from the Council's control," Octavia said, her tone venomous. Octavia had no patience for the Witch Council's politics. Lavinia shared her frustrations. They had barely made any progress in the last couple of weeks. If they'd known a warlock was on the loose as well... Perhaps they would have made more headway in finding the outlaws, and Michelle could have been spared a traumatic encounter with a demon.

"How long have you known about your rogue vampire?" Arran countered.

Touché. Lavinia considered. "Perhaps you agree it is in both of our interests to share information from now on."

"If the Council wills it," Arran said, inclining his head. It was the closest to agreement they'd come, so Lavinia moved on.

The faster they were able to find the warlock—and the rogue vampire—the sooner she would be certain Michelle was safe. For now, that meant working with the witches. They weren't untrustworthy, exactly. The issue was merely that they always had their own agenda, and one could never be sure what it actually was. But for now, collaboration was their best option. "What is the war—*dissenter's* pattern? What is their motivation?" she asked.

"Bloodwaster," the man beside Arran muttered to himself, and for a moment Lavinia felt her hackles rise. She didn't like the witches either, but she would not be insulted.

Then Arran clarified, "He seeks out those with the Mark, and kills them."

The Mark of the Fates. According to witches, they were a chosen people, marked for magic at birth. Lavinia didn't particularly know or care whether this was true or not. The only thing that mattered was that the witches believed it—and that the murderer who had targeted Michelle did as well. "And that's why you think the human in our keeping is a witch. Because he tried to kill her."

Arran nodded. Lavinia mulled over this information. She was certain Michelle wasn't a practising witch. She wouldn't have been ignorant of the Other World, and would have known to invoke the help of her coven, even if she hadn't been powerful enough to handle the demon by herself. But could she be marked somehow, have some latent ability that just had never been cultivated? Lavinia didn't know. It had seemed impossible only moments ago, but Arran's certainty planted the seeds of doubt in her mind. Perhaps he and the other council members were mistaken. Perhaps the killer himself was mistaken and had somehow mixed up Michelle with his real target. Innocent bystanders sometimes got hurt. When the killing started, rogues found that it was difficult to stop. Perhaps it was the same for warlocks and the demons who did their bidding.

"What else can you tell us about him?" Octavia asked.

"We are not currently willing to share our suspicions," Arran said smoothly.

"So you have an idea of who it might be?"

Silence met Octavia's question. Either they knew exactly who the warlock was, and they didn't want to share. Or, quite likely, they didn't know at all, and didn't want to admit to their ignorance. Whichever it was, the Council would wish to find the warlock first. They would have their own punishment in mind.

"Do you know where he is? This person you suspect?" Octavia pressed, but Arran shook his head.

"The raven will feast," the black-clad woman beside Arran added darkly.

Lavinia had no idea what that meant, but it was undoubtedly a threat. Witches had means of locating people who didn't want to be found. Then again, a skilled warlock would know what those means were and might know ways of counteracting them.

"Do you have any idea why the warlock might be working together with a vampire? Why they might kill together?" Octavia asked.

"No," Arran said. "We had been certain the warlock was working alone. In no small part because rogue vampires aren't known for their capacity for reasoning." He looked back and forth between Lavinia and Octavia. "No offense."

Lavinia gestured that none was taken. He wasn't wrong. Rogues were in the grip of bloodfever, having reverted completely to an animalistic version of themselves. Many of them lost all capacity for higher reasoning, acting purely on instinct. Many would kill their own kin, unable to recognise them as anything but obstacles standing in the way of their desires.

"We are willing to share information on the warlock's previous victims. The Council is amenable to extending a hand to the Sisterhood in order to restore the balance of power," Arran said.

"The Sisterhood thanks the Council," Lavinia said, but Octavia immediately followed with her own remark.

"And how will you do that? Will we have to dig it up like treasure? Postal dove? Magical sparks in the night sky?"

Arran gave her a stare that could wither a flower on its vine. "Email," he said drily.

"Thank you," Lavinia said again, hoping to move past the awkward silence that now reigned. "We will do the same." They had collated a file of increasing length on the rogue's victims. She would have to add the information on the murdered man in the alley later tonight before passing it on to the witches.

"One last thing," Arran added. "We will access the human, one way or another. If she is one of us, she *will* be brought into the fold."

Lavinia didn't reply. She turned around and marched towards Zachary and the car, not waiting to see whether Octavia followed or not, nor bothering to see what magic trick the witches would conjure for their grand exit. *Over her dead body.* Michelle wasn't going anywhere.

Chapter Nine

It was a quiet drive back to Thornblood. Lavinia wasn't in a chatty mood, and Octavia and Zachary followed her lead. Night had fallen by the time they got back, and Lavinia was glad for the comforting darkness. Being outside in daylight was bearable, but she never felt as alive as she did at night. They entered through the back door, Lavinia and Octavia going straight to Luce's ground-floor study. Even as she opened the door, she could smell Michelle's scent, intermingled with that of her Sister's. A tightness that she had carried within her all day relaxed. Michelle was safe. Of course she was—Thornblood was one of the safest places anyone could be. Why was she anxious about this?

Luce was in her office, as expected. She sat at her wooden monstrosity of a desk, bent over a stack of documents. Being the leader of the Sisterhood meant she carried huge responsibilities. While Vesta took on as many of the social demands from Luce's shoulders as she could, the main vampire families would continuously attempt to gain Luce's ear. Officially, the Sisterhood were the enforcers of law for all vampirekind in Britain. Unofficially, the Sisterhood had a significant influence on various aspects of inter-family politics and worked closely with the Justices. If there was anything civilian vampires loved to do, it was constantly vying with each other for scraps of power to hold over other families.

Lavinia didn't understand any of it, and didn't care for any of it. All she cared about was that everything stayed as it should be: that the balance between vampires and humans and all other supernaturals was sustained. That order reigned, and those who broke their laws were brought to justice and punished. What that looked like wasn't any of her business, really. She just found the murderer or saved the damsel. Perhaps punched some rogues or stabbed some demons along the way. It was a simple life, in a way. And that was exactly how she liked it.

She let Octavia take point at reporting their progress to Lucretia. Luce listened without interrupting and, when Octavia finished, said, "Sounds like this case is more complex than we thought. I am going to give you more resources to resolve this as quickly as possible. There is potential here for a scandal if the collaboration with the Witch Council goes awry, and an increased risk of revelation if the murders continue. We also don't need any more bad press for the rumour mill at the moment." She sighed.

There was a constant risk that humans would find out about vampires on a large scale. A handful of humans were not a problem—they were easily controlled and contained, and very few others would believe their stories. But any large-scale attention could easily slip out of their grasp, and should be avoided at all costs. Additionally, there were always those civilian vampires who thought the Sisterhood's methods were barbaric or outdated. Lavinia would invite every single one of them to try to argue with a blood-fevered rogue or scold a demon. The Sisterhood bore arms for a reason.

"I will pull in Vesta to help with the reputational damage control, and Proserpina for general support," Luce continued. "I want this handled quickly and quietly, if possible."

Lavinia nodded her agreement and was ready to leave when

Luce added, "Lavinia, can I speak to you for a moment?" Octavia gave Lavinia an inscrutable look and closed the door softly behind her.

"Sister?" Lavinia asked. What did Luce want to talk to her about that they couldn't discuss in front of Octavia? There were no secrets in their house. They lived and worked too closely for anything to stay hidden for long.

"The human," Luce started. "The witches want to assess her?"

"Yes. They think she might be marked by the Fates." She didn't say, *might be a witch.*

"And you refused? Why?"

Lavinia felt her face burn under Luce's intent gaze. "She's human. She was clearly completely unaware of the existence of demons."

"If that is so, there is no harm in them assessing her."

Lavinia opened her mouth to argue, then closed it again. She didn't know how to explain that the thought of Michelle being poked and prodded by a bunch of witches horrified her. That she felt an intense urge to keep her safe, keep her away from anyone who could pose a threat. She didn't trust the witches, didn't trust them to not manipulate the truth in some way that suited them. But to Luce, of course, Michelle's safety was merely a formality. A box to be ticked—*Human was not eaten by demon*, check—and Michelle could be released back into her life. But Lavinia felt a responsibility towards Michelle—perhaps misplaced, she admitted to herself. She felt a connection to Michelle that she could not explain.

"You will allow them access. You may set some terms, meet them in a place that you've secured, even bring some backup, but you will not stand in their way. Understood?" Luce said. Lavinia understood perfectly. This was an order, and she would not disobey. Could not disobey.

"Understood."

"Thank you, Sister." It was a dismissal, and Lavinia was glad to be released. The anxiety in her stomach that had only just loosened now returned.

While her mind was elsewhere, her feet propelled her forwards, honing in on the person at the forefront of her thoughts. She found Michelle in the library, leafing through an old tome. Lavinia drank in the sight of her. The light from the overhead lamps bathed her pale skin in a golden glow. Her mahogany hair cascaded past her shoulders, a couple of tendrils escaping from the lock tucked behind her ear. She wore a woollen green jumper that hugged her curves in comfort. The smallest of frowns creased the corners of her eyes as she squinted at the book in her hands. Michelle hadn't heard her steps and only looked up when she spotted movement from the corner of her vision. Lavinia had the small pleasure of seeing her unguarded response. Michelle's eyes, their irises a deep amber in the artificial light, lit up when she saw it was Lavinia, and smiled. Lavinia found herself enthralled by the splendour of that smile.

"Some of these books are ancient," Michelle said in awe, holding up the book. Lavinia moved closer and read the title page over her shoulder. *On the Origin of Species by Means of Natural Selection*, printed 1860. Her hair smelled like the shampoo Mrs. Frost left in all the guest bathrooms.

"This one must be worth loads," she continued.

"Probably," Lavinia said. "The library is Octavia's project. She bought most of them. I'm not much of a reader." She couldn't remember the last book she'd read. Proserpina had convinced her to read *Orlando* by Virginia Woolf when it came out, proclaiming it a masterpiece. That was a while ago, wasn't it?

"Of course," Michelle said solemnly. "You're too busy fighting off demons to read books."

Lavinia smiled. "Exactly. Too busy saving damsels in distress."

"My hero," Michelle said, without a trace of sarcasm. Her face turned serious. "I talked to Quintia earlier."

Oh stars. "I hope she behaved." Quinn wasn't known for her subtlety, and could sometimes act quite boorish. If she had somehow hurt Michelle's feelings...

"She was great." That was a relief, at least. She must have been on her best behaviour for some reason. "But she said that you're all... vampires." Michelle said the word softly, like a secret.

Just like that, the moment of unveiling had come. Lavinia was surprised that Quintia told Michelle. Usually she was keen on keeping their identity a secret. Lavinia's first impulse, too, had been to hide what she was. To let Michelle think that she was just a stranger—a human stranger—at the right place at the right time.

She had to admit that there had been a small fear, too. Lavinia wasn't sure she could handle Michelle's outright rejection or horror. It had been naïve of her to think that she could somehow thread the needle of keeping Michelle here, with her Sisters, while also appearing human. Lavinia had known, deep down, that bringing her here would reveal her true nature to Michelle. So she simply said, "We are. Most of us, at least. Zachary isn't."

Michelle looked down at the book cradled in her hands, but her eyes weren't focused on the text. Tension ran through Lavinia's shoulders, waiting for Michelle's response. Finally, she said, "I wish *you'd* told me."

"Oh." Was that actual hurt on Michelle's face? A stab of guilt shot through her heart. "I'm sorry. You'd already had enough shocks for one night. I didn't want to make it any worse."

"It's okay," Michelle said softly. "I think I just wish I'd known."

Lavinia shook her head. "You're right, I should have told you." At the very least, Lavinia should have been the one to tell her. This morning, perhaps, before she'd left for London. "It's no real excuse, but I don't have much experience with handling this type of situation."

"You've never told anyone you're a vampire before?"

Lavinia smiled, and she was glad to see a lightening in Michelle's countenance too. She didn't like seeing her sad—much less so if she'd been the cause of it. "Not recently. It never really comes up."

"But you do get out, right? Like, go into town and stuff."

"Quite often. But then again, there is no need to tell the sales clerk, is there?"

"True." Michelle closed *On the Origin of Species* and slid it back onto the shelf, placed snugly between two other ancient volumes. "I guess I never really thought much about it either. That there might be vampires just strutting around."

"I don't strut."

"Yes you do," Michelle said with a furtive smile. She turned more fully towards Lavinia. "Is there anything else I should know? Any more revelations?"

Lavinia's thoughts hurtled back to the meeting today with Arran and his acquaintances. At their insinuation that Michelle was a witch—or at least, had the potential to be one. That she had been targeted because of some latent power. Yet another piece of information that would slowly tear her away from the life of ignorance of the Other World she'd led so far. How much could she learn about the others that shared the earth with humans before she would no longer be able to fit in with her own kind?

Lavinia had heard stories of humans, particularly ones who hadn't grown up with the knowledge like familiars did, that couldn't handle it. Some would simply ignore anything that didn't fit their worldview. In a way, they were the lucky ones. Others started to doubt their sanity, lost their grasp on reality, or became outcasts for their insistence on telling their friends and family about vampires and witches and demons. That couldn't happen to Michelle—Lavinia wouldn't let it.

But then, Luce had ordered the witches to be allowed to test her. And just now, she had been hurt that Lavinia had kept something from her. Not with any ill intent, of course, as she hadn't really put much thought in it. Lavinia's job was to protect, but she hadn't considered how Michelle would experience that. Besides, even if she lied now, if she left her in the dark about the witches, it would only be a temporary respite. It wouldn't be long before the witches renewed their request, and Luce would grant it. It would be best, then, to rip off the Band-Aid, as the humans so charmingly put it.

"Well," Lavinia started.

"Should I sit down for this? I should sit down for this, shouldn't I?" Michelle sat heavily into the sumptuously upholstered armchair that faced the fireplace. Lavinia followed but found that she couldn't sit, restlessness spreading through her limbs. Instead, she clasped her hands behind her back, and paced back and forth along the length of the rug that delineated the seating area.

"Is it bad?" Michelle asked after watching Lavinia pace for a while.

"No, no," Lavinia said, intending the words to be comforting, but clearly failing in their intent.

"Now you're scaring me. Just tell me, please?"

Where to begin? "You should know that there are humans with... with a certain potential." Stars, she was botching this. "Some humans are born with what is called a Mark of the Fates. It means they can manipulate currents that are all around us." She gestured vaguely, then resumed her pacing.

"So it's like... magic? Is that what you mean?"

"Yes! They are witches. And unlike vampires, who are always only ever born to other vampires, any human can be touched by the Fates, regardless of their parentage. While it often does run in certain bloodlines, it doesn't have to, making it rather unpredictable at times."

"Right."

"And witches are governed by their own Council. They wish

to examine you, to find out whether you are marked by the Fates."

"Wait, what? They think I'm a witch? Why would they think that?" The incredulous outrage on Michelle's face softened something within Lavinia. But that didn't make the rest of what she had to tell her any easier.

"Because the warlock that set a demon loose on you was targeting witches. Only witches."

Michelle leaned back into the armchair. "Then he must have made some sort of mistake."

"I hope so," Lavinia said softly, mostly to herself.

"And they want to... test me or something."

"Yes."

"Will it hurt?"

Lavinia frowned. "I don't think so. I have never been present at one of their trials." Noting Michelle's alarm, she added, "They won't harm you. They know you're under our protection."

Michelle took a deep breath. "Good. Will you be there?"

Lavinia's heart jumped a little in her chest. "Of course." She couldn't imagine letting Michelle face a witch trial by herself regardless—but it felt wonderful to be needed. To be asked. To be wanted.

"I'm glad," Michelle said, and tucked her legs onto the seat. "I'm sure it will turn out to be nothing. I'm just a nurse."

Lavinia wasn't one to cast runes or look for omens, but Michelle's words sent a shiver up her spine. It felt like the words were tempting the gods—and they were vengeful if dared.

"Of course it will be fine," she said. But for the first time since she'd met Michelle, she wasn't so certain.

Chapter Ten

Michelle lay in bed that night, staring at the ceiling. She had opened the blackout shutters, allowing some of the light from the moon and the stars to spill into the room around the curtains. The absolute blackness with the shutters closed had created a claustrophobic darkness that made her nervous. Her muscles ached, protesting every time she shifted, but it was a satisfying ache. It reminded her of her own strength, allowing her to claw back the tiniest bit of control on this weird rollercoaster of a day.

She'd called her mum earlier and had given a rather pathetic attempt at an excuse for why she wouldn't be coming to her house for Sunday dinner this weekend. Mum, shrewd and an inveterate matchmaker, immediately asked, "Do you have a girlfriend? Can I meet her?" Unbidden, Michelle's mind flicked to Lavinia, and her protests sounded half-hearted even to herself. But then again, she could hardly tell her mum, "Actually, I'm currently holed up with a beautiful vampire and her Sisters in a safe house somewhere in the north. And by the way, they think I'm a witch. Funny, huh?"

She could easily imagine her down-to-earth mother immediately dialling the emergency hotline to report her missing, or to request some psychiatric help. If anything, it was probably best that she thought that Michelle had met some woman and had retreated into a love bubble.

She turned again, staring at the unfamiliar contours of the room. Strange, distant noises rose through the walls, the settling of the old house adding to her distraction. Mrs. Frost had made her a lovely dinner of risotto and a garden salad. She'd eaten by herself, apparently very much out of sync with the rhythms of the vampires. Her thoughts burst at the seams with questions about vampires, about witches, about demons, about anything and everything she didn't know. She ran her hands through her hair, untangling some strands. She sat up, looked at her phone. Half past four in the morning. She let herself fall back, counted some of her breaths, then rotated through some other relaxation techniques.

Nothing was working. Her eyes sprang open again as if of their own accord. Her body was tired, her mind exhausted, but rest wasn't forthcoming. Groaning and fighting sore muscles, she rose from the bed, her bare feet finding the soft carpet. She pulled on a pair of old leggings and pulled her jumper on over the T-shirt she'd worn to bed. She opened the door into the dark corridor. Nothing moved. No voices rose from downstairs to act as a beacon for her to hone in on.

She thought back to her first night here, and Lavinia's explanation of the layout of the house. She'd said her room was on the same floor, but in the other wing. Michelle padded to the grand staircase. She squinted at the light spilling from the chandelier on the ceiling as she passed into an identical but mirrored corridor on the other side. Unsurprisingly, a row of doors met her, most of them closed. Lucretia's warning about locked doors echoed in her mind. For a moment she cursed herself for her impulsive quest for company, then pressed on.

She wasn't sure what she was looking for—it wasn't like they had conveniently put little name tags on the doors. She continued, starting to feel rather silly. What was she doing, creeping around this house full of vampires in the middle of the night? She should just go back to her bedroom, try to fall asleep again. Surely, she'd succeed at some point.

Still, her feet carried her forward, following the bend of the corridor. Darkness encroached, and she wished she'd brought her phone to use as a torch. A click—a door opening? A shadow moved towards her.

"Ack!" Michelle jumped backwards, the image of a demon looming in her mind.

"Michelle?" A deep, smooth voice. Lavinia's voice. Of course. Lavinia stood in the door opening of what Michelle assumed was her room.

Michelle willed her heartbeat to slow, but her whole body had tensed for a fight. That should teach her not to skulk around like a thief in the night.

"Did you need something?" Lavinia asked. Her hand moved along the wall, and, with a soft click, illumination sprang to life around them. Lavinia looked as neat as always, her ponytail slicked back and hanging straight down between her shoulder blades. There were no marks of tiredness on her face whatsoever. Perhaps for vampires, half past four in the morning felt like one in the afternoon did for humans.

"Well," Michelle said. Why did she suddenly feel bashful? "I couldn't sleep. So I thought I'd come and see what you were up to." It sounded ridiculous when she said it out loud, and she immediately wished she could take it all back, retrace her footsteps, and just hide in the bedroom. Lavinia had to think she was pathetic—she surely had more important things to do than try to assuage her insomnia.

"I was meditating," Lavinia said. "I find it can provide some clarity sometimes."

"Oh," Michelle said. It wasn't hard to picture Lavinia sitting in perfect stillness for hours; there was something incredibly self-contained about her. Had she interrupted her? There was no trace of irritation on Lavinia's face.

"What do you usually do when you can't sleep?" Lavinia asked.

Well, she usually dropped off the moment her head hit the pillow. Being on her feet all day at work was exhausting, and dealing with people doubly so. "I don't know actually. It's never really been an issue before," she said honestly.

Lavinia contemplated that. It was odd how seriously she took everything. Warring emotions swirled within Michelle—on one hand, some embarrassment for making a big deal out of this. On the other, growing appreciation of Lavinia's kindness.

"Maybe I can watch some TV? There isn't one in my room, and I haven't seen one downstairs yet either..." Her voice trailed off. Maybe vampires just didn't watch TV? It was hard to picture them all relaxing. They always seemed to be either preparing to go somewhere or having mysterious meetings behind the closed doors of Lucretia's study. For a moment, Michelle pictured the warrior Sisters crocheting together or visiting a theme park, and she suppressed a smile.

"Of course you can. Let me show you the TV room." Lavinia immediately burst into action, clearly relieved to have something to do. She led Michelle deeper down the corridor. "There are actually two, but we rarely use the one on the second floor." She opened a door on the left-hand side and revealed a cosy room with a large sofa curling around two sides of the room, angled towards what looked like a very expensive and very large TV. Lavinia stepped inside and turned on a table lamp that cast a warm yellow glow across the soft fabrics that covered the room.

"Have a seat," Lavinia said, as she grabbed the remote control from the coffee table. Michelle planted herself on the sofa, tucking her bare feet underneath her. Before she could say anything, Lavinia had quietly placed a grey throw blanket beside her. Gratefully and feeling somewhat like a princess, Michelle spread the throw across her legs.

"Would you like anything to eat or drink?" Lavinia asked.

Would it be too much to ask for more? But then, Lavinia gave no indication of being annoyed or keen to get back to her meditation. "Maybe a cup of tea?" Michelle said. "Mint if you have it—anything without caffeine."

"Sure, I'll go get it for you." She handed over the remote. "There should be some of those digital subscription services on there. If you can't find anything you like, though, we also have a video and DVD library upstairs."

"I'll have a look, thank you," Michelle said. Lavinia slipped back into the hallway, and Michelle turned on the TV. Lavinia's words had been quite the understatement. The home menu showed all of the well-known subscriptions, and many she didn't recognise, some of them in foreign languages. If she couldn't find anything in here to watch, then she didn't know where she would. Although the idea of a videotape library did sound fun.

She navigated towards a familiar logo and found *Harrogate Homicides*. She hadn't watched the latest episode yet; she had planned to, when she was walking home only a day ago. It suddenly felt like huge swathes of time had passed since then. There was an insurmountable rift between the Michelle she had been before, and the Michelle who carried all of this knowledge of demons and vampires within her.

Lavinia returned with Michelle's tea, the liquid releasing steam with the refreshing scent of mint. Someone had placed a little biscuit next to the porcelain cup lined with delicate blue flowers. Mrs. Frost? Or had Lavinia done that herself?

"Found anything you like?" Lavinia asked. She put the cup and saucer onto the dark wood coffee table beside Michelle. Its polished surface gleamed in the lamplight. Doubtless another priceless antique. It was nothing like the glorified plywood stool

Michelle had set beside her narrow and saggy sofa at home.

"I did. It's called *Harrogate Homicides*. I love this show."

"Sounds very cheerful for a sleepless night, some nice, light murder," Lavinia said with amusement.

"It's a cosy mystery." Lavinia frowned, clearly unfamiliar, so Michelle elaborated. "Sure, there is a murder, but it's really fun. They always get killed in a ridiculous way, like being hit by a wheel of cheese during some summer fair or something. There are always silly village politics, and of course, the murderer is caught at the end of the episode." Lavinia didn't look convinced. "You should try it."

Before she could second-guess herself, or even really consider what she was asking exactly, she added, "Would you like to watch it with me?" Lavinia hovered between the door and the sofa; she hadn't brought a drink or biscuit for herself. All signs pointed to her not wanting to stay. But a sudden yearning overtook Michelle. She wanted to get to know Lavinia—to find the woman underneath the benign protective kindness she had shown her so far. She had been like a knight in shining armour, popping into her life at a moment of danger. Lavinia was a steadying presence—someone Michelle thought she could depend on, even if she'd only met her so recently. But beyond that, who was she? What were her hopes and dreams, her fears? Admittedly, part of Michelle was attracted by the novelty of her being a vampire, but it was more than that. She wanted to peek behind the calm exterior. Lavinia had seen her be so vulnerable, had already seen her cry. She wondered what Lavinia was like when *she* became undone.

She watched expectantly, therefore, for Lavinia to answer. Would she maintain her respectable distance, or would she soften, ever so slightly?

"You would like me to join?" Lavinia asked. She immediately cut to the quick, not hiding behind a sham polite refusal.

If Lavinia could be straightforward, so could Michelle. "Yes," she answered simply. "I would like your company." Her heartbeat rose as Lavinia moved closer, the sofa cushion dipping as she sat down next to her. Lavinia leaned back, one leg crossed over the other at the ankle. Michelle started the episode of *Harrogate Homicides*, relaxing into the familiar intro sequence. From the corner of her eyes, she could see the rising and falling of Lavinia's breath despite her stillness. She found herself almost painfully aware of her presence, making it impossible to concentrate fully on the show.

As the intrepid detective traced the events leading up to the victim's discovery at a children's Easter egg hunt, Michelle peeked at Lavinia under the cover of taking a sip from her tea. Lavinia had relaxed further into the cushions. It was impossible to lounge on a big squishy sofa gracefully, but she almost managed. Her left hand had crept up into her right sleeve, where she was massaging a scar on her wrist absentmindedly. Michelle wondered whether it still pained her—wondered whether she had more scars beyond the ones visible. Wondered who had tended to her wounds, or whether she'd had to face the recovery alone. Not wanting to stare or draw attention to herself, she turned back to the detective's interrogation of the elderly greengrocer whose answers weren't quite lining up.

"He's clearly lying," Lavinia commented as the detective and her right-hand man made their way back to the police station. "Did he commit the murder?"

"I don't know. I haven't seen this one before."

"Aren't you the expert?" Lavinia said slyly, and Michelle laughed.

"Fine. My theory is that it's the grieving widow. She didn't look all that heartbroken."

"Perhaps it was the detective herself."

"It was definitely *not* the detective—that's a completely

different kind of show."

Lavinia shrugged, unperturbed. "It could happen."

"Absolutely not," Michelle said. "You're excellent with a sword, but clearly you know nothing about TV."

Lavinia smiled. "True. I never watch any. I guess you will have to teach me."

Michelle smiled back, settling deeper underneath the throw blanket. Despite the strand of tension running through her—a pleasant thrum, feeding on her attraction to Lavinia—there was also comfort in talking to her, being with her. It was so easy to sit here with her and watch TV. It was almost like they were just two women, spending time together. No supernatural creatures. Just them and the simple pleasure of sharing their company.

The weight of the day settled within her. The tiredness that suffused her limbs dragged at her, pulling her towards sleep. Before the murderer was apprehended, before law and order were restored to Harrogate, Michelle's eyes closed, and sleep claimed her.

Chapter Eleven

Lavinia scrolled through the evidence Arran had sent, willing herself to focus on the list of names, locations, and brief background descriptions the witches had compiled. Over and over, her thoughts drifted back to last night. To how beautiful Michelle had looked, the soft glow drifting across her cheek as she slept. How her heartbeat had slowed, and how Lavinia's had matched hers in response, beating in tandem. Lavinia had sat there motionless for three hours, drinking in every dreamy twitch, realising that if Michelle woke up to find Lavinia staring at her, she might have found this alarming, while simultaneously finding herself incapable of moving and risking waking her.

Michelle had needed, no, *deserved* the rest. And Lavinia's obvious interest in the human, well, that was a problem for the future. There was no harm in spending time with her. Lavinia couldn't remember the last time she'd sat down and watched a television show. It had been years, probably. She was usually too busy, only taking the briefest of moments away from Sisterhood business on the holy days or when her Sisters forced her. She had never been drawn to flashy storytelling and melodramatic characters. But watching TV with Michelle, well, she found she actually enjoyed it.

The diffuse afternoon light filtering into the study had already shifted significantly since she had sat down. Time was slipping through her fingers like water. Lavinia had been comparing the locations where the warlock's victims were found with those of the rogue vampire's. A pattern was emerging. It wasn't a perfect match, but three victims of the warlock had been killed close to where the rogue had drained a human. The demon's attack on Michelle made a fourth connection. Too many to be a coincidence.

For some reason, the rogue and the warlock killed together—perhaps not always, but often. Try as she might, she had found no obvious links between the warlock's victims and those of the rogue, except for their locations. Four times already, they had hunted as a pair. But why? Why did they kill one each? What was the point? Rogues usually didn't need a motive, as they were consumed with an uncontrollable bloodlust and surrounded by humans who could slake their thirst. A rogue working together with a warlock...

She leaned back. Her fangs itched, an ache that only one thing could resolve. She had to feed, and soon. It had been too long, again. Some vampires revelled in their blood hunger, chasing the high of slaking their thirst. Lavinia had always found it a chore. Blood was sustenance, just like food was. It was unfortunate that pre-packaged blood didn't really work. Not only did the preservatives ruin the taste, it only gave the barest of boosts, never fully sating the hunger. A donor was necessary. She'd have to let Mrs. Frost know to arrange one for her.

Unbidden, Michelle rose in her mind's eye. The way her blood flowed through her veins; the little throb at the base of her neck. How satisfying it would be to sink her fangs into her soft skin, to taste her. To feel her sweet blood spurting into her mouth.

She swallowed, returning to Arran's information. The warlock had killed five people—two of whom Lavinia hadn't been able to conclusively match with the rogue's prey. All of the warlock's victims had been attacked by demons—all had their souls removed. This little bit of information was added in a footnote.

Lavinia didn't know what she found more disturbing: that demons could remove souls, or that witches were somehow able to tell when they had.

The five victims spanned various demographics and didn't have any obvious commonalities, besides the fact that they were all adults. For whatever reason, the warlock drew the line at killing minors. The youngest victim was nineteen, a student who was found inside his room in a shared house. None of the victims seemed to know each other; at least, there was no overlap in place of work or friend networks on social media. If the witches had an idea of how the warlock was choosing his victims, they hadn't deigned to share. She'd have to ask the witches for more information. Was there a distance limit on a demon summoning? Would the warlock need to be within a couple of blocks away to target someone, or would they be able to send a demon across London?

Crucially, though, how did Michelle fit into all of this?

As much as she hated to admit it, there was only one way forward. She wanted to shield Michelle from as much of this as possible. Michelle had been distressed on that first night they met, and that wouldn't happen again, not on her watch. But if Michelle could give any information at all that would set Lavinia on the right trail, Michelle would be able to go home.

Lavinia stepped into the corridor. Michelle's scent lingered in the air, but it had faded into a pale ghost of its usual full-bodied bouquet. She wasn't in her room, then. Taking the back staircase to the ground floor, she ran into Lucretia.

"Have you seen Michelle?" Lavinia asked.

"Kitchen."

"Thanks."

Luce stopped and turned. "Any progress?"

"Not yet."

Luce emitted a low humming noise from the back of her throat, half acknowledgement, half irritation. It wasn't anger with Lavinia—if Luce was angry with her, there would be much more than a grunt or two—but having Michelle around put everyone on edge. It had been just them for so long. Although Michelle was only one human, she disrupted their routines. Even Quintia had been on her best behaviour. That surely wouldn't last long. It would be better for everyone involved for Michelle to go back to her own life so they could return to their old ways.

Lavinia walked into the kitchen. Michelle sat at the counter, the spacious modern room making her look small. For a moment, Lavinia was stunned by her beauty. The line of her cheekbones, the way her chin curved, a perfect counterbalance for the hollow of her neck. Her skin glowed in the afternoon sunlight, and it looked oh-so edible. Stars, Lavinia really needed to feed.

Michelle looked up from her plate and tucked a strand of her mahogany hair behind one ear. "Oh, hey," she said, noticing Lavinia. "How are you doing?"

"Fine," Lavinia said, the answer coming automatically. Under Michelle's open gaze, she relented. "Frustrated, actually."

"How come?"

Lavinia leaned against the counter. Michelle popped the last piece of mango into her mouth. Lavinia had to tear her eyes from her lips and focused her gaze on the artwork on the wall behind her. It was some food-related still life in oil. She had never noticed it before. "The information we got from the Witch Council has been useful, but I've reached a dead end."

"Can I help?" Michelle asked, wiping her hands on a cloth napkin.

"Maybe," Lavinia admitted. "Would you mind having a look

at the victims and tell me if any of them seem familiar to you? If there is some sort of connection, we can narrow our search. Even for us, finding two killers among millions of Londoners isn't easy."

"Of course." Michelle hopped off the stool, picked up her plate, and took it to the sink. "Anything I can do to help. I've been thinking about why anyone would want me dead, but I can't think of anything. Why would they want *me*? They're some powerful witch, right?"

Lavinia shrugged. "A competent one at the very least, or the demon would have torn them to shreds the moment it was summoned."

"So why me? I don't know anything about magic at all." Michelle washed the plate with practised motions, shook the last couple of drops off, and wiped it dry with a dishcloth.

"I don't know," Lavinia said truthfully. "Also, you don't have to do that."

"Do what?"

"The dishes."

Michelle put the plate into the cupboard with its fellows. "I don't like being waited on. It's bad enough that Mrs. Frost does all the cooking and cleaning. The very least I could do is tidy up after myself."

"It's your funeral."

Her hand stilled, holding the door of the cupboard. "Why?"

"Mrs. Frost gets very grumpy when anyone messes with her kitchen."

"Mrs. Frost is always grumpy," Michelle countered.

"What was that about me?" Mrs. Frost's husky voice rang from the foyer. The old woman had the hearing of a bat.

"Nothing," Lavinia said, raising an eyebrow at Michelle. "We just love your food."

"You better," Mrs. Frost sniffed, marching into the kitchen.

Then she spotted Michelle, guiltily standing in front of the open cupboard. "What are you doing? Get away from there."

Michelle acquiesced immediately and closed the cupboard as if she'd been caught red-handed. She shuffled from behind the kitchen counter, hovering beside Lavinia.

"Come on," Lavinia said. "I'll show you the pictures."

"Please," Michelle answered, the tension only leeching from her shoulders once they left the kitchen.

"Damn humans. They're even worse than vampires," Mrs. Frost muttered after they'd left the kitchen, too low for Michelle's ears to hear.

Lavinia led Michelle to the large study. It was a sizeable room at the front of the house. Four generous desks lined the walls, allowing the Sisters to collaborate when necessary. Lavinia usually shared with their ninth Sister, but as she was currently on a long-term assignment, Lavinia could simply spread out the papers relating to the warlock/rogue case where she wanted. She laid out a couple of photos across the desk that she had printed out. In his email, Arran had included photos from the crime scenes as well as brightly lit pictures taken from the victims' various social media profiles.

"These are the victims of the warlock," she said. Michelle bent over them, carefully studying them in turn.

"Do you recognise any of them?"

"No," she said, after putting down the last photo. "I don't think I've met any of these people."

Lavinia nodded, not particularly surprised. "Thank you for having a look regardless."

"What about the other photos?"

"Excuse me?"

Michelle pointed to the neatly arranged pile of documents on the corner of the desk. A sticky note sat on top, the words *crime scene photos* scribbled on it.

"Don't mind those," she said.

"I want to help," Michelle insisted. "Show them to me."

"They're gruesome," Lavinia warned. There was no need to expose her to images of what could have happened to her if Lavinia hadn't been at the right place at the right time. Even vampire civilians didn't have the stomach for this kind of thing. Although vampires weren't squeamish about blood, many abhorred severe violence. The handiwork of a demon wasn't easy to look at. Although Lavinia had been a Sister of Twilight for over a century, she still couldn't fully detach herself from the suffering the victims must have experienced in their last moments.

"I can handle it," Michelle said firmly. "Before paediatrics, I did two years in the emergency department. The things I've seen... And those people were right in front of me, flesh and blood. A couple of pictures aren't going to be worse." There was a glint of determination in her eyes.

Silently, Lavinia handed over the second pile. Again, Michelle's gaze roved across the pages, taking in every detail. With the eye of a professional, she glanced beyond the injuries, studying the backgrounds of the photographs. She didn't blanch at the blood, the torn flesh, or the organs that spilled from the bodies. Michelle was a stranger to the hidden world of the supernatural, but now Lavinia started to appreciate that she wasn't a stranger to violence.

Michelle went through all of the photos for a second time but lingered on one page. The victim, a middle-aged man, lay in a pool of his own blood. His jumper had been torn by the demon's claws, which had raked through his skin as if through butter.

"Anything?" Lavinia asked.

"It's nothing," Michelle said, leaning back, placing the page with the others.

"Something caught your attention."

"Well... I don't think it would help with what you're trying to do. It's just the logo on the jumper. It's the logo of the animal shelter where my parents met."

Lavinia leaned across the desk, studying the photograph again. Splattered with blood, the dark green jumper sported an embroidered logo of a dog leaping into the air. No text accompanied it.

"It probably doesn't matter," Michelle continued. "It just stood out to me, that's all."

"It might be nothing," Lavinia agreed. There were bound to be commonalities between the victims that were just the result of coincidence. They all lived in roughly the same area, so their paths might have crossed in a myriad of ways that weren't what tied them together in the warlock's eyes. But still, even the smallest coincidence could set them on the path towards finding the murderer.

"Could you please write down the name? I think it might be worthwhile to have a look at it," Lavinia said, sliding a pen across the desk.

"Sure." Michelle picked up the pen and scribbled a couple of words on a sticky note. "But I'm coming too."

Chapter Twelve

"It's not safe," Lavinia insisted. They'd moved their argument to the foyer, where Quintia leaned against the staircase banister, smirking. At least someone found this all amusing.

"I don't care," Michelle countered.

"I do," Lavinia said.

Michelle took a deep breath to calm herself. "I appreciate that. But it's my choice."

"It isn't."

Michelle had had enough. She had been having this argument with Lavinia on and off for four days now, ever since Lavinia had shown her the photos of the warlock's victims. She'd been lying low for over a week now, letting the vampires take care of her. But it had been days—days of just hanging around their fancy house, eating their food, sleeping in their bed. The scratch on her cheekbone had scabbed over, new skin itching underneath. The initial terror of the attack had faded, and the fear had transmuted into anger.

How *dare* someone try to kill her. To try to end her life, and for what? Because of some arcane supernatural reason, even though she hadn't even known vampires and witches existed? She'd had a couple of days to come to terms with all of this (and if she was honest with herself, she was sure there was more of that to follow), but she knew one thing for certain: she was absolutely sick of staying inside and feeling sorry for herself. Her whole being was *itching* for action, to feel like she was dealing with the problem head-on. She couldn't hide forever, even though that was clearly what Lavinia wanted.

"How are you going to stop me?" Michelle challenged. "Are you going to lock me up, prevent me from leaving?"

Lavinia frowned. "Of course not."

"Then I'm coming. It's just an animal rescue, for God's sake."

"No." God, the vampire was infuriating. How dare she stand there, cool as a cucumber, telling her what she could and couldn't do? She might be gorgeous as hell, but that didn't stop Michelle from wanting to punch her right now.

"Besides, I have been training with Quintia."

"So I've heard."

Michelle clenched her jaw. Lavinia faced her, the clear jade of her eyes as unmoving as stone.

"She's not terrible," Quintia piped up from behind them. "She's weak, of course, but determined." Michelle didn't bother to turn around. This fight was with Lavinia, not her brash Sister.

Lavinia narrowed her eyes. "Show me."

"Are you joking?" Michelle said, incredulous.

"No." There was ice in her voice, a hardness that she had never used with Michelle before. Her heartbeat pounding, Michelle dropped into the position Quintia had shown her, and jabbed with her right fist, aiming at Lavinia's chest. Like Quintia, Lavinia easily deflected the blow, batting the momentum of it aside as easily as Michelle might a child's punch. Michelle stepped forward, not letting herself be discouraged. She wasn't helpless. *Jab.* She could stand up for herself. *Jab.* She was capable, goddamn it, even if she wasn't a supernatural creature blessed with ridiculous strength. *Jab.*

"What do you think that's going to happen? Is an army of demons coming for me while we look at some abandoned dogs?" Michelle's voice rose higher as she went through the series of stances Quintia had taught her.

Lavinia caught the last blow in her hand, cupping Michelle's fist. Michelle was suddenly aware of how close she had gotten. It was hard to draw a full breath as she stared at Lavinia, their bodies almost touching.

A faint flush swept across Lavinia's cheekbones. She wasn't as unflappable as she appeared. "Anything could happen," Lavinia insisted. "We don't know who wants you dead."

"*Exactly.* And if you don't let me help, you might never find out."

Lavinia recoiled as if she had been slapped. She dropped Michelle's hand. "You don't trust me to protect you." Her voice was suddenly quiet, nothing like the immovable wall of will she'd presented so far.

"I do. But you don't trust *me*."

"What? Of course I do."

Michelle pressed on, despite Lavinia's apparent hurt. If they were going to work together, they would have to be equals. She might have needed saving, but Michelle was more than just a damsel, and Lavinia better damn well know it. "You don't. If you trusted me, you would respect me enough to make my own decisions. It's *my* life we're talking about. I can't just sit here. I just can't."

An awkward silence followed. Quintia let out a low whistle. Michelle wasn't sure whether to laugh or cry. A fear gripped her heart. Had she pushed Lavinia too far? All she wanted was to be heard, rather than being bundled off to whatever location Lavinia thought was best for her.

Lavinia's shoulders dropped, deflated. Michelle had won, but the victory didn't taste as sweet as she'd expected. "I only mean to keep you safe," Lavinia said softly. There was an undercurrent to her words that hadn't been there before. A vulnerability. It felt private, precious. It felt like a declaration, but of what, Michelle wasn't sure. Lavinia lifted her hand, moved as if to touch her—Michelle desperately wanted her touch, found herself aching towards the gesture—but the vampire lowered her hand again, the ache unfulfilled.

"Right," Quintia's gruff voice tore through the moment. "We're going then?" She strode over, wrapped her arms around their shoulders and steered them towards the front door.

"You're coming?" Lavinia asked.

"Can't leave you two lovebirds alone. Might miss something good. Besides, I do agree that it's not particularly safe."

"Why didn't you say anything before?" Lavinia said, accusatory. Quintia bundled them out of the house. The late afternoon sunlight dappled the path leading to the car. Some leaves had drifted to the ground, crunching underfoot.

"Didn't seem like my conversation to have," Quintia said briskly. "If the human wants to gamble with her life just because she can't bear to be parted from you, who am I to stop her?" Upon hearing those words, Michelle frowned at Quintia, but the short-haired vampire didn't take any notice.

Lavinia only grunted in response. Michelle tried to read her mood. What was going through her mind right now? She wished they could talk more, in private. It felt like there was something left unsaid between them, causing them to stay in a holding pattern until it could be resolved. But with Quintia here, that would have to wait.

The animal rescue's main building sat on a small fenced-in grassy plot in North London. It was a pretty cheerless place—all twentieth-century concrete, function over form. An apologetically small sign on the fence read "Finchley Animal Rescue" over the silhouette of a leaping dog, the same logo Michelle had seen on the victim's sweatshirt.

It had been difficult to suppress the horror within her when she saw what the demons could do. They'd torn the man apart, rended his flesh. She'd seen plenty of bad injuries, some of them fatal, in the emergency department. Like many nurses, she'd learned to keep her mind on the task, rather than getting caught up in the display of suffering. Still, the photos had been the stuff of nightmares. Lavinia hadn't been wrong to want to protect her from that.

Hopefully, the visit to the rescue wouldn't be eventful. Quintia had told Michelle on the way there with a certain amount of glee that demons only roamed after nightfall, so the tenebris wouldn't be able to make an appearance. But then again, who knew what else a warlock could conjure up? As it stood, Michelle was very glad she had two vampires flanking her.

Quintia's levity had dissipated as they'd reached their destination. Both vampire women effortlessly slid into what Michelle thought of as their warrior mindset. It was easy to forget within the comforts of their own home that they were predators, but out here... Gone was Quintia's smirk, replaced with a coiled watchfulness. Gone was the softness in Lavinia. She looked more like she'd done on the night they'd first met: imposing, intractable. They wore no visible weapons, but Michelle was sure they carried some. Not that they even needed them, particularly. They were stronger and faster than any human she'd ever met.

And here she was, at her own insistence, to play detective trying to find her would-be murderer. This was all a terrible idea, but there was no going back now. Michelle squared her shoulders and pushed open the door into the rescue.

A lone receptionist sat behind a wood-panelled desk. The

bright fluorescent lights buzzed overhead as Michelle approached her. From the corner of her eyes, she saw Quintia wandering towards the couple of shelving units filled with dog toys and rabbit food. Trying to steady her nerves, Michelle greeted the receptionist, an elderly woman in a dark green jumper, her peppered grey hair pulled back into a full ponytail.

"I'm here to have a look at your dogs," Michelle said, putting her sweaty hands into the pockets of her coat to hide their shaking. Mrs. Frost had done an excellent job at washing out Lavinia's blood. She pushed that thought from her mind, feeling like the blood would somehow still stand out against the fabric for the receptionist to see. "We're hoping to adopt one."

Lavinia and Quintia had given her a quick rundown of how to approach their visit. Don't come out of the gate asking questions. Pretend to be a customer, draw the target into conversation. Most people would spill whatever information they had with minimal encouragement—but seem too eager, and you'll arouse suspicion and they'll clam up. It had all sounded very easy while they were in the car, but now Michelle suddenly felt as if she'd never spoken to another human being in her entire life. They must look ridiculously suspicious: three women, co-adopting a single dog? Michelle stood out like a sore thumb between Lavinia and Quintia—they were tall, muscular, and had an effortless grace. They looked like they should star in movies or rule an ancient kingdom, not walk around modern-day London. Meanwhile, she bumbled beside them, just as plain and ordinary as she'd ever been.

"Of course," the old woman said, squinting over the computer screen. "I can take you over to the kennel in a moment. Are you ladies a couple?"

"No, just housemates," Michelle said, a blush creeping in. It was the excuse they'd devised en route. It was true, in a way, which Quintia insisted was the best kind of lie.

"Hmmm," the lady hummed, laboriously moving the mouse for a minute while she completed some arcane forms on the computer. "Have you adopted with us before?"

"Not yet," Lavinia said. Superficially she looked relaxed, but Michelle could tell from the way she held herself that she was ready to jump into action at the drop of a hat. Behind them, a lock quietly clicked back into place. The woman didn't look up. Quintia had used the distraction of their conversation to slide through a door bearing a no-access sign. Michelle would be terrified of running into any of the rescue staff members, but vampires probably had their ways of going about undetected. They probably heard people coming from a mile away with their superior senses.

Meanwhile, Lavinia coaxed the receptionist, Nasim, into talking about her own pet. She leaned across the counter, swiping through dozens of nearly identical photos of a brown poodle.

"This is Bitsy," she said, showing another picture of said Bitsy lying on the sofa, head resting on her paws. "She's such a dear. Here she is chasing her ball. She does so love her ball." More Bitsy followed, and Lavinia and Michelle oohed and aahed wherever seemed appropriate.

After another three rounds or so of anecdotes about the minutiae of Bitsy's likes (sleeping, watching the birds) and dislikes (vacuum cleaner, the postman), Nasim finally remembered herself. "But let's get you two your own sweetheart. We are quite full at the moment, so there is a lot of choice."

Michelle and Lavinia followed Nasim as she came around the counter and led them outside and into the single-storey back building that housed the dogs.

"My father actually used to work here," Michelle said, trying to sound casual.

"Did he, dear? What was his name? Perhaps I know him."

"It was a long time ago. Twenty-eight years. His name was Paul

Warbrick."

Nasim stood still for a moment, collecting her thoughts. Then she narrowed her eyes, studying Michelle. "I remember Paul. You look a little bit like him. Such a shame what happened to him. I always told him, 'Paul, that motorcycle will be the death of you.' And then, well." She pursed her lips. "You must have been awfully young."

"I wasn't born yet when he passed away."

"You poor sweetheart. Such a shame. He was a lovely man. Wonderful with the dogs, just wonderful. There wasn't a dog he couldn't calm down. Seemed like magic, sometimes, the way he spoke to them. It was like the dogs *listened*. But that's silly, isn't it." Nasim chuckled to herself. "I didn't know he had a special someone in his life. Seemed more like the carefree type. He was kind, though. Always helpful. Not too good to get his hands dirty. It can be hard work at the rescue—it's a charity you see, and there is never quite enough money for everything. But we make it work. Here we are."

They'd come to a stop at the top of a long corridor, partitioned into individual gated rooms for the dogs. Several of them had started barking once they had come into earshot—another howled a plaintive note. It was a horrible cacophony, worsened by the relentless concrete of the building. Nasim led them around, showing off several dogs. Michelle petted a gentle Labrador, tried to coax a shivering bulldog from the corner of its kennel, and was scratched accidentally by an over-eager mutt with a shaggy black coat.

"We're just here today to have a look," Lavinia said while Michelle kneeled at the fence of an older dog, a one-eyed German Shepherd. The sign beside the fence said "Dora". "Can we come back sometime next week, when we've had some time to think?"

"Of course," Nasim said. "Always best to be sure. You may

want to ring ahead though—you're lucky I was in today. We're currently understaffed."

"Oh?" Lavinia said. Michelle envied the ease with which she said it.

"Horrible business, really. John, who used to work here. He was... *murdered*." The last word was a whisper. "It's been a horrible shock to all of us."

"Really?" Lavinia said, raising her eyebrows, mimicking surprise. "What happened?"

"Must be an absolute nutter. Sliced him with a knife, the police said. No idea why anyone would want to hurt the man. He was a bit odd, kept to himself, not the chatty sort. But great with the animals, always. A bit like your father, love," she said to Michelle. Dora the German Shepherd sauntered over from her bed and sniffed Michelle's hand. She was a handsome dog, her fur coat healthy and shiny.

"The police asked whether anyone would want to hurt him and I said to them, no, absolutely not. He minded his own business, and that's that."

"You don't think he was doing anything... illegal?" Lavinia prodded. "Like drugs?"

"Oh no, nothing like that," Nasim dismissed the suggestion. "Liked a spot of gambling now and again, but that's neither here nor there. Seemed pretty lucky, too. But never felt too good to work with the dogs. There are always so many poor sweethearts that need a new home."

Dora looked at Michelle with a single, plaintive brown eye, allowing the soft fur of her chin to be stroked.

"Been a working dog, that one. She was abandoned when she lost her eye though—no longer good enough for the farm. She's retired now, sweet girl." Nasim patted Dora's haunch. Despite the loud barks of some of her fellow creatures, Dora stayed quiet, looking almost melancholic.

"She's gorgeous," Michelle said. "Don't you think, Lavinia?"

"She is," Lavinia said, smiling. For a moment, Michelle lost herself in that smile; it was as if they were truly just two women, looking for a canine companion to complete their family. Then she had to remind herself that this was all a ruse. They weren't here for a dog, and they weren't together either. They were hardly even friends, really. And yet, there was that connection that ran between them, forged irrevocably the night Lavinia had saved her from the demon.

Nasim showed them some other dogs, but Michelle kept looking back at Dora, who sat at the fence, attentively following their every move. With an expert touch, Lavinia extracted all information Nasim had on the victim, which wasn't much. It seemed like he'd kept to himself mostly and, although Nasim loved to gossip, she didn't know much of substance. Still, they'd been in the kennel for over twenty minutes by now, allowing Quintia sufficient time to find out as much as she could.

"I think we should head home, have a think," Lavinia said to Michelle, nodding to Nasim. "Thank you for showing us around."

"Yes, thank you," Michelle echoed. She threw one last glance at Dora, still sitting at the fence, waiting for someone to take her home.

"I think she's already sold," Nasim said to Lavinia. "I know that look. Same one I gave my little Bitsy when she came into the rescue!" They walked back into the reception building. "And if you would like to hear more about your father, sweetheart, just let me know. It's just me and Bitsy at home, and we love to have some company over. I can't bring him back, but it's nice to reminisce sometimes, isn't it?" She gave Michelle's arm a squeeze. Once they'd reached the reception, she grabbed a leaf of paper from a stack on the desk. "And here is an application form for Dora. I think she would be perfect for you two."

Nasim waved at them through the window as they walked

back to the car.

When they were safely out of earshot, Michelle said, "Why do I feel like we're the ones who got played?" She looked at the adoption form in her hand.

Lavinia laughed, holding the passenger door of the car open for Michelle to get in.

Chapter Thirteen

Quintia updated them on her progress on the way back to Thornblood. Computer security had been non-existent at the rescue. Nasim hadn't thought to lock the computer when she'd left the reception and Quintia had been able to look through all of their records. She'd transferred whatever had seemed worthwhile onto a USB stick so they could look at it in more detail later. More interesting, at least to Michelle, was her report of the various smells at the rescue. Clearly, vampires had a keen sense of smell, closer to that of a hound than a human.

"That's offensive," Quintia said when Michelle said something to that effect. Lavinia was quiet, but Michelle could see the little quirk at the edge of her mouth that showed her amusement.

There hadn't been any witches at the rescue in the last week or so. ("What do witches smell like?" Michelle ventured, but neither of the vampires was able to give a clear answer. "They just have an... odour. Magic smells," Quintia said.) Nor was there any trace of any other vampires. The whole affair was somewhat of a disappointment to Michelle. Despite the implausibility, she'd hoped that she could have added some value to this whole solving-her-almost-murder mystery.

"This all looks so much easier in *Harrogate Homicides*," she muttered.

"There are always a lot of dead ends and setbacks," Lavinia said, throwing a short glance towards Michelle. She was a careful and diligent driver, sticking exactly to the speed limit. "So don't worry about it. We won't let go until we find who wanted to hurt you. Besides, there might still be something in the files Quinn got for us." Quintia grunted in assent.

But if there was a clue in the rescue's data, it didn't readily reveal itself. After the vampires' reluctant agreement, Michelle spent three days poring over every inch of the computer files that Quintia had taken. Meanwhile, while the vampires explored various leads based on rumours in the vampire community, or patrolled areas where they thought the killers might be hiding. She only caught glimpses of them: Quintia and Brigh, a shy but huge red-haired vampire, muttering in the kitchen. Lucretia called various meetings, the door closed solidly to keep out Michelle's curious eyes. Lavinia, too, was called away again and again, never giving them much of an opportunity to talk beyond the bare basics.

While the vampires were away from home, Michelle looked through the rescue's files, but there was nothing that looked even remotely suspicious to her. In the last couple of months, several dogs had been adopted. New adopters filled in extensive reports about their living circumstances, professions, and even how many hours they spent at home every day. Still, if there was a murderer among the families, they unsurprisingly hadn't declared it in their adoption forms.

The outing to the rescue had briefly suspended Michelle's cabin fever, but by the fourth day it had returned with a vengeance. She'd been forced to take annual leave from work, and her remaining balance of days off was dwindling fast. Still, she couldn't go home, either. Seeing the pictures of the warlock's victims had resolutely put that thought out of her mind. There was no way she could protect herself from that. It was better to run out of vacation days than die a gruesome death in her flat.

Complicating matters, friends and family became increasingly suspicious of Michelle's sudden disappearance. She constantly had to field phone calls, especially from her mum, and it became more and more difficult to find evasive reasons why she couldn't pop by for breakfast or lunch. She couldn't even pretend to be busy at work, as her mother would only suggest to stop by the hospital with a homemade meal to share in the cafeteria. Usually, Michelle loved that her family was close, but it was suddenly quite complicated now that she was the target of a homicidal person with magical powers.

"I think my mum is days away from reporting me missing to the police," Michelle said on Sunday. For the first time in days, Lavinia had stayed home, joining Michelle in combing through data they had collected, both from the rescue and files sent by the Witch Council. They had sat in companionable silence for over an hour, working side by side in the upstairs office. They had found an equilibrium again after their fight in the foyer, focusing on their joint efforts to find both the warlock and the rogue.

"How come?" Lavinia leaned back in her desk chair. She stretched her arms overhead to compensate for the bent-over position she'd been in for the last hour. Apparently, even vampires got stiff after a while.

"Look at this message." Michelle held out her phone, screen still cracked. She hadn't had an opportunity to get it fixed since the night of the attack, and it hadn't really been much of a priority.

Lavinia squinted at the screen, reading the message through the spiderweb of fractures.

Hi honey... feeling worried cos we havent seen you in so long... saw a horrid programme on the telly last night about human

"Who's Bob?" Lavinia asked. Her blonde ponytail had slipped over her shoulder. Though Michelle had been living at their house for over a week now, she had never seen Lavinia any less than perfectly put together. Hair neatly pulled back, the sameness of her white tees and jeans almost uniform-like.

"My dad. Or, I guess I should say, my stepdad. I never knew my biological dad."

"I remember you mentioning it at the animal rescue. That sounds difficult."

Michelle shrugged. "I never knew any different, really. Mum met my stepdad when I was four, so he's been around for most of my life. It never seemed that big of a deal when I was young—there was always plenty of family around so there wasn't anything missing, but for the last couple of years, I've been wondering about him more. What he was like." Michelle was surprised at the words tumbling from her, baring a secret part of her soul. She hadn't even shared these thoughts with her friend Iris yet, despite their long friendship. There was something vulnerable about admitting to missing a father she'd never even met. Like she wasn't *allowed* to, since she hadn't actually experienced his loss. But she often wondered about that unknown half of her.

"Humans often have stronger bonds with their parents than we do. More emotional. Perhaps because of your shorter life spans, you bond more intensely," Lavinia mused. "It's a tragedy he was taken from you."

A tragedy. You know what, it *was* a tragedy. Due to no one's fault, she'd been cut off from half of her roots, her history. The realisation hit hard. "Thank you," she said. It was a strange thing to say, perhaps, but she couldn't find any other words that felt right. *Thank you for seeing me.*

Quickly, Michelle changed the subject before she cried again. "What about your parents? What are they like? They're vampires too, right?"

"Yes, vampires are born, not made. The movies definitely get that one wrong." The fond smile that spread on Lavinia's lips gave a softness to her features that took Michelle's breath away. "I haven't seen Mother in a couple of years, but she lives with her two consorts in a vampire community in the Scottish Highlands. Vampires don't recognise fatherhood in the same way as humans do—I of course know who sired me, but we share no relationship. My little brother lives with Mother and her consorts still."

"I didn't know you had a brother." Michelle pictured a sturdy sixteen-year-old with Lavinia's blonde hair and high cheekbones. "How old is he?"

"Sixty-four," Lavinia answered, without a trace of irony.

Michelle's mouth dropped open. "Sixty-four?" Then, a thought hit her. "Wait, actually, how old are you?"

Without missing a beat, Lavinia responded, "Two-hundred-and-forty-nine. I'll be celebrating my quarter-millennium next year."

"You're kidding," Michelle said, disbelieving.

"Not at all. I was born in 1776 during the Revolutionary War. Very exciting times, according to my family, though I don't remember much of my infancy," Lavinia said serenely, as if it was of no significance at all to have been born in the eighteenth century.

"How old do vampires usually get? Or are you, like, immortal?"

"Oh, nothing like that," Lavinia laughed. "It may just seem like that to humans as we age at a different rate. Five centuries is a decently advanced age. Some reach their seven-hundredth birthday, but many don't. You have to understand, our infancy also lasts much longer than it does for humans. It takes us fifty years to reach adulthood. But we are very much alive and mortal, just like anyone else." Then she turned thoughtful. "Except the gods, perhaps. They may be immortal. I'm not a theologian though."

Michelle let that confusing statement pass. "But if you live for centuries, wouldn't you end up with tons of vampires? What if all the vampires just have dozens of children?" She struggled to wrap her head around the concept of Lavinia being more than two hundred years older than her. Talk about an age gap.

"Ah, it doesn't work like that. It takes three years from conception to birth, and it can take decades to conceive. It took Messalina, one of my Sisters, over thirty years. But if the subject interests you, you may want to talk to her. I know very little about the details. Science has never been my strong suit."

"Damn." Living for centuries. Being pregnant for years! Every little bit of information about the vampires opened up the chasm of difference between her and Lavinia. Their strength, their speed, their heightened senses... Lavinia and Michelle lived completely different lives, *were* completely different. It wasn't just the surface level stuff—you only needed to compare the easy luxury of the vampire mansion with Michelle's cramped one-bedroom apartment—but also everything else. Lavinia had been around for the Industrial Revolution, the crowning of Queen Victoria, and both world wars. She was more than three times the age of Michelle's grandma, a dizzying thought.

Lavinia lived in a world of supernatural dangers and violence, while Michelle had gone through life *aware* of human cruelty but never directly in its path of harm. Until now, at least. Part of her yearned for Lavinia, true; Michelle was mature enough to recognise the stirrings of desire, the trappings of a crush. And there was nothing wrong with enjoying her company, her physical closeness; to appreciate how gorgeous she was, or revel in the attention she'd given her.

But it would have to stay just that: an unrequited crush, a brief meeting of their lives until they returned to the spheres to which they belonged. Besides, there was no way someone like Lavinia would ever be interested in Michelle. Regardless of whether she was gay or not—and Michelle couldn't really tell, not getting any particular vibe from many of the vampires—surely she would only go for another vampire, a "consort" to live out centuries together with.

It was a sad thought, a dream-fracturing thought. At night, lying in bed staring into the darkness, she would sometimes indulge in fantasies. What if Lavinia swept her off her feet in more ways than one? What if she came through the door right now, confessing that she must have Michelle, and could no longer hide her feelings. Michelle conjured up various scenarios, each one more outrageous than the previous, all ending with Lavinia in her bed enjoying the best night of their lives.

But they were nothing but fantasies. In reality, there was a wall that separated them—a careful distance that Lavinia maintained even now. She was always kind, always ready to lend a hand in whatever way possible, but there was something in the way she carried herself, a certain distance that prevented any vulnerability from showing, except in the briefest of glimpses. No, it was best to keep her fantasies to herself, as ridiculous as they were. Lavinia was a friend, nothing more. Possibly not even that. Somehow, she couldn't imagine them staying in touch after all of this was over.

This was just a brief interlude, a strange adventure she was on, and she would return to life as it had always been.

Beside Michelle, Lavinia's head snapped up. Her nostrils flared. Her head tilted slightly, as if she was listening to something. Michelle didn't hear anything. Something must be wrong—never before had Lavinia looked so otherworldly, looked less human than she did now. Michelle held her breath, not wanting to interrupt.

"Stay here," Lavinia said, rose, and with inhuman speed left the room in three long strides. Usually so quiet, her footsteps thundered down the grand staircase, to be joined by those of her Sisters.

What the hell was going on? For a moment, Michelle debated whether to listen to Lavinia, but ultimately the decision to, at the very least, find out what was wrong triumphed. She would hang back, try not to get in the way. Heart beating loudly in her chest, she followed in Lavinia's footsteps, drawn to voices in the foyer. She turned the corner of the corridor and looked down onto a scene of blood and chaos.

Chapter Fourteen

Several of the Sisters crowded into the foyer. A woman leaned on Lavinia's shoulder, covered in blood. Red liquid seeped into the carpet, and crimson handprints covered the front door.

"What the hell happened?" Lucretia barked, marching into the fray.

"Found a lair of rogues," the wounded woman panted, ineffectively stemming the flow of blood gushing from a head wound with her hand. Another lay on the carpet, unrecognisable under a mask of gore. "Eight of the fuckers. Two of them got Pina good, I had to carry her from the car. She passed out about ten minutes ago."

A low rumble filled the room even through the din of several people trying to help all at once. It seemed to be coming from Lucretia. "Should have waited for backup," she said, with a voice that raised the small hairs on the back of Michelle's neck.

The woman, blood pouring down the side of her face, down into the neckline of her shirt, snapped back, "We were ambushed. Seemed like some of them were on guard."

Brigh bent over the unconscious vampire, who must be Proserpina underneath the pallor of blood loss and gore. Without speaking, she slid her hands under Pina's shoulders to lift her.

The crowd around Proserpina shifted, revealing a shaft of wood sticking straight out of her chest.

"Wait," Michelle called, taking the steps as fast as she could. "Don't jostle it." The vampires didn't listen, no one turning her way. She pushed past Quintia and held out her hand to stop Brigh from lifting Proserpina. Quickly, she sized up the positioning of the shaft. There was no way of knowing how deeply it had been buried into Pina's chest. It had missed the heart but could have punctured her lung. Her breathing was shallow and fast, sweat from her pale skin mingling with the blood.

"She needs a doctor," Michelle said, glancing at Lavinia. Michelle could stabilise her somewhat, but she needed to be in a hospital.

"None around here for miles," Quintia grunted.

"It would take at least another half hour to take her there, or for him to get here," Lavinia added. Her green eyes glowed fiercely in the afternoon light. There was a sharpness to her movements, an almost feline grace. Quintia, too, exuded a barely suppressed power. For the first time, Michelle truly felt like she was surrounded by predators.

"Why do you run around with swords but don't keep a doctor around?" Michelle muttered to herself. Lavinia heard her.

"We used to, but he left last month."

"Couldn't stand living with us," Quintia added.

"Can't blame him," Michelle said under her breath. Despite it all, Quintia chuckled.

No doctor around. A woman bleeding out on the carpet in front of her. No sterile equipment, no diagnostic tools. It was a fool's errand, but there was nothing to be done.

She slid her hand underneath Proserpina's back, feeling for a possible exit wound. There was none. That was good news, at least. The stake hadn't gone completely through. A blood-soaked towel lay on Pina's stomach, and Michelle pressed it back around the wound, stabilising the stake and stemming the flow of blood.

She looked up from her patient, looking into Lavinia's steady green eyes. "Get the doctor anyway. We need something hard to move her, she can't stay here in the doorway with everyone milling around. Do you have a board or something?"

Unquestioning, Lavinia turned around to Brigh, and said, "Call the doc, quickly." Quintia pushed past Lucretia and the vampire with the head wound, grabbed the kitchen door, and with one strong jerk, pulled it clean off its hinges. She turned and held the massive slab of wood up for Michelle's inspection. "This work?"

"S-sure."

Barely showing any strain from the door's weight, Quintia easily laid it beside Proserpina.

Michelle blinked a few times, then refocused. "Okay. We need to put her on the door but try to jostle her as little as possible."

Lucretia barked, "Hands!" and within moments, five vampires surrounded the patient, grasping her in their strong hands.

"We can slide it underneath her," Michelle explained.

"Lift!" Luce said, and Pina rose a couple of inches, her head barely even moving. Michelle kept her eye trained on her chest, willing the stake not to pierce the aorta or anything else vital.

"Slide!" The command followed, and within a second Proserpina lay securely on the door.

"Take her to the dining room," Luce said, and the vampires lifted the door between them.

"Be careful," Michelle warned, but it was unnecessary. Between them, they carried the wounded woman smoothly through the parlour and slid her, door and all, onto the dining room table as if she weighed nothing. Then, five pairs of eyes turned towards Michelle.

"Now what?" Quintia said.

The weight of expectation bore down on her. The vampires

loomed over her shoulder as she looked at Proserpina's injury.

"Can I have some scissors?" Michelle asked and, within a heartbeat, a pair of scissors appeared at her elbow. Careful not to nudge the stake, she cut through the cotton of Proserpina's shirt. The clothing stuck to her skin, thick with blood, but Michelle peeled it away to look at the wound more closely. From up close, she could see that the sides of the wood had been smoothed down and polished. Proserpina's breathing was shallow but even. Michelle leaned closer to the wound, and listened.

Five vampires leaned closer around her.

Michelle ignored them. No wheezing, and no bubbles appeared in the blood alongside the stake. Her lung might be punctured, but if it was, the stake was obstructing the hole, at least for now. If she removed it, the lung might collapse. It would have to be removed at some point, but the situation seemed stable enough for now.

There was no immediate sign of head trauma, nor of any other significant wounds. The knuckles of her right hand were scratched, but they were only surface-level abrasions. She had significant bruising along her arms, possibly having warded off blows, but Michelle didn't see anything that was particularly worrying besides the impalement. The blood around the stake was slowing, oozing and clotting around the wood.

"A light?" she asked. Lavinia pulled her phone from her pocket and turned on the light before handing it over.

Drawing up Proserpina's eyelids one by one, Michelle checked the pupil reflex. They contracted normally under the light. She looked pale and clammy, having lost a significant amount of blood.

"She's going to need a blood transfusion," Michelle said. "Is that something vampires can do?"

Lucretia bent to Quintia. "Get Zachary. Tell him we need some blood."

She showed Lavinia how to press the towel against Proserpina's chest wound. Michelle turned to the other vampire. She was leaning against the wall, looking like a character from a horror movie with the blood streaming down the side of her face.

Michelle beckoned her over and slid out a chair for her at the table. "Here, have a seat."

The blood poured from a cut that slashed diagonally from her forehead to her temple. Like all head wounds, it bled profusely, but at least it didn't seem particularly deep. It might need stitches—but then again, she'd seen how fast Lavinia's wound had healed. She might not need stitches at all.

There was no debris in it; it was a clean slash, as if made by a knife. One of the vampires had put a first aid kit on the table, and Michelle gratefully helped herself to some wipes, cleaning the skin around the wound.

"Can you tell me what happened?" Michelle asked, trying to remove the sticky blood from the woman's dark skin. It had soaked into her hair as well, leaving the bright blue splattered with brown, matted patches.

"Rogue caught me with a knife. I didn't quite get out of the way quickly enough."

"Did you hit your head in any way?" The box also contained a pile of sterile bandages. She tore one from its plastic, placed some gauze on the cut, and put some pressure on the wound.

"Nah," the woman said.

"Any dizziness? Blurred vision? Ringing in your ears?"

"Bit lightheaded," the vampire admitted.

Michelle checked the vampire's pupil reflex—normal—and asked her to perform some simple memory and coordination checks.

"I don't think you have a concussion, so the dizziness might just be from the blood loss," Michelle said. "But to be honest, I don't know much about vampire physiology." They looked human enough; their blood looked normal, if slightly stickier than human blood. But that didn't mean they were the same beyond what she could see. There had to be differences, or vampires wouldn't be as strong or fast as they were. "It's best to drink plenty of fluids. You may want to take it easy until the dizziness passes."

The vampire nodded and stayed in her seat. Michelle always liked a good patient who followed advice. She patted the woman's shoulder and, at that moment, Quintia came back into the room with Zachary in tow. Strangely, they weren't carrying anything. Did they fetch Zachary to instruct him to drive somewhere to retrieve vampire blood? Would they need a specific kind?

However, no one spoke, and the man slid out of his jacket and rolled up one sleeve.

"What are you—" Michelle said, when Zachary leaned over Proserpina, extending his bare arm. The woman still lay unconscious, unaware of the man leaning over her.

"Got to get her going," Lucretia muttered, and Zachary turned, showing her his arm. Casually, Lucretia bent over, opened her mouth, and *bit*.

Blood welled up from the wound, and Zachary went back to his previous position. Cupping Proserpina's chin, Quintia gently opened her mouth. A drop of blood trickled onto her tongue. Another. Michelle stared at the scene unfolding in front of her. Nothing happened for a moment. Then, Proserpina rose an inch off the table, latching onto the arm, teeth sinking into flesh. Her throat worked, swallowing, swallowing, but her eyes stayed closed. A brief flash of pain spread across Zachary's face. Then, a deep tranquillity followed. The moment felt strangely intimate, like Michelle was intruding on something private.

After a minute, Proserpina unlatched, her head bobbing back onto the board, her mouth open. Her breathing deepened, closer to a natural sleep. A faint blush had crept across her cheeks.

Now it was Michelle's turn to feel dizzy. She dropped down heavily onto one of the chairs. It was one thing to understand intellectually that these women were vampires. That they looked like humans, but were somehow other. That they had their own habits and customs, even rules, and lived in a world separate from the one she knew.

Still, it was a whole other thing to watch one of them suck blood from their driver.

Chapter Fifteen

Lavinia joined her Sisters in a lightning-fast conference, leaving Proserpina in Michelle's capable oversight. Zachary, too, stayed in the dining room, enjoying his post-feed bliss. Luce rang the Magistrate from the phone in her study, briefly outlined the situation, got the confirmation she wanted, and hung up.

"We got authorisation to clean up the nest," she said, somewhat redundantly. All of them could easily hear the Magistrate's words through the handset's speaker.

Outside of the window, the sunset painted bright red and orange across the sky. "Does anyone need to stay with the wounded?" Vesta asked.

"Octavia, you stay here. I'm not risking you in the field with a head wound." Octavia nodded sharply, the bright white bandage bobbing.

"The civilians should be safe here. Octavia said they weren't followed. Worst case scenario, the humans sit tight until we return. A couple of rogues aren't blasting through the front door any time soon." Luce's fist jammed the button expertly camouflaged among the paintings lining the wall, and all over the house the emergency shutters clattered closed, cloaking the room in darkness. Seconds later, emergency lights flickered to life overhead, bathing them all in a soft reddish glow.

The Sisters filed out in a flurry of activity, not bothering to present their human-like front. Their Sisters had been hurt, and whoever was responsible would pay for it with their life.

Lavinia ran down the stairs, taking four at a time. The armoury was next to the gym, holding the Sisterhood's wide assortment of weapons. Lavinia strapped on her armour, the Kevlar-reinforced leather moulded perfectly to the contours of her body. She tied her sword sheath around her waist, slid her twin daggers into their thigh holsters. Beside her, Quintia grabbed her quarterstaff, weighing it in her hand for a moment, swinging it experimentally in a couple of short jabs, before moving to adjust the straps on her leather bracers.

Returning to the ground floor of the mansion, Lavinia found Michelle standing beside the still unconscious Proserpina, taking her pulse with her index and middle finger. She looked up when Lavinia strode into the room, her eyes widening.

Her mouth opened, as if she meant to speak. Then she closed it, swallowed, and said, "What's happening?"

"We're leaving. How's she doing?"

"Okay for now. The blood she drank must have helped. The chest wound is no longer bleeding much."

"The sun is setting. She might wake up once the moon rises." Lavinia could already feel the tingle of power creeping across her flesh, suffusing her muscles, her bones. The prospect of battle under the stars electrified her, drew her outdoors. But then, there was also Michelle, gazing at her with dilated pupils, grounding her in the present.

"Please be careful," Michelle said, and grasped Lavinia's hand. The soft heat of her hand was a shock on Lavinia's sensitised skin. Their fingers intertwined, the call of the moon and stars singing in harmony with the touch, sending a pleasurable shiver down her spine. She had never felt anything like it.

"Always," she said. Her voice was low with the unexpected cocktail of sensations. Battle was no longer on her mind. Her bloodlust transfused into something different, something even more potent. Lavinia looked at Michelle anew, drinking her in: her soft brown eyes, creased at the corners with laughter lines. Her mahogany hair shone gold in the light of the emergency lamps. Her full lips were slightly parted, revealing just a sliver of the pearl of her teeth. Michelle's heartbeat drummed in the palm of her hand, and her scent suffused the air. Lavinia's teeth ached, she pulled their joint hands slightly closer, narrowing the distance between them until their bodies stood flush together…

The reinforcements of the front door opened, the clank reverberating through the house. The ugly sound ran as a shock through them both, reminding them where they were.

"I have to go," Lavinia said. Michelle nodded, and with an effort that seemed herculean, Lavinia let go of her hand. It was an acute loss. All she wanted was to close that distance between them again, breathe her in, feel her skin against hers. But battle called, and Lavinia had a duty to fulfil.

She didn't look back when she joined her Sisters on the front steps. She couldn't risk looking back. If she did, she would want to throw herself at Michelle's feet. The stars hummed overhead, the night clear and crisp. The moon was rising, its sickle shining brightly on the navy-blue horizon. Luce, Quintia, and Vesta stood at her sides. They drank in the power of the night. Their senses sharpened. Their muscles trembled with unspent energy.

The rogues wouldn't know what hit them.

The rogues were holed up in a run-down cottage nestled between two hills. Octavia had shared the coordinates, leading the Sisters straight to their doorstep. If the rogues had been smart, they would have fled the scene the moment Octavia and Pina had retreated, but rogues weren't guided by reason. They were animalistic, instinct-driven. And when their territory was invaded, they dug in deeper, entrenching themselves.

It certainly wasn't a very promising fortress. The cottage had been made of the rough-hewn grey stone common in the area, but its roof had partially collapsed years ago. Ivy and brambles covered parts of the ruins. It would have seemed uninhabited, one of the many abandoned ancient buildings that were found throughout the valleys of the Pennines, their gardens overrun and almost inaccessible. It could have been one of many of those innocuous places, home to foxes and other wildlife, if it wasn't for the smell of blood. Vampire blood.

Lavinia drew her sword from its sheath. The only sound was a slight breeze rustling in the foliage overhead. The leather grip fit perfectly in her hand, the silver-plated blade meticulously crafted by the Blacksmith catching the pale light of the moon. The sword had been presented to her when she joined the Sisterhood, so many years ago. It would taste the blood of rogues again tonight.

Several paces away, Vesta crept through waist-high grass. Luce and Quintia had gone around the back of the cottage, cutting off any possibility of escape. No lights burned within the cottage. Perhaps they were afraid. Perhaps they didn't have any lights at all. Not that they needed any. The stars were bright tonight, casting enough light for Lavinia's eyes to see every blade of grass in sharp relief.

A shuffle and a hushed word sounded from within. They were still here, no doubt about it. The Sisters could have tried to lure them out, but that would defeat the element of surprise. In front of Lavinia a window gaped into the night, its glass panes broken decades ago. Its wooden shutters hung decayed from rusted hinges, providing no protection whatsoever. Nothing was visible through it. The Sisters creeped forward, the grass of the overgrown garden whispering at their touch. Vesta would take the equally rotten front door.

They were in position. Lavinia held up her hand, meeting Vesta's burning eyes for a moment. They counted down together. One breath. Second breath. Third.

They flew forward.

Lavinia leapt through the window, landing on something soft and uneven. She rolled over her shoulder to arrest her momentum. A grunt arose from behind her. She'd jumped straight onto one of the rogues. Vesta kicked through the rotten wood of the door, the remains of it slamming against the wall. Not waiting to see the rogues' response to this, Lavinia swerved and stabbed the rogue she had landed on straight through the heart. Her sword disappeared into his chest, a look of surprise on his haggard features. A cry rose from behind her, and she ducked as a piece of furniture whistled overhead. A stool they had found in some corner, probably. Lavinia pulled her sword free and faced the second attacker.

She only had enough time to see two bloodshot eyes surrounded by dark, matted hair before the rogue dashed forward with a bone-curdling shriek. Her dirty, wiry arms lifted the stool overhead again and again, bashing the piece of furniture at Lavinia in a desperate frenzy. Lavinia warded off blow after blow, pieces of wood shattering against her armoured forearm. Bruises were forming underneath, but the ferocity of the attack distracted her from the pain. She pressed on, swiping her sword, but the rogue easily leapt from its path. With one final crash, the stool split in two, and, with a roar, the rogue wielded the two pieces as if they were daggers.

"Vin!" Vesta shouted, and Lavinia stepped out of the path of a third rogue barely in time. He stumbled across the floor, clutching a rusting knife in his hand. The female rogue used

Lavinia's momentary distraction to lunge, aiming the chair leg at Lavinia's torso. Lavinia partially redirected the blow with her left arm, but the wood still connected in a glancing hit, tearing through the leather at her side. They were fast, these rogues. Strong, too.

Behind the female rogue, Quintia struggled to hold one of them down while Luce aimed her spear at them. Before the spear impaled them, they struggled free, tearing away from Quintia's hands. The spear's metal tip struck the empty ground where they had lain only a moment ago.

There was no time to consider this, as the man who had stumbled past her now zeroed in on Lavinia. As she warded off his lightning-fast attempts to stab her with the pommel of her blade, the woman circled her, trying to find her back exposed. Lavinia stepped backwards, keeping them both within view, swiping with her sword to make the man jump away. The cottage was small, only two rooms connected through an archway, and there was little space to manoeuvre. She had to move, or she would risk being pinned against the wall.

She kicked out at the female rogue, surprising her as she had been expecting another attack from the sword. Lavinia's foot connected squarely with her solar plexus, and she staggered. Again, the man lunged, this time aiming at Lavinia's unprotected face. She dodged, not quite enough, the knife slicing open skin at her cheekbone. She ignored it, using the moment of his overextension to draw a dagger from her thigh holster and stab upwards, through his neck. The man fell forward, hot blood pouring over Lavinia's boots, twitching as he died.

His death produced a frenzy in the female rogue. Without a care for her safety, she jumped at Lavinia, the full weight of her body slamming Lavinia into the rough stone of the cottage's wall. Sharp pain bloomed across the back of her hip, a piece of stone crashing against bone. The sharp smell of sweat and old blood filled Lavinia's nostrils as the rogue snarled at her, revealing short, misshapen fangs. The teeth clacked inches away from Lavinia's neck, her shoulder muscles straining to keep the woman from reaching her target. The woman's hands formed claws and tore at her face, her armour, fingers reddened by Lavinia's blood.

The rogue was so close that her sword was useless, and Lavinia dropped it onto the floor. She lifted her left leg, forcing her knee into the woman's stomach, whipped out her second dagger, and stabbed at her chest. The woman's frantic writhing caused it to miss its intended target, and glanced across the ribs, slicing upwards instead of finding the heart. Blood splashed across them both, hot and acrid. The woman pulled back her arm, and Lavinia could see the punch coming, but couldn't defend herself without either dropping the dagger or running the danger of the rogue's fangs latching onto her exposed neck.

The rogue's knuckles smashed into her cheek, bashing her head back against the stone wall. Ice-hot agony screamed through her head, blackening the corners of her vision. She couldn't pass out, not right now. Grasping the woman's torn overalls in one fist, she stabbed with the dagger once more. This time, it struck right. The pierced heart beat once, twice, then stilled. The woman's head lolled sideways, her eyes glossed over. Lavinia pulled the dagger from her chest and let go of the overalls. The rogue's body fell to the floor in a heap.

Within minutes, the fight was over. Bodies littered the ground, blood seeping into the packed earth underneath. The four Sisters stood among the carnage, blood-splattered and weary. The stars outside no longer sang of battle but chimed a requiem. Lavinia's head throbbed with every heartbeat, pain lancing through her right leg when she leaned on it.

"Let's bury them," Luce said.

The Sisters of Twilight were moved into action once more. Lavinia grabbed the male rogue from the floor, tore her dagger from his throat, and laid him outside in the light of the moon and stars. Eight bodies were retrieved, laid neatly beside each other. They took turns digging into the rocky earth. The still bodies were lowered into the grave and covered with the fragrant night soil. Eight rogues—the largest nest Lavinia had ever seen. Eight lives lost to the call of boundless blood. It was a horrible shame to see their broken bodies put to earth like this.

They beat the dirt from their hands as much as they could, having mingled with the fresh blood into a paste. Together, they started back to their home, back to the veneer of domesticity the house provided.

Behind them, the grave of the rogues lay unmarked, their blood soaking into the earth in the quiet hills of the Pennines.

Chapter Sixteen

The light of the mansion shone like a beacon in the night sky. Lavinia and her Sisters walked through the gate. It was an unobserved and silent victory march, a quiet homecoming. They strode into the foyer, greeted by their Sister's blood congealing on the rug. It would take Mrs. Frost ages to get that out, Lavinia thought, her thoughts fragmented by fatigue. The immense energy that was expended during battle, the adrenaline careening through her arteries—all of that was gone now.

All that was left was mud, and her cuts and bruises clamouring for attention. Luce patted her shoulder, a sisterly gesture of solidarity, before making her way to the study, probably to report back to the Magistrate. Quintia, prickly Quintia, held her hand for a moment, then disappeared into the bowels of the house to tend to her weapons before washing the stink of battle from her body. Vesta nodded to Lavinia, then followed Quintia. A soft noise caused Lavinia to raise her head, to tear herself from the recollection of the last hour.

Two wide, soft brown eyes peered at her from the dining room archway. Her wavy chestnut hair had been braided and lay coiled over one shoulder. Lavinia drank in the sight of her, enjoying a moment of pure aesthetic pleasure after the ugly reality of bodies torn asunder. Here was Michelle, like a drink of water to a woman parched of the good and the beautiful. Then the edge of her fear reached Lavinia. The whites of her widened eyes gleamed.

"Lavinia," she said, her voice low, a tremble at its edge.

Suddenly, Lavinia felt every spatter of mud and blood on her skin, her armour. Felt the violence still clinging to her like dirt. No wonder Michelle was afraid of her. This was the real her—the warrior, the soldier. This was who she was, who she had to be to protect vampirekind. Lavinia, her Sisters. They were the ones who got their hands dirty, who cleared out nests of rogues like the infection they were. It was honourable work, a coveted position in vampire society, but this was its dark side, its reality.

Every night the Sisters risked their lives, their bodies, and their souls. Some Sisters couldn't live with the violence, the battle song. They had each other, at least; there was always a Sister's shoulder to lean on. Everyone else was kept at a distance, for good reason.

And now Michelle had seen the real her. Her understanding of the Sisterhood was written clearly in the shocked lines of her face.

"I'm so glad you're alright," Michelle said, and she rushed forward, her hands cupping Lavinia's face. "Are you okay? Did you get hurt?"

Michelle's gentle words, her soft touch, were like a balm to Lavinia's soul. Michelle saw her, but she wasn't horrified. She was still here—she looked at her with kindness and worry in her eyes, not revulsion. Lavinia flinched when Michelle's finger grazed the cut on her cheekbone. "Only a little. Nothing serious."

"Thank God."

For a moment, Lavinia allowed herself to melt into her touch. "How are you? How is Pina?"

"Fine, we're both fine. The doctor got here about half an hour ago. He removed the stake from her chest. It was absolutely horrifying—a human would never survive anything like that. But he said she'll recover. Together with Octavia, he moved her to her bedroom upstairs."

"Good. That's good." Lavinia sighed. Pina was receiving the care she needed. She'd been avenged, swiftly and with minimal complications. They would all live to see another night.

And Michelle was still here, after all of that.

"You should see the doctor too, just in case." Michelle's eyes were serious. There was an edge in her voice which demanded to be obeyed.

Lavinia had no fight left within her. "Fine."

The doctor, a middle-aged vampire called Benjamin, gave Lavinia a brief once-over, taking a bit more time on the cut at the back of her head and the bruise on her hip.

"Heavy contusion around the hip joint. That'll be sore for a week or so. No heavy lifting or running, definitely no fighting. You might lose control of the joint if you push it too far. The cut on your head looks like it will heal within two or three nights, but be careful not to reopen it. You may wish to bathe in starlight for an hour a night to speed up the healing."

"Thank you, doctor," Lavinia said, inclining her head.

"Sister," he answered, bowed, and quietly left the room to check on his other patients.

Michelle pulled a face after he had closed the door behind him. "So formal."

Lavinia shrugged, the movement pulling at the leather armour sticking to her back. She really needed a shower. "Vampire customs don't change as quickly as human ones. Most of us can remember when the curtsy was common like it was yesterday."

Michelle shook her head, as if in disbelief. "I still forget how old you all are."

With the pressure of battle fading, Lavinia's hunger returned with a vengeance. It wasn't the hunger for food, for sustenance, but for blood. She closed her eyes, suppressing the thirst. It could wait.

"Are you all right? You look a little pale."

"I'm fine."

"Do you need to bathe in the moonlight, or whatever the doctor said? Does that help?"

"It helps with regeneration, but I'm alright for now. Just hungry."

"Want me to get you some food?"

Lavinia smiled, softening at the earnest care Michelle was offering. She could easily see her now as she would be at her job. Kind, compassionate, but with a backbone of steel that wouldn't abide any nonsense. She must be an excellent nurse. Had already proven to be a great nurse for Pina, actually.

"Hungry for blood," she explained, almost apologetically.

"Ah," Michelle said, realisation dawning. She was quiet for a moment, then said tentatively, "Should I see if Zachary is around?"

"No, thank you," Lavinia said. "He will need some time after providing for Pina. We don't take a large amount of blood, but it can take its toll."

"Right," Michelle nodded, her brows furrowed. She looked adorable when she frowned, the skin above her nose wrinkling. Goddess, Lavinia must have gotten star-struck, she was turning sentimental.

"What if," she said slowly, "you take my blood?"

Now it was Lavinia's turn to frown. "You can't do that."

"Why not?"

"Because." It was a childish answer, Lavinia realised, but the tangled ball of feelings within her wouldn't unravel sufficiently for her to express why it horrified her to accept Michelle's offering, so freely given.

Michelle wasn't taking it. "That's not a reason."

Lavinia sighed in frustration, picking at her gut feeling. "It wouldn't be right."

"Do I need to do something special? Or do you only drink a particular kind of blood?"

"It's not that." Lavinia looked at her. She was wearing the maroon jumper again. It must be her favourite. Lavinia thought it might be hers too; it brought out the warm tones of her skin. "I'm supposed to be protecting you."

"And you are," Michelle said emphatically. "Trust me, I'm incredibly grateful. There are a lot more things out there than I ever realised, scary things, and I know you're doing everything you can. But you have to let me take care of you, too."

A pang shot through Lavinia's heart. "That's not how this is supposed to go." She had always had these clear boundaries, this impenetrable wall. Being part of the Sisterhood was more than a job; it was a calling. And whenever they came across civilians, they did what they could, accepted their thanks, and faded back into the night. Never before had she gotten attached.

But then again, Michelle had been special from the very start. Lavinia had never brought a human to Thornblood. Looking back at it now, why had she done that? Why had she had this feeling in the pit of her stomach that she had to keep Michelle close? Why had it only grown stronger over the last couple of weeks?

"The only thing that matters is what you need. And if you need blood, and I have blood to spare, well..." Michelle shrugged. "I don't see why you can't take it. Assuming that I won't get a nasty infection from your saliva."

"No, no. I'm sure the good doctor could tell you why exactly, but that's not an issue." Lavinia closed her eyes for a second and took a deep breath. She could hear Michelle's heartbeat thrumming steadily, her blood rushing through her arteries and veins. She let herself imagine the taste of her on her tongue, how it would feel gliding down her throat. Drinking blood was a sensory pleasure like no other, except perhaps sex. There was an intimacy in feeding on someone's blood, someone's life force. Most vampires had trusted familiars to provide for them. For rogues, drinking blood was a dynamic of predator and prey, of rapacious taking. It was a perversion of the symbiotic relationship between vampire and willing donor, which strengthened intimacies and often created familial-adjacent ties, like with Zachary and his family.

Drinking from Michelle would be yet another step closer to a dangerous precipice. Lavinia couldn't afford to lose herself in this human, as enticing as she was.

"Maybe later," she hedged, cursing herself inwardly for her cowardice for not rejecting the offer outright. Still, part of her was not quite willing to let go of the dream of piercing Michelle's soft skin with her teeth, of her gasp as the short burst of pain would turn into pleasure. "I'm going to have a shower first." She had to wash off all the gore.

Michelle narrowed her eyes. "Alright," she said, her tone somewhat sceptical. For a second, Lavinia felt as if her motivations were crystal-clear to Michelle, that she could see through her with ease. Like Michelle could read her mind.

Of course that was impossible, but it was a disconcerting feeling to be so scrutinised by a human. Lavinia was used to carrying a whole world of knowledge within her that most humans would never uncover, unless introduced to it through legacy. Yet here Michelle was, having stumbled into her world through twist of fate.

She shifted her stance, her hip complaining. The doctor had been right—there was some instability there. She wouldn't be in any shape to fight for at least a couple of days. In normal circumstances, this wouldn't be much more than a nuisance. Her Sisters would take over any tasks that needed to be done until she recovered. She would have a dull week of desk work, no one's favourite, causing nothing worse than some boredom. But right now, they were looking at some kind of unprecedented warlock/rogue duo whose killings were becoming increasingly frequent. On top of that, an unusually large group of rogues had settled close to the mansion and had somehow evaded detection until now.

There was no obvious connection between the two events, but they both contributed to a sense of unease building within her. She wanted to be ready for when the other shoe would drop. And though she didn't know in what way, she was sure that it would, and soon.

Lavinia walked up the central staircase, Michelle following closely behind.

"I won't fall," Lavinia said, noticing Michelle's focused expression.

"Not on my watch, you won't," Michelle agreed.

Under Michelle's vigilant gaze, they made it upstairs safely.

"Do you need any help?" Michelle asked when they reached Lavinia's room.

Pride rose momentarily, and Lavinia opened her mouth to say she was fine, she could handle it all. She had done so for centuries and would do so forevermore. She had gone into battle more times than she could count, was covered in scars she could no longer recall how she had gained, and had always managed herself. She had always borne her wounds stoically, without any complaint.

But then, there was no judgment in Michelle's expression. It was a kindness, an offering, and one that didn't need to be rejected out of pride. Accepting help wasn't weakness, Lavinia knew that; she accepted the help of her Sisters with grace and thankfulness, never giving it a second thought. That was what it meant to be part of the Sisterhood, after all.

Maybe she could take this help, too.

"Would you mind helping me take off some of this armour?" she said, swallowing the urge to return to the safety of her self-sufficiency. "The straps can get difficult." Particularly after she'd scratched and bruised her knuckles as she had done tonight.

"Of course," Michelle said without any hesitation. Lavinia turned the doorknob and let her into her rooms. They were spacious, the windows looking out over the rocky cliffs that surrounded the house. The clean white of the walls glowed brightly under the overhead lights, starkly illuminating the sparse furniture. Lavinia took off her sword and its sheath, and removed the daggers. She laid them out on the desk. She'd clean them later, removing the flecks of dried blood from their surface. Lavinia took the plain wooden desk chair and turned it so she could stretch her legs before her.

She showed Michelle the straps of the various parts of her armour, from the narrow bands holding her bracers tightly around her wrists, to the larger straps that kept her breastplate in place. It was an ingenious system, the various parts overlapping so the straps were rarely, if ever, exposed. Together, they unravelled the armour, removing it piece by piece, peeling the stained reinforced leather from skin and clothing. Michelle laid out the pieces on the desk with reverence.

Lavinia rose, unburdened by the weight of her armour. "Thank you." There was a depth to the words that she hoped were conveyed.

"No problem at all," Michelle said. Lavinia—for a second—considered closing the distance and kissing her, resolving that tension between them. But her clothing stuck to her with dirt and blood and tugged at her with every movement. With a sigh, she turned to the bathroom instead.

Chapter Seventeen

Michelle heard the shower turn on in Lavinia's en-suite bathroom. She was glad to have a moment to catch her breath. The night had passed in weirdly proportioned time. First, they'd had that moment when Lavinia said goodbye, which had left her breathless. Then, there had been the absolute agony of waiting in the quiet house with two wounded vampires, tortured by the thought that perhaps Lavinia would be next to be carried through the door, unconscious. She has tormented herself with thoughts of all the ways in which Lavinia could get hurt, how the other vampires would return, carrying their fallen Sister. It had been a relief when the doctor had arrived, though that was only short-lived, lasting only until he told her how he planned to remove the stake from Proserpina's chest. That process had been nerve-wrecking in a different way. All of Michelle's instincts had screamed at her when he'd grasped the slick surface of the wood with a tea towel and removed it from her chest with one swift, squelching movement.

He had assured her that vampires were very resistant to infections and that there was no danger from that source. Still, seeing this procedure done on a dining table, without any sterilised tools or even an IV with a blood infusion to help replace the blood pooling freely into Proserpina's chest wound, had made Michelle queasy. Vampire medicine was not for the squeamish.

Lavinia had returned safe and sound, though somewhat battered and bruised. For a moment, she almost hadn't recognised her in the bright light of the foyer. That glint of otherworldliness that flashed forth occasionally had been on full display, her green eyes blazing with a bright, unnatural sheen. Then Michelle's perception of her adjusted, stretched, and she was Lavinia again, Lavinia her protector, and also just plain Lavinia, who brought her cups of tea and had watched her detective show with her. She understood now, or at least thought she did, how being a warrior was in her nature. Dressed in her armour—even splattered with blood as she had been—she looked *right*.

She had also looked terrifying. At the same time, Michelle found herself absolutely captivated by her, attracted to her like a moth to a flame.

There had also been a softness to her as Michelle had helped Lavinia remove her armour. She had held up her arms patiently while Michelle undid the straps that had gotten sticky with blood. It was an intriguing dichotomy, the unyielding warrior and the softness underneath. Michelle felt dazzled by Lavinia, by her complexity, by her apparent otherness and her simultaneously recognisable humanity.

She was glad to have a moment to herself in this oddly sparse room to digest all she had seen and experienced in the last couple of hours. She sank down onto the unrelenting wooden chair at Lavinia's desk, listening to the familiar pitter-patter of the shower.

She should probably leave, but oddly, she felt protective. Lavinia had come back to her. She would keep her right under her nose, where she could keep an eye on her and make sure she was okay. It was an irrational thought—this was Lavinia's own home, and Michelle's presence probably didn't make much of a difference, but she indulged herself and took in this inner sanctum of Lavinia's.

There truly wasn't much to look at. The windows were large, but the night outside obscured any potential view. The curtains were of a pale grey, barely providing any variation to the room. The walls were completely white. The main feature was a simple king-size bed framed in a pale wood that matched the chair and desk. The sheets, neatly made, were also white. A couple of doors, one of which she assumed must hide a closet from view, branched off from the room. Finally, there was a nightstand with a single drawer topped with a minimalist modern lamp. Michelle had seen roadside hotels with more personality.

Yet at the same time, it didn't surprise her, this empty environment. In a way, it was incredibly *Lavinia*, to have pared everything down to the absolute essentials. Lavinia was never frivolous, in word or deed, always moving with a purposefulness that awed Michelle, who often felt like she had floundered through life. In a way, she envied it, but sitting on the unforgiving surface of the chair, she also thought there was an element of self-denial here that made her a little sad.

There was no pleasure here, not a single item designed for more than utility. There were signs of life here and there, of course, a pen that hadn't been returned to its drawer, a half-full glass of water left on the windowsill. But Michelle couldn't shake the feeling that something was missing here, a warmth that she had seen so many times in Lavinia that wasn't reflected in her space.

The shower had stopped running a little while ago. No further sounds came from the bathroom. Michelle waited for another five minutes, time creeping by slowly, until she decided to get up. She was probably being overbearing, but still she knocked gently on the door. Vampire or not, she wasn't taking any chances with that head wound.

"Lavinia? Are you alright?"

No answer.

She knocked again with a little more force. "Lavinia?" She wouldn't have passed out on the floor, would she? She had seemed fine before—a bit bruised and battered perhaps, but steady on her feet regardless.

"Come in," Lavinia's voice filtered through the door.

Michelle turned the doorknob and stepped into a spacious bathroom. The fresh scent of lemon hung in the humid air. Condensation coated the expanse of mirror above the double sinks, a walk-in shower and a standalone bath completing the scene. Lavinia sat on the edge of the bath, wrapped in a cream bathrobe. Her wet blonde hair lay loose across her back, darkened to a deep brown by the water that had soaked it.

"I can't see the wound on the back of my head properly, even in the mirror," she said with a shy smile. "Would you mind terribly giving me a hand?"

"Let's have a look."

The shower had washed away the majority of the blood that had clotted around the cut, but some still clung to the scalp around it. It was almost uncanny how good the cut looked already. A crust had formed, and there was practically no redness surrounding it. If she'd had to guess, she would have said it was three days old. The ability of vampires to heal wounds was nothing short of miraculous. If only the injuries of the children on the paediatric ward would heal half as well.

"Shall I wash your hair for you?" Michelle asked.

"Please, if you don't mind."

"Not at all." It was the least she could do. A certain sense of a debt unpaid had hung over her ever since Lavinia had intervened and saved Michelle's life. Tonight, again, she had risked her own life to protect others from harm. All Michelle had been able to do was sit around and eat their food, until today. It had felt good to take control of the situation earlier, to flex that muscle that had lain dormant since she had been to work last.

And now, this was something she *could* do, something she knew how to do. A way she could be useful, even if it was only to provide a small sense of comfort and support to Lavinia right now. It wasn't much, perhaps, but it was enough.

She got Lavinia a stool to sit on and let her lean her head backwards over the rim of the bathtub. She ran the showerhead until it was the right temperature. Carefully, she lathered Lavinia's hair with the shampoo that she found on the side of the bath. Lavinia closed her eyes as Michelle's fingers ran across her scalp, gently loosening the debris of her fight.

"Does it hurt?"

Lavinia hummed a negation. "Stings a little."

The water ran pink as Michelle rinsed the shampoo from her hair, a small trail of blood appearing along the bottom edge of the cut. Lavinia didn't seem to mind much, not budging or flinching as Michelle lathered it again.

It was intimate, to be so close to her. Michelle was used to helping people in their most vulnerable states. Over the years, she'd helped people of all ages wash, eat, and even perform the most basic human functions. As a trainee nurse, she'd initially been somewhat hesitant touching people, but that was a shyness that quickly abated under the immense pressure of the work that had to be done. She learned that it was impossible not to form personal connections with patients, some fleeting as they were discharged after only a couple of days, and some more sustained.

In a way, the intimacy of this moment, washing Lavinia's hair in her bathroom, was familiar. At the same time, it was absolutely nothing like being at work. Michelle tried to keep her attention on the task at hand: the methodical massaging of Lavinia's scalp to remove the dirt that had somehow made its way into her locks, the slow untangling. Over and over, her glance wandered to Lavinia's face, which had relaxed into a serene calm. In some ways, Lavinia had been somewhat unreachable ever since they had met. But tonight, something had shifted between them. She couldn't put her finger on how it happened, or what any of it meant. All she knew was that she was inexorably drawn to her, wanted to be close to her. It had started as a somewhat awestruck crush, but now it was growing into something more.

She rinsed Lavinia's hair one last time, the water running clear down the white porcelain of the bath. She grabbed a towel and carefully squeezed any last moisture from her hair, mindful not to pull on the wound.

"There," she said, draping Lavinia's clean, thick hair across the back of her bathrobe, running her hands through them one final time. She found it surprisingly hard to stop touching it now that she had started.

Lavinia sighed. It sounded a little bit wistful. Lavinia opened her eyes, and Michelle started. "Your eyes." Lavinia's pupils were dilated into wide black. There was only a thin rim of the green of her iris visible.

Lavinia blinked, the pupils tightening slightly. "Sorry." Her voice sounded a bit odd, too.

"Are you alright?"

Lavinia smiled, tight-lipped. "Fine." Something had changed in the last couple of minutes, but what? Only moments ago, Lavinia had been relaxed, loose-limbed. Now there was suddenly an edge to her gaze, a sharpness to her movements as she stood up and tightened the bathrobe more closely around her. Lavinia's glance met Michelle's, then wandered down to Michelle's neckline. To where her heartbeat was pounding under the surface of her skin.

Oh. *Oh.*

"You're..." Michelle swallowed. "Hungry?"

Lavinia looked away, shrugged. She busied herself with rearranging the scant few items beside the sink. She obviously wasn't an adherent to a twelve-step skin routine. Like everything else with her, simplicity was everything.

The action was clearly meant to give her space to collect herself. To rebuild the walls she upheld so tightly. Michelle could see it happening in real time. How Lavinia suppressed the hunger that must be intensely physical. How she turned from view to regain that calm that she presented so meticulously. Once again, the real Lavinia, that wonderful blend of warrior strength and vulnerability, would disappear from view.

Michelle wasn't going to let that happen. There was a reckless desire to keep the real Lavinia within her reach that made her step forward. She laid her hand on Lavinia's robe-clad arm. She wasn't thinking about the consequences of the choice she was making in offering herself in this way. Didn't consider how dangerous it might be. There was no thought of safety in her mind. All she wanted was to be near Lavinia.

"Take me," she whispered. Lavinia froze. Michelle could see their shadowy silhouettes in the fogged-up mirror. She tightened her grip on Lavinia's arm. "Drink from me."

Lavinia turned slowly. All the green had fled from her eyes, replaced with limitless black. That uncanny gaze searched Michelle's as if seeking a handhold as they both lost themselves in each other. Michelle certainly felt like she was drowning, drowning in the magnetic gaze pinning her in place. She held on to Lavinia, fearless. She trusted her. Trusted her with her life, in a way she had never done before. With anyone.

Lavinia gently took Michelle's hand between hers. "You're sure?" she asked, her voice low. It had a slight lisp.

Michelle nodded, unable to form words. It was intoxicating, letting herself trust with such abandon. Lavinia's arm curled around her waist, pulling her closer. Their heads curved together, and for a second, Michelle thought Lavinia would kiss her. But then Lavinia's head tilted, nuzzled Michelle's neck. Michelle closed her eyes, leaning into Lavinia's touch.

A sharpness of teeth, a pressure, a flash of pain. Lavinia's fangs penetrated the skin at the tender spot at the base of her neck. There was a dizzying sense that she was falling, like on that cusp between being awake and asleep, but Lavinia's arms held her close. Pain receded, and intense pleasure came in its place. As Lavinia drew blood from her, Michelle lost herself in the sensation, the heady contrast between the softness of her lips on her neck and the pressure of teeth, of her overwhelming presence all around her. Time ceased to matter, as everything became enclosed to this one point. She surrendered herself to the feeling, to Lavinia. The distance between them had been obliterated, and Michelle rode the waves of unexpected pleasure.

Finally, an eternity later, an ending that came way too soon, Lavinia's fangs pulled back. There was a slight wetness—her tongue licking the last traces of blood from Michelle's neck. Still, Lavinia held her in her arms, and Michelle snuggled close into the embrace.

Chapter Eighteen

It was difficult to tear herself away from Michelle, but their little oasis within reality was shattered by Quintia's shouting for Lavinia from outside of Lavinia's door.

"Coming!" Lavinia answered for Quintia's sake. "Are you hungry?" she asked in a smaller voice, pulling back slightly so she could see Michelle. A deep red flush braced her cheeks, her eyes bright.

The taste of her blood was still on Lavinia's tongue. Strength was trickling back into her veins, suffusing her with a feeling of well-being that had been lacking for a while. She really should have fed earlier. But then, it was hard to regret her actions when they had led to this moment.

"Not really," Michelle answered. Then she wrinkled her nose. "Okay, maybe a little. It's been a long night."

She looked so damn adorable in that moment. Before she knew what she was doing, Lavinia leaned in and kissed her forehead, as fleeting a touch as from a butterfly's wing. Michelle closed her eyes briefly, and the flush on her cheeks deepened.

"Just give me a moment," Lavinia said, and tore herself from their embrace. It was an instant loss, and her body yearned for the feel of Michelle in her arms immediately. She walked into her walk-in closet, pulled a white T-shirt from a pile of identical white T-shirts. Slowly, rational thought was returning now that she'd created a bit of distance between her and Michelle.

The sharp scent of fresh blood still clung to them both, mingling with Michelle's own smell, that now-familiar scent of floral notes with a hint of warm spice. Stepping into a pair of soft grey leggings, she couldn't decide whether she'd just made a horrible mistake. There was no place for a human in Lavinia's life. There was hardly any space for anyone else at all beyond the Sisterhood and her own family, let alone someone from a different species. But she couldn't help but grin in the privacy of the twilight of her closet. If it had been a mistake, it had been an amazing one that she would refuse to regret.

"Come on," she said, walking back into the brightness of the room, and led Michelle to the staircase at the end of the west wing corridor. As they walked, Michelle's hand brushed Lavinia's. Without looking at her, she slid her hand into Michelle's, their fingers entangling. They didn't let go until almost at the dining room door, a handful of voices filtering through the wood that had been returned to its rightful place.

The door opened to a familiar scene. Lucretia sat at the head of the table, arguing with Quintia over whether she should have a larger helping of the roast pork that lay on a silver dish between them.

"You don't eat enough," Quintia urged.

"None of your business," Luce countered.

"You skipped breakfast this morning."

"I didn't know you were my keeper."

"Take it." Quintia threatened the sovereignty of Luce's plate with a piece of pork dangling from a pair of tongs. Luce easily warded the incursion off with a clash of cutlery.

"No."

While they argued, Vesta scrolled on her phone with one

dainty finger while she loaded her plate with green beans, seemingly without looking.

"No phones at the table," Messalina beside her said, frowning.

Vesta launched into a defence of her behaviour, quoting several different families who were at a tipping point in their struggle for power, rattling off a list of names that apparently meant as little to Messalina as they did to Lavinia. Octavia, however, nodded along with Vesta's explanation. The clean gauze wrapped around her head contrasted starkly with her electric blue hair, now free from blood. Slipping between the cacophony of voices, Mrs. Frost put another steaming bowl of fragrant food onto the table before disappearing back into the kitchen.

Lucretia was the only one to look up at their entrance. "Sit down, you two." Lavinia pulled out a chair for Michelle beside Messalina and sat down opposite her, next to Vesta.

"I don't think we've met," Messalina said, addressing Michelle. She extended her hand. "Messalina. I've heard so much about you."

"Michelle." They shook hands.

"I didn't hear you come in," Lavinia said, holding out her plate for Vesta to share some of the green beans.

"I just arrived. I came as soon as I could. I wish I had been here with you all." Messalina's eyes spoke of fatigue. She had pulled back her black hair into thick twists and still wore the flexible, lightweight armour suitable for missions where little fighting was expected.

"You're stationed in Scotland. We can't be everywhere at once," Lavinia said.

Messalina sighed and held out the dish with roast pork so Michelle could serve herself. "Don't I know it."

"How's Gus?" Finally, the fray at the head of the table subsided, a relative quiet returning to the room. Beside Lavinia, Vesta slipped her phone back into the pocket of her flowing dress.

"Gus is my consort. Augustus," Messalina explained to Michelle. "He's fine. Wanted to come, but with the little one... It's not always easy."

Lavinia nodded. Messalina was the only one in the Sisterhood who had a child. It was a challenging life, and adding a young child into the mix made everything even more complicated. Gus was a wonderful consort, understanding of the risks Messalina took, but even then, the competing demands took a heavy toll on her.

"You've got a kid?" Michelle asked.

Messalina nodded, her eyes filling with pride. "A daughter. Messalina, the sixth of her name."

"How old is she?" Michelle ventured tentatively. Lavinia thought back to her facial expression when she'd told Michelle about her little brother's age and smiled to herself.

"Eight years old now. She's still so small but getting stronger every day. She wrestles with cousins twice her size and wins. She might make an excellent warrior someday."

"Minerva be willing," Vesta said.

"Minerva be willing," Messalina agreed. "What about you, Michelle? Do you have any children?"

"Oh, no," Michelle laughed. "Unless you count all the ones on the ward. I'm a paediatric nurse. But I never really thought much about having any myself."

"Neither did I, until I met my Gus," Messalina said.

The door behind Lavinia clicked open, and Proserpina shuffled in. The table fell quiet for a moment and then burst into cheers.

"She's up!" Octavia exclaimed.

"About fucking time," Quintia grunted, but a crooked smile softened her words.

With a groan, Pina lowered herself slowly into the dining chair. She looked like hell. The bandage around her chest was stained with blood, and her olive complexion still looked sallow. Her usually bouncy, curly hair lay flattened against her head, and Lavinia could see the tremor in her hand as she held up her plate for Lavinia to ladle some stew onto. Still, looking like hell was miles better than being unconscious and impaled.

Mrs. Frost appeared at Pina's elbow and silently placed a glass of water in front of her. "Thanks, Mrs. Frost," she said. "I feel like the queen with everyone serving me. I should get stabbed more often."

The table erupted in laughter, breaking the tension.

"Alright ladies," Luce said from the head of the table. "Bless the moon and stars that we've survived another damn night. Let's eat."

This was all the incentive everyone needed, and the Sisters attacked their meals as if half-starved.

"I meant to thank you, Michelle," Pina said, gingerly stabbing a potato with her fork. "Not that I was awake for any of it, but the doctor told me of your assistance. He spoke highly of you. Without you, one of these idiots might have just ripped the stake out of my chest without any precautions."

"Hey!" Quintia exclaimed, her mouth half-full.

Pina levelled her eyes at her. "Do *you* know anything about medicine?"

Quintia swallowed. "Nah. I just know not to get stuck by the pointy end."

"Dickhead," Pina murmured, but it sounded like a term of endearment. "Still, thank you."

"That's alright," Michelle answered with a blush. "I didn't do that much."

"Oh, she's humble. I see why you like her, Vin," Pina said. In a conspiratorial voice to Michelle, she continued, "Lavinia here is also terrible at taking any kind of praise. I think you two are a great fit." Michelle's blush deepened. She gave a sly little smile to

Lavinia. The red of her bite mark peeked from beneath the maroon of her jumper. Lavinia suddenly recalled Pina's words on the first night she'd brought Michelle here. *You like her*, she'd said. She had been right, of course. Pina was always right about this kind of thing. Still, there was no reason to be so smug about it.

"Stop it," Lavinia said, shooting a warning glance to Pina that said, *don't push it*.

Pina waved her fingers in the air. "Just saying. I can't help but notice that you're looking exceedingly *healthy* tonight, my dear Vin."

"Pina," Lavinia said, this time cranking up the threat in her voice.

"You fed?" Vesta asked. "Goddess, Vin, finally. You were getting increasingly grumpy."

"I wasn't." Lavinia refused to lift her eyes from her plate, not meeting the teasing glances of her Sisters.

"You were almost as bad as Quintia."

"Hey!" Quintia said, not having been part of the conversation but realising immediately she was being made fun of. When Vesta explained, she said, "Actually, fair enough."

"Well, I fed, and that's the end of it," Lavinia said. She glanced at Michelle, whose colour was still high. She didn't question the squeezing feeling in her chest whenever she saw the bite on Michelle's neck. The protective, possessive voice within her whispered, *she is mine*. The bite hadn't been a claiming—it had been a gift freely given. She tried to hold this thought firmly in her mind. "Let's talk about anything else."

Michelle cleared her throat, putting her fork down. "Actually, there was something I wanted to talk about."

"Yeah?" Lavinia said.

"It's my mum's birthday on Saturday. I'm very grateful to you all for letting me stay here so far, but I would like to go. She's really worried about me, and showing her I'm fine would help a lot, I think."

Lavinia chewed on a bite of roast pork, the tender meat deliciously savoury, considering Michelle's words. Usually, she would have dismissed the idea outright. Michelle was safest here, so here she should stay. But they had gone to the animal rescue, hadn't they?

"It's during the day," Michelle added. "Just coffee and cake."

"You can't go alone," Lavinia warned. She wasn't ready to let Michelle out of her sight. Not when there were still so many unknown threats to her life.

"I was hoping maybe you could come with me? As my guest, I mean."

Lavinia glanced at Luce at the head of the table. Luce was bent towards Vesta, who whispered in her ear. "I'm not sure," she hedged.

"I think you should go," Pina said, gingerly nibbling on a green bean.

"Really?" Lavinia turned towards her. She would have expected caution from Pina, especially after her warning on the first night she'd brought Michelle here.

"You'll have to take it easy, right? And no demon will be busting through the doors while the sun is up."

"But what about the rogue?" It wasn't just the threat of a demon that worried Lavinia. If the warlock killed alongside a rogue, who could say whether or not he considered Michelle a target, too? And while rogues, like all vampires, were weaker during the day and usually hunted at night, there was nothing to stop them from wreaking havoc among a bunch of humans. With her injuries, she wouldn't be able to protect them as well as she usually could.

"Maybe take some backup?" Messalina offered. Lavinia considered the possibility, but it didn't seem particularly viable. Would Luce allow so many resources to be taken away at a time when they were on high alert? For a human to attend a party? It seemed unlikely.

"I'll go," Quintia grumbled from the other side of the table. "If Luce agrees, of course."

Lucretia, apparently having followed their conversation somehow even while listening to Vesta, proclaimed her permission across the table. "Fine. We are grateful for your help tonight, Michelle. We will make sure you can visit your mother for a day." She turned to Quintia and mumbled. "Get you out of my hair for a damn second."

"You'll miss me."

Lucretia sighed. "Probably."

"There you go," Messalina said. "Official stamp of approval and all." The Sisters and Michelle all turned back to Lavinia, waiting for her answer.

"Alright," she said. "We'll go to your mother's birthday party." It would make Michelle happy, and although a small voice within her said it was an unnecessary risk, a larger part of her wanted to give Michelle whatever she wanted.

Michelle smiled warmly, and seeing her glow of pleasure set off a cascade of tender feelings in Lavinia. Stars, she would do anything to make her smile like that. Even more pleasing, however, was seeing her here, at the table, talking easily to Messalina and the others.

She hadn't quite realised how isolated Michelle had been since she'd come here. The others had, by and large, avoided her. Perhaps unconsciously, there had been a strong separation between *us* and *her*. Michelle had been on the other side of a divide that had seemed impossible to bridge. Now, though, they were warming to her. Perhaps the distance between their lives wasn't so insurmountable as it had seemed at first.

"Lavinia," Michelle whispered to her as they left the dining room after puddings had been eaten with relish. "I'm really glad we're going to my mum's birthday and all, but there is just one thing."

"What is it?" Lavinia leaned close, enjoying the tickle of Michelle's hair on her cheek.

"I don't know how I'm going to explain bringing two women to my mum's birthday. If it were just you, I would pretend that we were dating, and it would be no big deal, but..." Lavinia finished Michelle's thought: but it would look very odd if Michelle showed up with what was effectively a vampire bodyguard detail.

"Quintia can guard the perimeter," Lavinia said reassuringly. "She won't mind. But I do think someone should always be within sight of you, just in case."

"Oh, that's good," Michelle said, taking a deep breath of relief. "That's okay. Will you be my date?" she said, a teasing hint in her words.

"Of course," Lavinia answered, her heart constricting. It wasn't real—they weren't actually dating, but her heart didn't understand the difference. Still, even if they were only pretending to avoid any prying questions, Lavinia would try to be the best fake date she could be.

Chapter Nineteen

Michelle slept deeply into the afternoon of the following day. The ecstasy of letting Lavinia drink her blood had worn off, but the memory filled her with a delicious shiver of satisfaction. She caught herself running a fingertip along the raised scabs where Lavinia's fangs had pierced her skin. It was odd, how right it had felt. She'd thought it would be disturbing, having someone drink your blood. But now, she felt like she understood. Thinking of Lavinia drinking from anyone else, though... That created a pang of envy that was difficult to rationalise.

Michelle didn't have much time to muse on this though, as when she finally rose that Monday afternoon, she found that Arran had left a message for her. She had been summoned, sorry, *invited* to meet a bunch of witches.

"What if I don't want to go?" she'd asked Lavinia when the vampire had shown her the cream-coloured envelope that had arrived that morning. Michelle felt relieved that the message came as a simple letter rather than anything more supernatural and disturbing, but the message felt ominous nonetheless.

Lavinia had shaken her head. "I don't think you'd want to find out." When Michelle had asked more questions, she'd only said that she didn't know much about witches. Vampires and witches avoided each other whenever they could.

"Will it be dangerous?" None of Lavinia's warnings made Michelle feel more confident about this meeting.

"Not to you, I don't think," Lavinia had said. That didn't particularly help assuage her fears either. It all felt like a confusing case of mistaken identity. Lavinia had told her they would be testing her for some kind of magical abilities, which was ridiculous. She didn't have any magical powers.

If she had, she wouldn't have been living in a tiny apartment for the last five years. Wouldn't she have been able to magic herself to richness? Shouldn't she have felt, you know, *special* or *different* in some way? Michelle had always felt perfectly ordinary. She was never the smartest kid in class, nor did she particularly struggle more than the other kids. Nursing school had been tough, but she worked hard and got her degree. She was special, say, to her mum, but to the rest of the world, Michelle was just... normal. If she'd been harbouring these amazing magical powers, wouldn't she have known, somehow?

They were meeting the witches in some field half an hour's drive away. Michelle had asked whether it wouldn't make more sense for the witches to come to the mansion, but Lavinia had explained that Thornblood was protected by various measures that prevented magic. "Iron in the walls, underground salt circle, that kind of thing," she'd said, like any of that meant anything to Michelle. Additionally, the vampires didn't trust the witches not to spy on them or to try to find faults in their anti-witchery protections. The witches, on the other hand, seemed not particularly keen to be surrounded by a brood of warrior vampires on their own turf either. So, a neutral space was negotiated, away from human eyes.

"Couldn't they have chosen anything indoors?" Michelle asked as they walked the last couple of hundred yards through a grey drizzle of rain. It beaded on her coat, somehow soaking her hair.

Lavinia shrugged beside her. Vesta simply said, "Witches."

It had been decided that Vesta would accompany her, in addition to Lavinia. Lavinia herself refused to budge from Michelle's side, and Michelle was incredibly grateful for her familiar presence now. Vesta, too, was formidable in her own way. She was almost impossibly beautiful, with waist-length blonde hair and alabaster skin, wearing loose flowing dresses that somehow just skimmed above the dewed grass. She was what Michelle imagined a goddess would look like, and she found herself somewhat awed by her presence. Michelle had also seen several daggers disappear between the folds of Vesta's dress. She might seem serene and angelic, but Michelle was certain she could hold her own in a fight.

Despite Vesta's pristine beauty, Michelle found her eyes being drawn to Lavinia. She marvelled at the green of her eyes, brought out by the grasses and hedges they walked past. Of the two, she very much preferred Lavinia's clean handsomeness, a slightly more down-to-earth loveliness, than Vesta's ethereal beauty.

They made their way to a muddy path striated with old knobbly roots. The track slid between two rows of tall hedges, and they entered a clearing sheltered by the far-reaching branches of oaks, their leaves yellowing in the October breeze. Three figures stood in front of the majestic trunk of a willow. The witches, Michelle assumed, though they looked just like anyone else. It was almost disappointing, in a way. All morning, images of pop-culture witches wearing pointy hats and floor-length black cloaks had darted through her mind. Lavinia had also warned her that the witches might resort to tricks, like appearing out of thin air. A nervous laugh tickled the back of her throat at the solemn looks of the three figures, one a child, one a bearded man in his twenties, and an older woman. They looked no more sinister than a family on a day's outing in the woods.

The urge to laugh faded when they stopped within a couple of paces from the witches. It wasn't just that Michelle feared what would happen now, although she did. Nor was it the solemnity with which the three gazed at them. There was something uncanny about the space itself. There was no sound besides the whisper of the leaves of the tree—no birdsong. Even though Michelle was a London-born city girl through and through, she had spent enough school holidays camping in the British countryside, and none of it had felt like this. It was like a blanket cloaked them from the surrounding area; like they were *enveloped* by something, some energy. She couldn't explain it rationally, but she could feel something like electric static tingling and raising the tiny hairs on her arms.

Lavinia gently pressed a steadying hand onto her back. She hadn't even realised she'd lost her balance.

Vesta spoke first. "As per the council's request, the Sisterhood presents Michelle Hughes."

"Thank you," the man in the middle said. He was tall, and his red hair and beard shone golden in the grey light. With his flannel shirt and heavy work boots, he exuded the rugged air of a man comfortable in the outdoors. "Michelle, my name is Arran. These are Althea," he gestured towards the older woman at his right hand, "And Balor." He indicated the child on his left side. The boy looked to be about eight and wore a simple moss-green tunic over loose trousers.

Michelle didn't like the way he looked at her: there was something in his face that didn't suit the youth of his body. There was nothing of the energetic clumsiness of the child in the way he stood, or the disdain in the corners of his mouth. The worst, however, were his eyes. They were completely black, showing not even a sliver of iris or white. Michelle forced herself to look back at Arran, a cold shiver running down her spine.

"Hello," she said uncertainly.

"All witches potentate are tested through the same three trials:

earth, soul, and sky. If you have any magic in your veins, it will answer the call. If there isn't..." He shrugged. "We will be on our way, and you may return to the Sisterhood."

"And if I do? Have magic, I mean."

"Then you will be subject to our laws and will complete an apprenticeship according to our custom." Lavinia's hand on Michelle's back twitched. Michelle, too, tensed. Arran's words sounded pretty damn ominous. She had no intention of going anywhere with these people, least of all the creepy child.

"The first trial is earth, which will be administered by me." He gestured for Michelle to step forward. As she did so, Lavinia's hand slid away from her back. She wished she could go back, flanked by the vampire warriors. They were intimidating in their own way, but they made her feel safe. These witches, on the other hand, she didn't trust at all.

"Hold out your hands, palms up." Michelle did as he directed. Arran took two stones from his pocket and placed one in each of her palms. They were crystals of some kind, still somewhat warm to the touch. One was a chocolate brown, roughly textured. The other was a beautifully polished and clear violet. She held each of them, feeling the slight weight of them in her palms. She looked back at Arran, who frowned.

Was she supposed to do anything with them? Make them move or something, like telekinesis? Before she could contemplate this further, Arran snatched the stones back. "Right," he said, and returned to his companions. Michelle couldn't tell whether he was disappointed or merely annoyed.

"The next trial is air, which will be administered by Althea."

The older woman stepped forward now. She wore her grey hair in a braid down her back, and her grey eyes reminded Michelle of the stone of an ancient fortress.

"Your hand," Althea said, and this time a soft white feather was placed in her palm. Its barbs waved gently in the breeze, but the feather didn't lift off into the wind. Again, Althea observed her for a moment, then took the feather back.

These trials were incredibly puzzling. Was she supposed to know what to do with these stones and the feather? Were they expecting some sort of magic trick? If that was the case, they were certainly barking up the wrong tree. All of Michelle's life had been perfectly ordinary until a couple of weeks ago.

Althea returned to her place without a further word, but she wore a sour expression. Michelle felt like she had somehow disappointed her.

"The final trial is that of soul, administered by Balor."

Michelle repressed the urge to step backwards as the creepy child approached her. She held out her hand again, expecting some other thing to be placed on it. Instead, the boy grasped her right hand in his, his black eyes boring into hers. Thoughts flitted through her mind: the sound of drawers opening and closing, nimble little fingers leafing through pages, the searching beam of a lighthouse converging, converging.

The thin layer of sweat on Balor's warm, small hand clung to hers. A rustling of leaves, snatches of long-lost voices. Then Balor, without warning, cast her hand away from his. His unnerving eyes slid away from her, as if she were of no more interest to him than a speck of mud. He stepped back to his fellow witches, and Michelle stopped herself from wiping her hand on her jeans. It was ridiculous, but somehow it now felt *unclean*.

The witches didn't speak to each other to compare notes or impressions. They didn't need to, apparently.

"The trials have concluded," Arran said.

"And?" Whatever these tests had been, Michelle was pretty sure she had failed. There had been no majestic surge of amazing power, or latent trickery that she could suddenly access. She had no idea what that would look or feel like. All she knew was that she felt just like she always had, except perhaps some additional embarrassment over standing in the middle of a clearing with a couple of vampires and triad of witches.

Balor answered, his voice eerily high yet resonant. It was as if every word had an echo that chased his speech. "Your magic is infinitesimal. It is a spark without a flame, a minute flicker of desperation."

"Does this mean I have to come with you?" Michelle didn't voice her second question: *does this mean I'm a witch?*

Althea sneered. Arran, only barely more political, said, "No. It would not be worthwhile to train you. Perhaps the flame could have been ignited in you when you were still malleable and young. It will now stay dormant."

Barely a witch then. Perhaps not even a witch at all.

It was an incredible relief. While Michelle liked *Practical Magic* as much as the next person, she couldn't imagine going with *them*. She briefly imagined having to live with the creepy child, his unrelentingly black eyes following her throughout her day. It was the stuff of nightmares. "Right. Well. Thank you for your time." The platitude came out rather limply, but she didn't know what else to say. The witches, now that the main event was over, seemed to have lost any interest in her. Arran turned to Vesta.

"Regarding our shared enemies. We are closing in on the warlock. Once they are caught, we will share any further information we can glean from him with the Sisterhood to seek out the rogue they are in communication with."

Vesta inclined her head. She made it look graceful and natural. "The Sisterhood thanks the Council for their generous openness regarding this issue. We look forward to a return to normality and our accustomed peace and prosperity."

"Indeed." Arran nodded to Vesta and Lavinia and, without any further glance to Michelle, the three witches turned, walking straight into the solid tree trunk they had stood in front of. Michelle blinked twice, not trusting her eyes. As they stepped into it, the bark somehow became translucent, as if made from the thinnest of weaves, and the witches were swallowed up into its depths. Michelle had seen some weird things over these last couple of weeks—hell, she had even *done* some strange things, like offering her blood to a vampire—but this took the cake.

Lavinia shook her head. "Told you. Damn witches."

"Not here," Vesta warned. With a graceful gesture of one arm, she broke the hold that this show of the impossible had cast on Michelle and guided them out of the clearing. Walking back to the car, Michelle fell into step beside Lavinia. "The witches freak me out."

"They unsettle me too. Many of us think they do so on purpose."

Michelle shivered, and not because of the grey drizzle steadily drifting from the clouds. "I'm glad I don't have to go with them."

Lavinia glanced down at her, her green eyes darkened by the leaden sky. "Me too."

Chapter Twenty

Michelle stretched across the sofa in the TV room. The movement made the cushion underneath Lavinia shift and caused a lance of pain to stab through her hip. The doctor hadn't been lying when he said it would take some time to recover. She could walk, but any kind of high-risk situation was out of the question.

The Sisterhood was on high alert since the nest had been found so near their base. Rogues were reckless, and they occasionally lived together in small family groups caught in some kind of shared blood rage, but the Sisters had never seen a group so large in such a remote area. Nor had there been any reports of humans suffering mysterious deaths, one of the signs that rogues might be hunting in a region. Somehow, they had not only hidden themselves, but had also managed to feed covertly. Lavinia couldn't shake the feeling that there was something different about these rogues. Her Sisters were out there right now, scouring the surrounding hills for information on what the hell was going on.

Instead of being there with them, Lavinia had been benched over the last week, forced to take a break while the skin of her scalp knitted back together and the bruising in her hip healed.

Normally, she would have been impatient to go back out there. Realistically, she was still somewhat restless at the thought of not backing up her Sisters. But the enforced time off also meant spending time with Michelle, which was an absolute pleasure.

"I can't help but feel somewhat rejected," Michelle said. She leaned over Lavinia to grab another strawberry from the plate on the coffee table. Lavinia could have handed her the plate, of course, but Michelle seemed content with the arrangement, and so was she. They had chosen to sit in the TV room, which was smaller and cosier than the downstairs rooms. Few of the other Sisters ever went here, giving them a sense of privacy that was often lacking in the Sisterhood's headquarters.

"Rejected?"

"The witches. Them telling me I'm such a terrible witch that I might as well not be one at all."

"Would you want to be one?" It had been a weight off Lavinia's shoulders when the witches dismissed Michelle. Lavinia hadn't wanted to consider the possibility that Michelle might be one of them. Her perspective on the insurmountable difference between human and vampire had slowly been shifting. The chasm between vampire and witch, however, still prevailed. If she had indeed been one, Michelle would have been forced to be taken into the fold of the Witch Council, and they would have been drawn into different directions by their different allegiances.

At least now Lavinia could hold onto the small and distant hope that somehow Michelle might not have to be completely lost to her after all of this was over. Perhaps they would find a way for their paths to cross, sometimes. For now, though, she would enjoy every moment with her that she could find.

"Not really. I mean, I don't know. It really depends on what witches can do, right? Would I be able to magic away illnesses? That would come in very handy at my job."

"I think they probably get sick like everyone else," Lavinia said. "Vampires do, too."

Michelle sighed. "Probably."

"And worst of all, you would have to be... with *them*."

"Excellent point. What was up with that kid? Should he really be involved with things like that?"

"Well, I met Balor for the first time over forty years ago," Lavinia said.

"No way." Michelle started upright—another jolt through Lavinia's hip. Still, Lavinia wouldn't move away or sit on one of the armchairs. She was exactly where she wanted to be.

Lavinia nodded. "I don't know what the witches call... what he is. We call them the forever children, because they don't age. It is said that it is a bargain they make, where they choose magic over the growth of a normal human life. I don't know of any making it past sixty. Balor is quite old for his kind."

"So they make a *child* do that to themselves?"

"I don't know whether they have a say in their own creation or not, but yes."

Michelle slumped back into the cushions. "God. I'm starting to see why you all don't like them."

"Don't like who?" Proserpina sauntered into the room. Rest had done her good. Her olive skin had regained warmth, and she moved with more ease. She, too, was relegated to staying inside until she had regrown her torn lung tissue and restored her cracked ribs. She still slept through most of the day, the hours that she was awake extending slowly. When the weather was clear, she and Lavinia lay on the grass for an hour at the height of night, allowing their bodies to heal under the moonlight's rejuvenating rays. Lavinia had taken over some of Pina's duties around the mansion's defence, checking the security systems, both visible and invisible, that protected the Sisterhood's headquarters until Pina was well enough again.

"Witches," Lavinia said. Pina picked up a strawberry from the plate on the coffee table and popped it into her mouth. The soft thickness of bandages around her chest still filled out Pina's loose hoodie, but Lavinia was pleased to see her friend's steady recovery.

"Fucking witches," Pina agreed. Then she looked at Michelle. "No offence."

"Apparently I don't count, which is fine by me," she replied.

"Then I stand by it." Pina sat down on one of the armchairs and folded her legs underneath her. "I don't know how you can stand it, Vin. I'm bored out of my mind."

"Teaches you not to get impaled by a chair leg next time," Lavinia said mildly.

"I swear, those rogues were the most coordinated I've ever seen. And so fast."

Lavinia nodded. She had been thinking much the same.

"How can you tell someone is a rogue, and not like, just another vampire?" Michelle asked.

Pina lifted one perfectly manicured finger. "Well, first of all, a vampire in their right mind would never threaten a Sister of Twilight. But with a rogue, it's more than that. They have a certain smell, all sour and bitter. They feed until their victim dies, and that death clings to them. It's in their eyes, their movements. It's hard to explain, but once a vampire truly gives themselves up to their thirst for blood, they leave their senses behind. They usually barely speak—reasoning with them is impossible. It's like they have reverted into an animalistic state."

"And they never come back from it?"

"Never," Pina said.

"Couldn't they be locked up or something?"

"Annihilation is the only justice vampires know," Pina said.

"It just seems so…"

"Cruel?" Pina supplied.

"Yeah. Maybe."

It wasn't like humans had a much better track record. Lavinia could well remember the festival atmosphere of the London public executions of the early nineteenth century. Then, due to changes in ideas of morality, they had been curtailed, held behind closed doors. Now, the Brits no longer killed their murderers but kept them to live out their lives in crumbling estates. Lavinia wasn't a moral philosopher. All she knew was that rogues were a danger to civilians, vampire and human alike.

"You have to remember a rogue could live on for centuries. As they descend deeper, they become increasingly engulfed by their frustrated desires. Quite frankly, keeping them alive only to suffer would be torture," Pina said.

"It's an imperfect response," Lavinia agreed. It was certainly dirty work, and dangerous. "But it's the only one we have right now." If there was a way to bring a rogue back from the brink, that would be vastly preferable. No one had ever been able to. Many rogues killed their family members, or even loved ones, if they stood between them and the objects of their obsessions.

"You should talk to Octavia about this. She lives for this kind of shit." Pina lowered her voice to mimic Octavia's, pinching her eyebrows. "Pina, we need to dismantle the matriarchy, or true equality will never prevail." She returned to her normal voice. "She doesn't have to tell me, I was born under a different star."

"What does that mean, born under a different star?" Michelle asked.

Pina picked up another strawberry and turned it between her fingers. "I think you humans nowadays would call it 'trans'. The name might have changed over the centuries, but the idea stays the same. I wasn't born Proserpina, fifth of her name. I was renamed at twenty-five at my request. I would not have been able to be a Sister of Twilight if I hadn't. Still, there will be no sixth of her line. As I cannot birth my daughters, my line will end with me."

It was an unfairness that Pina and Lavinia had spoken about occasionally, in the early hours of dawn over a couple of bottles of wine. Pina's mother and her consort had been thrilled to meet their daughter, but some difficulties remained, particularly around the rigid roles within the matriarchal vampire society. Only the birth-giver could continue a line, regardless of their gender. Change might happen eventually, but vampire society moved at a glacial speed, nothing like the breakneck pace of its human counterpart.

"Anyway," Pina said. "Changing the subject. What are you two lovebirds up to?"

Lavinia glared at Pina, but Michelle seemed unbothered. "We were just watching one of my favourite TV shows. We'll be going to my mum's birthday in a little bit."

"I can't believe you managed to rope Lavinia into watching TV with you. Usually she has to be dragged kicking and screaming towards anything that has even a whiff of fun to it."

Lavinia frowned. "I'm not that bad."

"Of course not, sweetheart." Pina patted her on the arm, sending a cheeky wink to Michelle. "We love you anyway." Michelle laughed and, at the infectious sound, Lavinia couldn't suppress a smile either.

"However, I can't believe you both would abandon me in my hour of need." Pina slumped dramatically backwards into the chair.

"You'll be fine," Lavinia responded.

"Always so pragmatic, Vin." Pina lifted her hand to her forehead as if in a swoon. "I am a delicate flower."

"Delicate my ass. I've seen you knock out a pair of rogues twice your size within a minute."

"Well. They had it coming."

"That, I agree with." Lavinia glanced at the screen of her

phone. "We gotta go."

Pina sighed. "Fine. I'll go annoy Quintia. I can always get a good rise out of her."

Lavinia stood, the tendons in her right leg straining. She extended her hand to Michelle and helped her up. The feel of her skin made her heartbeat rise. "Quintia's coming with us as well."

Pina's expression of horror was comical. "But if she's gone too, that only leaves me with…"

Lavinia patted Pina's shoulder affectionately. "Exactly. Hope you have a great time annoying Mrs. Frost instead."

Michelle and Lavinia left Proserpina, who sat with a sour expression. It was one thing to goad their hot-headed Sister— quite another to tease the indomitable housekeeper.

Michelle's mother lived in a narrow terraced house on a quiet street in East London. The façade was warm brick, blackened with soot from traffic. They had walked from a nearby parking garage, as the street was already packed to the brim with parked cars. Quintia had taken up her position a hundred yards away, where she was currently leaning against a lamp post, smoking a vape and scrolling on her phone. Quintia didn't actually smoke. The vape was filled with water only, but it allowed Quintia to arouse less suspicion. With her leather jacket, piercings, and permanent scowl, Quintia never particularly blended in, unless the mission required her to be posted at a metal concert. Usually, she drew some measure of attention wherever she went. It just mattered what *type* of attention.

Lavinia could hear voices vibrating through the walls. Four, maybe five people were already inside. The muscles in her neck twitched. Her palms were sweaty, although the autumn temperature was mild, bordering on chilly. Was she nervous? She glanced at Michelle. Her pupils were dilated slightly, and her heartbeat raised. Michelle was tense too.

It was an unexpected conundrum. There was no reason to be nervous. Perhaps if this had been a real date, where Michelle's family was to meet her chosen partner, this would indeed be an important event. But it wasn't a real date, and they weren't partners. Actually, Lavinia had somewhat lost track of what they were to each other. Friends? Certainly. She loved to spend time with Michelle and found her a kind and engaging companion. Lovers? There had been a chemistry between them, and Michelle was very attractive. Possibly the most attractive woman Lavinia had ever had the pleasure of meeting. Unlike some of her Sisters, she wasn't often drawn to romantic or sexual connections. Michelle had awakened a hunger in her that she hadn't felt in decades. Hell, if she was honest with herself, maybe even centuries.

Yet, they hadn't quite crossed that boundary either. Michelle had willingly offered her blood to Lavinia, and Lavinia still felt that power coursing through her veins.

She didn't know what they were to each other. Perhaps that didn't matter. What mattered was that she was here for Michelle, keeping her safe while she spent time with her family.

Thoughts of the rogue and warlock, still at large, crowded Lavinia's mind. She couldn't carry her sword. Instead, she had taken her daggers. One was strapped to her calf inside her boot, the other in a holster at the small of her back, its outline hidden underneath the texture of her knit jumper. The slight discomfort of the holster was familiar, a reassuring reminder of her preparedness. Nothing would disrupt Michelle seeing her family, not if she had anything to say about it.

"Ready?" Michelle asked, a shy smile forming.

Lavinia nodded, the movement sharper and more soldier-like than she had intended. The door was unlocked, and Michelle led her into a cramped foyer. Lavinia had to step almost into Michelle's arms to close the door behind her, cutting off the intrusion of the cool air into the warm house.

"Mum runs a shoes-off household," Michelle said. She slipped out of her trainers, stacking them onto a shelving unit intended for that purpose. Lavinia looked at her boots, the concealed weapon held within. She could leave them on and face the wrath (or mild disappointment) of Michelle's family. It was the rational choice. Keeping Michelle and her relatives physically safe from any potential attack was more important than social rules. On the other hand, it would immediately mark her as a stranger, someone not to be trusted. Someone who would not be suitable for their daughter.

Lavinia stepped out of her boots and left the dagger concealed inside.

Chapter Twenty-One

When they stepped into the living room, Mum was the first to greet them. "My dear!" she shouted across the room, squeezing past Bob and Michelle's Aunt Sarah and Uncle Damien. She descended on them with arms spread wide like a bat. "I thought you would *never* come. I even said to Bob, I don't think she's coming now that she's got this fabulous girlfriend. We will be left all alone! She won't think for a moment of her old mother, who just wishes to spend her birthday with her family." Michelle hugged her, wondering whether there was a genuine edge to her mum's usual dramatics. Mum truly had been worried. There was real relief in her expression. "And you must be Lavinia! I am so *thrilled* to meet you! Michelle hasn't brought a girlfriend home in so long, and Bob and I have been wondering... well, we've been wondering whether she would ever tie the knot!"

"*Mum,*" Michelle complained. It was one thing to be worried, quite another to harass Lavinia. Lavinia was currently in Mum's patent grip, smiling calmly under the onslaught. She envied Lavinia's ability to stay cool. "But now she has you, and we've heard *such great things about you*. We're so happy that you're here, aren't we Bob?" Michelle's stepfather Bob stood behind Mum, smiling sheepishly. When Mum got on one, it was best to just wait for it to pass. "You'll have to tell us everything, we want to know everything about you! And between us two," Mum's voice dropped down into what could hardly be called a whisper. Everyone in the room heard her next words. "We are so glad that you're taking care of our Michelle. She's been so lonely, all by herself in her apartment."

"*Okay*," Michelle said with emphasis. "That's quite enough of that. Let's get Lavinia a drink, shall we, Mum?" With some effort, she pried Mum's hands from Lavinia's arms. But the implication that she was being a poor hostess was like catnip, and she finally released the bemused vampire into the benign care of Bob, while Michelle dragged her mother into the narrow kitchen.

"Could you dial it down, just a little bit?" she hissed when they were alone.

"Oh honey, we're just so happy for you," Mum said, filling the kettle for a new round of tea. "She's gorgeous, isn't she? Tall and statuesque. Like an Amazon, and with that beautiful blonde hair. I can see why you like her."

"Well. Yes. I do," Michelle stuttered. Perhaps this had all been a terrible idea. It had seemed so straightforward. While someone was after her for some unknown reason, Lavinia had to be around. It would be easy to explain her presence if they were dating. But she hadn't quite expected this welcome, though now she was here, perhaps she should have. It was all just an excuse; she wasn't dating Lavinia. And now it seemed like Mum would be devastated if she found out it was fake.

Michelle didn't want to be the bearer of bad news, especially on her birthday. She would have to bear their enthusiasm, and at some point in the future, invent some reason why they had broken up. She could pretend to be dating Lavinia for one day, couldn't she? "Just, please, don't scare her off."

Mum waved away her concerns. "How does she take her tea? Or does she drink coffee?"

"I think she'd prefer water, actually. She's not huge on hot drinks."

"Well, go and ask her, I don't want her to think we're rude."

"Sure." Michelle went back into the living room, where Lavinia had been given the best seat on the sofa. She looked to be in conversation with Bob, while Aunt Sarah and Uncle Damien listened from the dining room chairs that had been set around the coffee table.

Lavinia looked up the second Michelle took a step onto the living room carpet.

"Would you like a drink? We've got tea, coffee..." Michelle asked.

"Just water, please," Lavinia said.

"Could you bring the coffee pot too, please, sweetheart?" Bob added.

"Of course." Michelle went back into the kitchen. "Just water for Lavinia."

Mum handed her a glass of tap water, giving her a knowing smile. "Seems like you two are on the same wavelength."

Michelle suppressed the urge to roll her eyes. "It's just a drink, Mum."

"Well, it's the little things that are important. The big things will follow," Mum retorted.

"I guess," she said non-committedly. She didn't have the heart to say that, for them, there would be no big things. Their lives were just too different. Hell, Lavinia was a *vampire*. And not just a normal one, either—she was like a vampire commando, running straight into deadly danger. Michelle was glad that the weather was cold enough to wear a turtleneck, the collar hiding the two scabbed-over puncture wounds visible on her neck. She blushed thinking of Lavinia holding her close, her lips on her skin, the heat of her mouth. In a way, it had been more intimate than a kiss would have been.

"Ohhh, you're blushing," Mum cooed. Michelle grabbed the freshly made coffee and fled the kitchen and her mum's teasing smiles.

She found herself ensconced on the sofa with Lavinia, feeling uncomfortably like a teenager bringing a first girlfriend home. Luckily, Lavinia impressed Bob with her knowledge of history.

"Gosh, I never knew that there'd been rumours of Queen Victoria having an affair after her husband's death," he said. Michelle wondered what he would think if he knew that Lavinia had been sixty already by the time Victoria claimed the throne. He would probably be ecstatic, to be fair.

Mum was pleased with Lavinia's good manners and attentiveness towards Michelle, absolutely beaming in her armchair when Lavinia offered Michelle the plate of biscuits so she wouldn't have to reach. After half an hour of intense scrutiny, it was a relief when her half-siblings arrived, a brood of children of varying ages in tow. The children demanded attention, and Mum and Bob easily slipped into the roles of doting grandparents.

"Sorry about all of that," Michelle said under her breath when the showing off of a favourite toy had solidly drawn the family's attention away from them.

"Not at all," Lavinia said.

It was strange. She often seemed otherworldly, or strangely remote. Right now, on the worn sofa in her mum's terraced house, she looked like she could have been anyone. She looked like someone Michelle could have brought home to meet her family for real, not as some guise for her protection. She hadn't realised how easily Lavinia could assimilate into the domesticity of normal people despite her decidedly abnormal life. She deflected any probing questions, telling them she worked in private security at events, and easily spoke of her family as if they weren't centuries old. Some of the assumptions Michelle had made about her were crumbling.

It had been easy to dismiss her feelings for Lavinia when she hid behind the thought that they could never be together: that they were just too different, that it could never work. Bit by bit, that thought was becoming more and more brittle. Was it really true that it could never work? What if it could? Would Michelle *want* to be with her? The repercussions of these questions were too big to consider now, surrounded by her eager family members. She would think about all of that later, when she was alone.

Aside from her feelings about Lavinia, there was another subject weighing on her mind. While the others were busy in a conversation of their own, she turned to her mother.

"Mum, I—I wanted to talk to you about Dad."

"Of course honey, what about him?" There was no discomfort about the topic visible on her mother's face. Whatever grief had been there once upon a time had faded over the decades.

"I've been thinking about him more recently. I was wondering if you could tell me anything more about him."

Mum shook her head slightly, "It was such a long time ago, dear."

"I know."

"Well, as you know, we only dated for a month. We met at a party, and I gave him my phone number. He would pick me up on his motorcycle, and we would have the most wonderful adventures. Went for picnics, or he would take me out dancing. We had such a lovely time, and it was a surprise when he stopped calling. He wouldn't pick up when I rang him either. I figured at first he had found someone else, you know how these things go sometimes, especially when you're young. But then I saw his name in the newspaper obituaries. It was a shock, that was." Her gaze softened. "I can still remember it like yesterday, how I sat at the breakfast table at your grandparents' house."

"Did you ever go to his funeral?"

"Oh, no, it had already happened by the time I found out. Why?"

Michelle shrugged. "Just wondering. I've realised recently that I know so little about him. And even less about his family—which I guess is also my family."

"I think he mentioned an older brother once or twice... But I can't think of his name, or if he even said it at the time. I'm sorry, honey. I thought about reaching out and telling his family, but by the time I knew you were on your way, it all happened so quickly, and it never really came about. I never meant to keep you from them, you know."

"No, of course, I understand." Michelle patted Mum's hand. "Don't worry about it." She wasn't angry, couldn't be angry at her mother, not about this. It must have been hard enough to be a single mother and raise Michelle by herself. She had only ever tried to do right by Michelle. She had always told her the truth about her father, though she had softened the grim reality of his death when she was younger.

Now, though, she had started to wonder. Lavinia had said that magic *could* run in families, though not necessarily. Michelle had some magic, as little and useless as it was. Could it be possible that her father had had magic, too? Would he have been a witch? What about her other family members? Did she have aunts, uncles, perhaps cousins that she had never even known about? It was odd how these questions had lain dormant in her mind for many years, only to be shaken loose now that so many parts of her life were in flux. She'd asked many questions as a kid and could remember very well how she'd follow Mum around asking about his favourite colour or his favourite animal, which Mum bore with exceptional patience. Over time, the questions had petered out, and the routine of everyday life had taken over. She had never known her father and never would, and that was that.

But now she was coming to terms with a whole new world of warrior vampires and witchy trials and demon attacks, and it turned out that perhaps she had never been as separate from these things as she had initially assumed. Perhaps it had always been her world, except that she had been torn from it by one reckless drunk driver swerving into the opposite lane one night almost thirty years ago.

Although Lavinia and Michelle had planned to set off early to make the long drive back to Thornblood in daylight, Michelle's family predictably placated and enticed them with an endless supply of food and drink, making it impossible to leave. When they finally extricated themselves after promising several times that they would be back, that Lavinia would certainly come again, and that they would drive safely, the sun was already low on the horizon.

"Hope that was alright," Michelle said as they walked along the quiet street.

"Of course. Why wouldn't it be?"

"They can be a bit... much." There was a reason she didn't take many women to meet her family. Okay, fine, part of the reason was that she barely dated. Who had time for that? She was lucky that her family was so accepting and so excited to meet whoever Michelle decided to take home. On the other hand, they could be a bit intense about it. She wouldn't put it past Mum to be picking out wedding invitations right about now.

"They were very kind," Lavinia said. "And they care about you very much."

Michelle smiled, relief spreading a sudden lightness throughout her. "True. And they liked you." Her family was nice, but it hadn't just been politeness—they had genuinely liked Lavinia.

As they crossed the street, a shape moved in the corner of Michelle's eye. Quintia appeared as if from nowhere, making her jump. Lavinia seemed completely unbothered—she must have heard her approach.

"Anything?" Lavinia asked.

"All quiet. I followed a drug dealer on his rounds to amuse myself for a little bit, but nothing that concerned us," Quintia said, falling in beside Lavinia.

"Good."

"I got you some cake, Quintia." Michelle held up a stack of takeaway containers, now repurposed to hold an impressive array of cake and biscuits. "I didn't know what you would like, so I brought different ones."

Quintia took the box and grunted. Lavinia elbowed her in her side. "I mean, thanks."

It had gotten too late to make the drive back, Lavinia said, so they would just stay over in her apartment for the night.

"You have an apartment?"

Lavinia looked at her in surprise. "Of course."

"Sorry, I just thought that you all lived at the mansion."

"Most of the time. It's just convenient to be there, as it's where we operate from. We all have our own places too, though."

It was only a short drive to the leafy modern suburb of Lavinia's apartment. They parked underneath a tall apartment block that shone in the setting sun, its abundance of glass reflecting the last yellow rays. The elevator that carried them up into the building required both a passkey as well as a password before its brushed metal doors would open. They rose smoothly upwards, and the doors opened into a broad and brightly lit corridor. Despite clearly aiming at a richer clientele than Michelle's apartment building—instead of hard-wearing plastic flooring, the corridor was all smooth, shining marble—it had the same air of transience. Even money couldn't make a corridor more than a place you'd rather pass through as fast as possible.

Lavinia repeated the ritual of key and password at her front door, the keypad turning green and buzzing briefly when she pressed a button.

"Come on in," she said, and held open the door.

Chapter Twenty-Two

Michelle wasn't sure what she'd been expecting, especially after having seen Lavinia's room at Thornblood. Perhaps that room, with its bare walls and lack of personal items, had just been some kind of temporary base, while her actual apartment would breathe "home". Nothing was further from the truth: if anything, there was even less of Lavinia visible here.

It was a beautiful place, in that stark modern minimalist way. Everything consisted of clean lines and sharp angles, the walls white, the carpet an unobtrusive cream. A marble-topped island stood in the centre of the kitchen, which led into the open-plan living room. It had everything you would expect from a modern apartment: a comfortable-looking grey sofa, a large TV on the wall facing it. Floor-to-ceiling windows opened onto a concrete balcony that overlooked the city. It was stunning, in a way, and certainly a far cry from Michelle's messy and cramped apartment. Yet at the same time, it seemed like a transitory place: impersonal, as if it was waiting for a touch of life. It was the kind of place you'd hire for a brief holiday stay.

Quintia clearly read some of her thoughts from her expression. "Vin doesn't do decorating."

Lavinia pulled the hair tie from her ponytail, running her

hands through her long, blonde hair. "I just haven't had the time."

"How long have you had the apartment?" Quintia asked. There was a glint in her eye that made Michelle think she already knew the answer.

"Twenty-three years, I think."

"Over two decades, can't find an hour to put a fucking painting on the wall." Quintia slapped her on the back. "You're absolutely hopeless. Anyway, I'm going to hang out in the guest room to get away from the both of you. All of your pining glances disgust me." With those parting words, she shouldered her bag and sauntered into one of the bedrooms at the side of the apartment, slamming the door shut behind her.

Michelle walked to the windows. They were five storeys up, and the view of the city was stunning. The cityscape unfolded before her, roofs stretching in all directions. The high-rises of the inner city stood proudly on the horizon, the last pink tones of the setting sun gleaming on their façades. "The view is amazing."

"It's one of the reasons I chose this one," Lavinia said, moving to stand beside her. They stood in companionable silence for a moment. "Do you think I should decorate more?"

"Oh." Michelle glanced at her. "Do you want an honest answer?"

"Please."

"It's up to you, of course, but it does seem a bit... sterile. Is there nothing you would like to put anywhere? No pictures, or keepsakes, anything?" She thought of the relentless shades of white. "Maybe a plant?"

Lavinia smiled, a little sadly. "I never really thought about it. My focus has always been on my duties, my Sisters, and my family. Perhaps I have been remiss in the other parts of my life."

Michelle moved closer so their shoulders touched. "I think it's amazing, the things you do. Risking your life for others. For me." The last yellow of the sun disappeared beyond the horizon. The sky was darkening, but there was still enough light to see by. "You're really brave."

"Thank you," Lavinia said, her voice so low it was almost a whisper. "Michelle, I want to..."

A small movement caught Michelle's eye. She looked more closely, peering through the fading light. There—there it was again. A flicker, like a light reflected in glass. It seemed suspended in the air. The flicker grew, reformed, and shaped itself into a tear. "Lavinia," she said, a primal fear rooting her feet to the spot.

Something was coming through. Smoke roiled on its surface. Within the blink of an eye, it had squeezed itself into reality, unfolding into the monster of her nightmares: the demon that had attacked her that night only a couple of weeks ago. Its flaming eyes glowed with malice, its monstrous arms outstretched towards her, lunging for her. She tripped backwards, trying to get away, her cheek burning with the memory of searing pain.

Steady hands caught her before she could tumble into the coffee table. "It can't reach you." Lavinia's calm voice in her ear grounded her, cutting through the blind panic coursing through her veins. "I won't let it hurt you." Michelle forced herself to focus on Lavinia's arms around her, on her steady body behind her. She took one shaking, shallow breath, then another. The demon was stopped in its forward progress, claws still outstretched. It couldn't press on, stopped by the glass.

"Why can't it come in?" Michelle asked, clutching at Lavinia.

"The windows and walls, even the foundations and the roof, have all been inlaid with salt. We are basically in one large protective circle that demons cannot cross. Unfortunately, there was no easy way to treat the balcony, so it falls outside of its protection." Lavinia's arms tightened around Michelle, feeling her shiver. "The whole building is secure. It's not as sophisticated as Thornblood, but it'll keep out any demons."

"So it really can't reach us?"

"It really can't," Lavinia said confidently.

The calm in her voice made Michelle relax the tiniest amount. She realised her fingernails had been digging into Lavinia's upper arm. "I'm sorry," she said, embarrassed.

"Don't be. Don't ever apologise for being afraid. Our fear protects us."

Michelle tore her eyes away from the demon and its hateful gaze. "You never seem scared at all." Only a couple of days ago, she had run headlong into danger, sword in hand.

Lavinia laughed, a small chuckle that reverberated through Michelle's body. "I am afraid all the time. Afraid that we will be too late to save an innocent bystander. Afraid that one of my Sisters might get hurt or be killed. Afraid that the world might change in such a way that we can no longer live in the shadows and will be forced into the harsh light of the human public eye. There is so much to fear." Her voice was low and soft. Lavinia's face was so close that Michelle could see every eyelash encircling her half-closed eyes. "Do you fear me, Michelle?"

"No," Michelle answered immediately. "No," she repeated. It was the truth. She was afraid of many things, including the demon currently clawing at the glass of the balcony window, any contact throwing up bright sparks into the rising dark. Her heart beat in her throat, and fear coursed through her veins, but *this*, being in Lavinia's arms, felt right. This felt... safe. There was no doubt in her mind. "I'm not afraid of you."

"Good," Lavinia whispered. Then she bent towards Michelle and kissed her.

Their lips touched and it was as if every feeling that she'd had over the last couple of weeks, every thought, poured out between them. There was no distance, no holding back. Everything narrowed completely into the softness of her lips, the feel of them moving against hers, the sweet scent of her skin. It was everything she had dreamt of in secret moments, everything she'd hoped for—and more. They might be vampire and human, but in this moment, they were simply two women, kissing.

They explored the kiss with a hunger and a sense of urgency. Michelle wrapped her arms around Lavinia's waist, revelling in the feel of her. The muscles of her back moved underneath her fingertips, their strength noticeable even through her soft jumper. Their kiss deepened, and she slid her hand underneath the edge of the fabric, luxuriating in the velvety suppleness of her skin. She pressed her body against Lavinia's, her pliant curves against Lavinia's muscular firmness. Lavinia's kiss slowed, her lips nipping gently at Michelle's.

"What's wrong?" Michelle said, pulling back an inch, reluctantly breaking contact. Lavinia's green eyes seemed almost black in the scant light.

"Nothing," Lavinia breathed. "I just... have never..."

Michelle's mind ground to a halt. "Wait—you're a virgin?"

Lavinia chuckled, the movement travelling between their bodies. "No, it's not that." She stroked her hand down Michelle's back in a way that made a delicious shiver travel down her spine. "Just never with a human."

"Oh. That makes sense." Her thoughts slowly sped back up to their usual pace. "I don't think it's any different," she offered, smiling sheepishly. Vampires might be very different on the cellular level, but their anatomy... that seemed familiar enough.

"No, you're probably right," Lavinia said, a faint smile on her lips. Those soft, kissable lips.

Michelle nestled closer into her arms. "You don't need to hold back," she whispered, planting the tiniest kiss on the corner of Lavinia's mouth. "Don't hold back."

Lavinia captured her lips with hers, an avalanche of sensation travelling through Michelle's body like lightning. With one smooth movement, Lavinia picked her up. Michelle wrapped her legs around her waist. Lavinia carried her with ease, stepping away from the window.

"Wait," Michelle said, "What about the demon?" She didn't bother looking towards the balcony, where the creature undoubtedly still clawed at the building's defences.

"The demon can go to hell," Lavinia growled, and kissed her again. Michelle dissolved in her arms, letting herself be carried away by the gorgeous vampire, shutting the demon and her fears out with the slam of the bedroom door.

Chapter Twenty-Three

Lavinia awoke in a haze of contentment. Michelle lay cradled in her arms, still asleep, her breaths deep and slow. The first rays of sunlight peeked around the curtains, bathing Michelle in a soft glow. It was a blissful lull, one of those delightful moments where time slowed down and it felt like everything was as it should be. Michelle was here, in her arms. Lavinia let her eyes drift shut again, nestling into the warm, drowsy embrace.

The doorknob turned, and Quintia barged into the room with the subtlety of a rhinoceros. "Rise and shine," she said, throwing Lavinia's clothes at her. "Assholes have been at it again."

"What?" Lavinia said, not quite following. Her mind was full of Michelle, and only Michelle. Of the feel of her, the taste of her. There was no room in her thoughts for Quintia's emergency.

"The murderers. You know, the ones that've got it out for your lover over there? They've killed again. Octavia just called. She's waiting for us." Those words were enough to shatter Lavinia's reverie.

Michelle stirred and opened her eyes, blinking the haze of sleep away. "What's happening?"

"I have to get up," Lavinia said, extricating herself from their tangle of limbs with regret. She placed a tender kiss on Michelle's forehead. "You can stay here. Get some more sleep." They hadn't gotten much last night, after all.

Michelle rubbed the sleep from her eyes. "No, no, I'm coming."

"Alright," she said, looking at Quintia, who simply shrugged. Michelle would be safe enough in the apartment, but Lavinia preferred to have her close.

Quintia gave her a quick rundown as they hurried into their clothes. A vampire had found three dead bodies only fifteen minutes away. Octavia was already at the scene. The police couldn't be far behind, so if they wanted to have a look before the humans got involved, they would have to leave right now.

Michelle looked somewhat pale in the bright light of morning as they neared the building where the bodies had been found. It was a house at the end of a street, its windows boarded up and its tiny patch of a front garden overgrown with waist-high weeds. Lavinia squeezed Michelle's hand briefly, and she gave a grateful smile in return. Lavinia's heart clenched. She would do anything for this woman. When she finally got to the warlock who was targeting her, they would fall by her sword.

They entered the building through the back. The door had been nailed shut at one point, but now hung open limply. They stepped into a dark kitchen, scant light making its way around the boards covering the windows. The stench of blood pervaded the air so thickly that Michelle coughed. It mingled with the damp mustiness of the mould clinging to the walls, its black tendrils burrowing through wallpaper and stone.

It was exactly the kind of space a rogue would use, and underneath the freshly spilled blood was indeed the unmistakable scent of a rogue: the sour bitterness of a vampire gone wrong. Quintia took point, climbing a wooden staircase, passing through a corridor of bare floorboards covered in dust and debris. She led them into what must have been a bedroom at some point, but what was now a scene of carnage.

Three dead bodies lay in the room. Octavia stood in the middle of the space with her arms crossed, surveying the scene. No furniture was left behind by previous inhabitants to clutter the empty space. The smudged wallpaper hung down in strips, the damp having loosened the adhesive until gravity won its battle. One body lay so close to the door opening that they had to step over it. "Careful," Lavinia muttered, helping Michelle avoid the pool of blood that had spread underneath it.

"What have you got so far?" Quintia asked.

"Three bodies, all human. Two female, and the one by the door is male. Looks like the male was killed by a tenebris, the other two have clear marks of draining."

"So those were killed by the rogue."

"Exactly. They were found by a civilian vampire passing by. His name is Claudius, son of Claudia, seventh of her name. He smelled the blood while he was walking across the street and got curious. As he went to the back door, he heard someone exit the house through a window at the front of the house. Once he realised what had happened, he called the Magistrate. They let us know."

"Did the civilian hear anyone else?" Lavinia asked, kneeling beside the body at the doorway. It was difficult to guess the man's age. His face was covered in deep scratches, blood obscuring his features.

"No," Octavia said. "Which brings us to our problem."

"What problem?" Quintia asked. "Besides all of the murdering."

"Smell them," Octavia answered.

It was difficult to penetrate the stench of blood to take in the more subtle scents that lay underneath. Lavinia sniffed the man. There was the rogue, unmistakable in its bitter note. Human blood, of course. The brimstone of a demon, an uncomfortably sulphurous odour. Then, the scent of the human himself: soap, beer, sweat, and a hint of cinnamon.

She swapped positions with Quintia, examining the woman. One of them lay beside a summoning circle carved into the floorboards with a knife. It was surrounded by symbols that meant nothing to Lavinia. They carried the odour of witchcraft, the unmistakable smell of spice that all magic brought with it. Michelle stood in the corner, staying out of the way, while Lavinia and Quintia investigated.

"I don't get it," Quintia said. "Humans, check. Rogue, check. And it reeks of magic."

"There are only four," Lavinia said slowly.

"Four what?"

"I can only smell four individuals. Plus the demon, of course."

"So?"

"If this is the work of a summoner *and* a rogue, there should be five," Octavia said.

Quintia frowned. "But that's impossible."

"That's what I thought too," Octavia said, troubled. "But I have been here for half an hour, and I am sure of it. No other person beyond these three humans and the rogue have entered this room over the last couple of days."

"What does that mean?" Michelle asked, her voice somewhat choked. The room really did reek. Lavinia wished she could whisk her away and keep her from these horrible realities.

"Logically, it means that the rogue and the warlock are one and the same. There were never two people working together. Except that vampires have no magic. Vampires can't be witches. No vampire has ever been born with those capabilities."

"Until now," Lavinia said quietly.

Octavia nodded. "Until now."

Quintia swore. Lavinia didn't say anything, but she agreed with the sentiment. Rogues were bad enough as they were. They had a level of animal cunning, able to hide in the corners of society until they were caught. But none of them had the foresight or capability to manipulate magic and summon demons. Lavinia had always assumed complex thought was beyond the mind of a rogue. Apparently, everything they thought they knew had been wrong.

"What do we do now?" Quintia asked.

Octavia answered, "The way I see it, there are two positives. First, we now know what we are dealing with, even if we don't understand it. Second, we can follow the rogue's trail. All of us have his scent now. He won't be able to hide as easily anymore."

"True," Quintia growled. "Let's go after him." She breathed deeply, eyes closed, committing the scent's profile to memory. Then, in a whirlwind of movement, she was gone.

"We will need to let the witches know," Lavinia said, turning to Octavia. "Even if we're wrong, and the warlock somehow managed to successfully cloak their scent, we can't keep this suspicion to ourselves." Better safe than sorry. Lavinia wasn't keen to find out what the witches would do if they considered the treaty between vampires and witches to be broken. It had been a messy couple of centuries before the treaty was agreed upon.

Octavia nodded. "Agreed. I will call Vesta, let her run point on the communication with the Witch Council. Quintia will be tracking the rogue already, and we will join her on her trail. I imagine Luce will want to send reinforcements. If this is truly a rogue who commands magic, we need as many of us as we can spare."

Quintia's absence manifested as a minor itch on the edge of Lavinia's consciousness. She had to join the hunt, join her Sister. There was only one issue: Michelle.

Michelle still stood in the corner of the room, looking lost in the shadowy interior. She had wrapped her arms around herself tightly, and the shallow and fast heartbeat that thrummed through her veins spoke of her distress. Lavinia ignored the call of the hunt and approached her, cupping her cheek, stroking that buttery skin with her thumb. "Are you alright?" she asked softly.

"Yeah. I think." Michelle's eyes were wide, a wisp of panic moving below the surface. "What will happen to these people?"

"When we're done here, we notify the human police. Call from a payphone, tell them we heard or saw something suspicious. They will take everything from there."

Michelle closed her eyes for a moment, leaning into Lavinia's touch. "Who are they?"

Octavia spoke up from behind Lavinia. She had politely pretended not to hear their conversation, but even the quietest whisper would still be audible. Privacy among the Sisterhood was a polite fiction. "Their names are Stacey Jones, Taylor Richmond, and Elliot Warbrick. All of them still had their wallets with them. I had a look while I was waiting."

Michelle frowned. "Warbrick? That's my dad's name."

"Do you recognise him?"

Michelle shook her head. "I don't know anyone in his family. And he's too..." She swallowed heavily, "wounded to be able to tell whether there is any resemblance. I have only ever seen a handful of grainy pictures of my dad, anyway."

"Could be a coincidence?" Lavinia offered.

"It's not a common name at all. I never met anyone with that last name." Her eyes whipped to Lavinia. "What if it's not a coincidence?"

The puzzle pieces of the case in Lavinia's mind tumbled, reshaped into a different picture. The warlock—the rogue—was killing people. *Their souls have been taken*, Arran had said. What if, somehow, he was *harvesting* them? What had seemed random at first might not be so at all.

Michelle had a small amount of magic, the witches had said after their assessment. What if, for whatever reason, someone was going through her bloodline, picking off those people who weren't under the protection of the Witch Council? It would explain why the witches themselves struggled to make the connection. Lavinia had no idea whether that was even possible, stealing another person's magic. The only thing that really mattered was that someone might be after Michelle, not just because she was at the wrong place at the wrong time, but because of *her*. Because of a heritage that she hadn't even been aware of until recently.

"I think you're right," she said slowly. "I fear it might not be a coincidence at all."

Michelle took a shaky breath. "What happens next?"

Lavinia leaned forward and brushed a fleeting kiss onto her forehead. "We will find who is responsible. Quintia will already be tracking him, and my Sisters and I will join her. It won't be long until we find him. You can stay in the apartment, where you'll be safe. I'll be back as soon as I can."

"What about your leg?" Michelle asked.

The scent of death and violence had pushed any worries about her injury from her mind. Now she was reminded of it, the ache returned. "It'll be fine," Lavinia said. "I rested it for a couple of days. Don't worry about me."

Michelle smiled wanly. "No promises."

"Come. I'll take you to the apartment," Lavinia said, wrapping her arm around Michelle's shoulders.

"Zachary is outside too. Could you take him as well?" Octavia asked, looking up as they passed.

"Of course," Lavinia agreed.

To leave the room, they had to step over the man killed by the demon. The man who might be related to Michelle. When they reached him, Michelle looked at him for a moment. She bent down, lightly touched his shoulder. "I'm sorry," she whispered under her breath.

Chapter Twenty-Four

The ruined face of the murdered man haunted Michelle as Zachary drove them back to Lavinia's apartment. Could it be possible that he had been a relative of hers, however distant? Why was someone trying to kill them? Was there some kind of family secret she knew nothing about, a birthright that had drawn a killer to them? More than ever, Michelle's parentage felt like a gaping hole, a blind spot in which danger had festered. Had she been naïve? Had she been too trusting that nothing more sinister than a chronic illness or two had been lurking in that part of her heritage, such as a possible tendency towards high blood pressure or eczema?

They arrived at the apartment much too quickly. Lavinia brought them upstairs, letting Zachary go in ahead. Without a word, Michelle hugged Lavinia, wrapping her arms around her tightly. "I'm scared," she said, her voice muffled by Lavinia's shoulder.

"I know," Lavinia said, stroking the back of her head. "We will get him, whoever he is. You'll be safe here, and Zachary will keep you company. I'll text when we have any news."

"Okay," Michelle said. She forced herself to let go of Lavinia. A part of her wanted to stay in her arms forever, to shut out any of the fears and anxieties of the real world. In her arms, everything was as it should be.

Lavinia kissed her gently. Michelle leaned in hungrily, grasping at the comfort of Lavinia's lips against hers. "I—" she said, starting a sentence without knowing how it would end. Before she could sift through her confused mind to find out what she had meant to say, Lavinia gave her a final kiss and was gone.

Michelle stood by herself for a minute, feeling like she had missed an opportunity to say something important. Something that could change both of their lives.

"Would you like some tea?" Zachary called from the kitchen, releasing her from her paralysis.

"Yes, please," she answered, walking into the room. All that was left for them was to wait. Wait for the seconds and minutes and hours to pass while the vampires risked their lives, hunting a vampiric serial killer with magical powers. She needed the strongest pot of tea she could find.

"It will be fine, you know," Zachary said, glancing at Michelle. She must be radiating worry right about now. Her nerves practically vibrated with nervous energy. She couldn't bear to sit, so she rummaged through Lavinia's cupboards looking for some mugs. "I know this must seem terrifying, but they do this kind of thing all the time."

The image of Lavinia in her body armour covered in gore rose before Michelle's mind's eye. The wound that had torn through her scalp, the bright bruises against the pale skin of her thigh. Lavinia might be a warrior, used to running headlong into danger, but that was not a comforting thought at all. All Michelle wanted was for her to be safe.

Instead, Lavinia was out there right now, trying to find someone who had killed a dozen people already and was somehow able to send demons to their doorstep. Lavinia was a hero, sure, but right now Michelle wished with all her heart that she wasn't in need of one.

The cupboards were as bare as Michelle had expected, their gaping depths somehow depressing her even further, and it didn't take long for them to find the mugs and teaspoons. Their emptiness only reinforced the feeling of absence of Lavinia, that sweet steady presence that felt so natural, so *right*. It was terrifying to think that they could be torn asunder, that Lavinia might not return from their hunt.

She tried to shake these thoughts from her mind. "What is it like, working for them?" she asked instead, sitting on the edge of an armchair. Zachary had sunk into the sofa, his legs outstretched, crossed at the ankles. Michelle envied his coolness and ease. It stood in stark contrast to the anxiety coursing through her. Still, it might be hours of waiting. She would drive herself crazy if she dwelled on it too much.

"It is both magnificently mad as well as surprisingly mundane," he said. "It's hard to explain. It's easy to forget that they're not human. They look like us. Talk like us, for the most part. They eat, and sleep, and are flesh and blood like us. But at the same time, they can suddenly seem incredibly *different*, almost alien. They've got their own culture, their own customs, many of which make absolutely no sense to me. They're intensely hierarchical in a way that feels like a thing of the past. But that's it, isn't it? It's not even that far in the past for them. Many of them knew my great-great-grandfather and talk about him like he died only a couple of years ago. Probably feels like that to them."

"Has your family been with them for that long?" Michelle asked, surprised.

"A couple of centuries, I think. Should ask Octavia, she's really into history. Or Vesta, she never forgets anyone's family tree." He took a sip of his tea. "It becomes a way of life. We're not bound to them in any formal sense. I don't want you to think we're forced to serve them or anything like that." He flashed a brief smile. "No oaths of blood or anything that exciting. They're generous, though. Paid for my university education, and that of my sister. Got my grandma the very best care available, no questions asked. Dad's slowing down a lot now as well, so although he is supposed to be the groundskeeper, Lucretia has been gently pushing him to take on more help. I could leave, get a different job, whatever. But I don't know, there is something about working for the Sisterhood. It's not just that they're vampires, or that they're richer than anyone else I've ever met. There is something incredibly magnetic about them. I feel a bit like a moth drawn to a flame, sometimes. They shine so brightly, so brilliantly." He shook his head. "I don't know. It's hard to explain. You must think I sound crazy."

"No, not at all," Michelle said. "Actually, I know what you mean." *They shine so brightly.* He was exactly right. Michelle herself had been caught up in it so quickly, so easily. She had let herself be carried off into their household, had accepted their judgement on what was best for her. Had been star-struck by Lavinia: not just by her beauty, or her courage. There was a quality to her— somehow, she was like any other person, but *more.*

Zachary studied her for a moment. "Lavinia really likes you, you know."

A blush crept along her cheeks. It was embarrassing to talk about Lavinia like this, almost like she was a teenage crush. "I like her too."

"I'm not sure you understand. She *adores* you. She would kill for you, cut down anyone that even dared to stand in your way." He was quiet for a beat, looking for words. "Lust comes easily to vampires. They have no qualms about gender, mostly, and often have an endless string of bedfellows whenever it suits them. They're a lot less inhibited about that, is what I'm trying to say.

"Lavinia is different, even among her Sisters. She holds herself away from those kinds of things. I have no idea why, and it's not really any of my business. I just want you to know that I have seen how she looks at you, and it's the look of someone who would tear the stars from the sky if she thought it would bring you joy. She will worship you if you let her."

He fell silent as Michelle digested his words.

"It's a dangerous thing, to be loved like that," he said quietly. "Just be careful. You have to be sure. She won't be able to live with any less."

Michelle didn't answer, and he didn't seem to expect her to. He disappeared back to the kitchen, leaving her alone with her thoughts. She tried to sort through her feelings about Lavinia. Of course, she thought she was amazing. It wasn't difficult to be smitten with her. Last night had certainly made that last piece fall into place. Everything had felt so *right*, so blissfully perfect that their night together now seemed like a distant dream. For one night, there hadn't been questions about their future, about what would lie beyond the realm of their touch and desire. It had just been about them, in the heat of the moment, finding their release together.

Now, though, sitting in the harsh reality of their lives, it wasn't so easy or clear-cut anymore. If she was honest with herself, completely honest, tearing away the hesitancy and what-ifs and rebuttals that her rational brain offered up, there was an irrefutable truth that had slowly been emerging.

She loved Lavinia. She loved her with an intensity that scared her. The thought of an ending between them, a reversion to their own separate lives, was heartbreaking. Michelle had never been impulsive, always taking the safe route through life. She took a safe path through school, went into nursing as a stable job. She was dependable, level-headed. Lavinia made her feel dizzy, off-centre, but in a delicious and heady way. A life with Lavinia, if that was even a possibility, would be a life of extremes.

There was Lavinia's own steadiness, her fundamental goodness. But then there was also that other side of Lavinia's life, which would always bring danger, violence, and death to their doorstep. Lavinia had dedicated her life to the Sisterhood. Michelle wasn't sure whether it was even possible for them to leave or give up that role. Either way, she could never ask that of Lavinia. The Sisterhood was who she was—and if Michelle wanted to be with her, she would have to deal with the anxiety that came with it. She would have to be at home, wishing for Lavinia's safe return, as she was now. Would she be able to do that if it meant being with Lavinia? She stared out at the London skyline covered with grey clouds. What would it be: a predictable life, or an adventurous one?

Chapter Twenty-Five

Lavinia met her Sisters in the overgrown backyard of the house where the three bodies still lay inside. Luce was there, flanked by Octavia, Messalina and Brigh, the youngest member of the Sisterhood at only one-hundred-and-twenty-two. She was tall, even taller than Luce, and thickly muscular. Her natural red hair was cut short, and the gold of her eyebrow piercing stood out against her pale freckled skin. She had joined the Sisterhood only a decade ago. Still, within that short time, she had proven herself to be a reliable fighter. There had been whispers in society that Brigh had only been offered to the Sisterhood for political gain, a concession to the old families of the British Isles who complained of the Roman lineages dominating vampire society. Whatever the gossips said, whatever the intentions of the people surrounding Brigh had been, Lavinia knew one thing for sure: Brigh was a Sister of Twilight just as much as any of them.

Despite the cloud cover, Lavinia could feel the sun bearing down on them, draining their powers. It would be another six hours until sunset. Night would be both a blessing and a curse, a double-edged blade. They would regain their natural strength, but so would the rogue. They would have to be careful.

"Are they safe?" Luce asked Lavinia as she joined them.

"I took them up to the apartment." She hoped Zachary could help keep Michelle calm. She had to be quite upset after what she'd seen. Lavinia wished she could have stayed with Michelle, her heart aching to be at her side.

"Good." Luce surveyed the surrounding houses, making sure they hadn't drawn any unwanted attention. "Quintia is scouting ahead. Vesta is with the witches right now and will bring them here if they ask to see the bodies. We don't know what they'll want to do beyond that. Pina is holding down the house."

"She must hate that," Octavia said with a smirk. "Missing out on all of the action."

"Needs must. I won't risk her in the field, especially as we don't know what we'll be dealing with here. How's your leg, Vin?"

Lavinia tested the hip joint, putting her full weight on it and exploring the limits of movement. There were some stabs of pain, but no weakness or lack of control. "Good enough," she said.

Luce's dark eyes bored into hers for a moment. "Fine," she said. "It's your call."

"What's our plan?" Lavinia asked.

"I've already spoken to the Magistrate and gotten clearance to use whatever force necessary. The rogue poses an unacceptable threat to our safety and to that of the humans, and should be eliminated. They said to be careful to appease the witches, as this falls into a grey area of our treaty.

"The way it looks now, we will follow the rogue, pin down their location, surround the area, and go in armed. We will have to blend in while we seek." It was one of the realities of modern life that humans were absolutely *everywhere*. Gone were the times when the vampires could easily move about without notice. This was London, and while Londoners were used to some level of eccentric behaviour, wearing full armour in broad daylight would draw too much attention. They would wear running clothing for now, an easy disguise. Later, they would have to regroup and arm themselves before confronting the rogue, wherever he had hidden himself.

Quintia returned and led them down a warren of streets behind the house. The scent of the rogue was easy to follow now that its contours had been imprinted onto their memory. Even the cacophony of smells of the city couldn't easily obscure a scent trail once it had been latched onto by several master trackers.

Octavia ran point, following the scent. Brigh and Quintia explored side paths. Luce, Lavinia, and Messalina brought up the rear, pushing the group onwards. With the six of them, they could easily branch off, testing various strands and doublings of trails, as the rogue had moved erratically through various paths to attempt to confuse any pursuers. Still, together, they relentlessly held the bitter, sour stench of the rogue's sweat central in their mind as they scouted through passageways filled with mould and walked past busy thoroughfares.

After an hour, during which they had traversed over nine miles through the metropolis, Luce received a text from Vesta. "The witches are at the house," she said. She held up the phone for them to read the rest of the message. It simply read: AND THEY ARE NOT HAPPY!!

They continued their hunt, a watery sun appearing overhead during the afternoon. Its rays sapped Lavinia of some of her strength, but there was no resting now. The only way to keep Michelle safe in the long term was to find the killer. As much as she loved having her close, Michelle was not a bird to be caged, kept in Thornblood while demons roamed outdoors. She deserved to be free to go and do whatever she wished. If that might mean she would no longer need Lavinia... then she would have to accept that.

Around three o'clock they lost the trail for half an hour. It reached a dead end along the Thames, the scent disappearing into the murky water near some docks and warehouses. Aware he might be followed, the rogue had entered the river, one of the few ways to break off a trail of scent. The Sisters split along the riverbank, three taking the north bank, three the south. They fanned outwards, determined to find the place where the rogue had left the river again.

Lavinia jogged along the path on the embankment, taking in the air of the city. The movement loosened some of the tight muscles around her hip. It felt good to have the wind in her hair, to burn off some of the tension that had been building up during the day. She wondered how Michelle was doing, whether she was okay. But along those lines lay another worry, an anxiety that went beyond this hunt. It felt like today had set something into motion that could only end in two ways: either they would kill the warlock-rogue, or they would die trying. They were hurtling towards a confrontation, drawing ever closer. There was no doubt in Lavinia's mind that they would find him. There would be no hiding, even in a city of millions. Failure was not an option. The Sisterhood would prevail.

But what lay beyond that? Lavinia's footsteps pounded rhythmically along the pavement, her breaths coming deeply and steadily. Michelle would want to go back to her job, her life. Lavinia would miss her. She would miss her cheerfulness, her smile. She wouldn't be there anymore to bring her tea, to watch her favourite shows with her. Michelle had taught her to relax, to enjoy their time together. Michelle brightened every day, gave it shape and meaning. She had tasted her blood, and more, and it had awoken a hunger within her that could not be stilled.

Suddenly, eternity seemed unbearable without Michelle in it.

A whiff of bitterness lay on the wind. Lavinia stopped, resting her hands on her waist as if winded by her run, in case any curious humans were paying attention. She used the opportunity to close her eyes, drawing her attention to the air passing through her nose.

There. The rogue had come this way. It was subtle, diluted by the stench of the sewage in the river water. Still, even a swim couldn't completely mask the scent. Lavinia pulled her phone from her pocket and quickly shared her location with her Sisters.

The hunt continued.

The phone rang. Michelle jumped, the device buzzing in her lap. *Lavinia.* In her hurry, it almost slid from between her fingers. "Hey," she said breathlessly, once she had succeeded in accepting the call.

Lavinia's familiar voice sounded through the speaker. "Hello, this is Lavinia."

So formal. Michelle smiled, softening. "Are you okay? Have you found him?"

"Not yet, but we're getting close. Octavia thinks the trail is fresh, now. He was here only a couple of hours ago or so." There were voices in the background. The other Sisters, arguing about something.

"That's good," Michelle said. It was good, wasn't it? The Sisters getting closer. Yet at the same time, that also meant they were getting closer to danger. She wished there could be another way, some way that didn't involve blood and violence. Then she remembered the three dead bodies lying in a dilapidated London house. There would be no other way.

"Are you well?" Lavinia asked.

Michelle willed her voice to be steady, to not let the tears that lay unshed behind her eyes escape. "I'm fine," she said, and almost believed it herself.

"And Zachary?"

Michelle glanced through the window onto the balcony. Zachary leaned on the metal balustrade, a cigarette in his right hand. He took a drag, enjoying the view of the city.

"He doesn't seem very bothered by any of it," she answered truthfully. "He's been looking through all of the takeout menus. I think he might be planning some kind of feast for tonight."

Lavinia chuckled on the other end of the line. Michelle wished she could hold onto that sound, keep it close. What if this was the last time she'd ever hear it? She pushed that thought away. If the others could keep it together, so could she.

A voice—Michelle thought it might be Quintia's—said Lavinia's name. "I have to go," Lavinia said. "I'll check in with you when I know more."

In a heartbeat, the connection was broken. Michelle stared at the black emptiness of the screen. It looked like death.

Chapter Twenty-Six

They found him.

Hours more had passed, hours in which they had drawn closer to the killer without rest. It was unnerving how the rogue, driven by paranoia, had created a confusion of a trail across London. It wasn't normal rogue behaviour—but then again, this wasn't a normal rogue.

For a brief interlude, the hunt had taken them down into the sewers, and for a moment Lavinia had feared that they would have to crawl through tunnels and tunnels of stinking filth to reach their target. Luckily, it seemed like this had just been another attempt at shaking off any pursuers, and they had climbed back into the relative freshness of the open air after half an hour.

And now the trail had ended. They were on the outskirts of London, the iconic high rises of the inner city barely visible along the horizon. It was an industrial estate, all warehouses and small factories. Lorries thundered down a road close by, making the ground vibrate.

"Are you sure he's in there?" Quintia asked sceptically.

"Pretty sure," Octavia said.

"That's not what you said five minutes ago."

"Maybe you should stop asking."

Quintia huffed, holding the binoculars in front of her eyes. "I don't see anything." Vampire eyes were powerful, but not omnipotent. The Sisters lay on the rooftop of an empty warehouse, closed for the day, looking over the estate to a building on the far side. It was a good choice from a tactical standpoint. It lay on the intersection of a pair of roads and had doors along three sides of its walls. Not easy to surround. Unless you brought seven of your Sisters.

"There was some movement a little while ago."

"What if it's just some bored human security guard?" Quintia challenged.

"Look closely at the doors."

Quintia repositioned the binoculars. "Shit," she breathed.

Lavinia knew what her Sister would see. Sigils had been painted in black onto the sheet metal of the doors. Some kind of ward. Whoever was hiding inside that building most definitely wasn't an innocent human.

Lavinia crawled back, letting herself drop from the ledge of the roof onto the ground. The leather of her armour creaked. They had all changed into their battle gear, their weapons at the ready. They were only waiting for one thing: for the witches to finish their ritual.

Three of them sat cross-legged in a small circle in the shadow of the building. One of them was the forever child, Balor; she didn't recognise the other two. The scent of magic wafted from them, the warm smell resembling cinnamon or cardamom. Whatever they were doing, it wasn't visible.

Lavinia left the witches to their meditative trance and walked up to Arran, who paced back and forth between some parked trucks.

"Anything?" she asked. His normally unflappable demeanour carried a dark cast. Perhaps there were things that disturbed the witches, too. A vampire who could use magic probably fit the bill.

"Not yet," he said. "They're trying to break through the wards."

"Is that possible?"

He shrugged. "There will be a crack somewhere. And once pressure is applied to the weak point..."

Lavinia suppressed the urge to shudder. Give her a sword and an enemy, and she could rise to the challenge. This battle of the mind, probing invisible magics, was something she wanted nothing to do with. It was a good thing the witches were on their side—kind of.

Time crawled, the shadows lengthening as the sun made its way to the horizon. Still, the three witches did not move. A breeze picked up, blowing through the strands that had escaped Lavinia's braid. Somehow, the wind didn't affect the three witches: their clothes remained perfectly still, not even a hair tossed about. Lavinia went back onto the roof to escape their eerie unnaturalness, preferring to keep watch away from them.

She could see Arran pace back and forth, back and forth from the corner of her eye. Then, he suddenly stood still, snapping his head towards where the rogue was hiding. "They found it," he said, almost conversationally, though no one stood close by.

The vampires crowded around Arran, his three companions still sitting, motionless. It seemed to Lavinia like nothing had changed except for an air of anticipation.

"How long do we have?" Luce asked.

"About five minutes. Once the wards fall, you'll have to move quickly. He will notice them being broken."

"Alright. Vesta, Brigh, you take the east door. Vin, Octavia, the south one. Quinn, you're with me. Messalina, you will take float and make sure there isn't some exit we don't know about. Once we engage, you can approach. Clear?"

They all nodded.

"What about... them?" Brigh asked, inclining her head in the direction of the witches.

"We will do what we can from here," Arran said. "We may move in, should that be necessary." The vampires were about to march off to their positions before he added, "Don't be alarmed. If you see some things." Without any further qualifications to that ominous statement, he stalked off to resume his restless pacing. Lavinia lifted her eyebrows at Luce, who pulled a face that said, *don't ask me.*

With Octavia by her side, Lavinia snuck towards the south-facing door. It was more of a gate, large enough for a small vehicle to drive directly into the warehouse. Their footsteps were lost in the whispers of the wind and the rumble of the nearby road. The breeze came from the northeast, hopefully masking their scent until it was too late. The dark sigils looked jagged, foreboding. Lavinia crouched, checking her weapons: the sword at her side, the daggers strapped to her thighs. Beside her, Octavia pulled her twin short swords.

The wind tugged at her braid. They sat unmoving, awaiting the signal. It was the quiet before the storm, this pocket of time. Lavinia thought of Michelle and was glad she was safe. After tonight, she would be safer still.

Lavinia's heart beat steadily in her chest, a war drum keeping time. *One, two, three, four.* The others would be in their positions now. *Five, six, seven, eight.* The five minutes were almost up. No movement from inside the warehouse, no sound. *Nine, ten, eleven, twelve.* Her muscles clenched, ready to face whatever was coming.

The dark symbols on the gate burst into bright, green flames, flashing briefly. *That'll do it.* Lavinia charged at the gate, Octavia behind her. Picking up speed, she crashed through the gate, the sheets of metal tearing from their hinges. Something whirled towards her, and Lavinia ducked instinctively, hoping that Octavia was doing the same. The end of her braid singed, the stink of burned hair filling the air. *What the hell was that?* Behind her, the remainder of the gate blasted outwards, heat radiating from the glowing metal.

Before Lavinia had a moment to think, another projectile moved at her at incredible speed. She only had just enough time to see it coming from the corner of her eye: a ball of flame, hurtling through the air. She dropped to the ground, rolled over her shoulder, and landed in a crouch. This time, she was prepared when another fireball grew and raced towards her. Its centre was a bright blue, with licks of orange on its surface. It blasted through the hole where the gate used to be.

"It's coming from that sigil," Octavia yelled behind her. Lavinia scanned the floor ahead. Rows of haphazardly stacked wooden pallets and mouldy cardboard boxes littered the floor. *There.* On one of the cardboard boxes, an angular design had been painted. A bloody handprint overlapped the design, the blood still fresh and gleaming. As she watched, another fireball formed in the air above the sigil, appearing as if from nowhere.

Before it could finish its growth, she dashed forward, lifting her sword. The fireball whirled around itself, the orange flames covering its surface, and was released. Training her eyes on her goal, she dodged out of its path, leapt and slashed through the cardboard, her sword cleanly tearing through the sigil. There was an audible *pop* as the spell collapsed.

Lavinia took a second to survey the battlefield. The stench of magic suffused the air, mingled with the scent of the rogue's blood. On the east side of the building, Vesta and Brigh were engaged with their own magical trap as thick, sinuous vines burst through the concrete to tear at them. Brigh was hacking at one of the vines with her battle axe, new tendrils appearing for every one that she destroyed. Vesta was slowly marching forward, pulling vines that had wrapped themselves around her from the ground as she strained to reach the sigil that was undoubtedly close.

The west side of the building was obscured by a hill of stone pebbles. From the noise cascading through the building, Quintia and Luce had been engaged as well. There was no sight of the rogue yet. Her nose couldn't detect his location as his scent suffused every part of this building, nor could she hear his heartbeat through the noises of battle. She ran on, Octavia's footsteps following closely behind. They jumped over a pile of debris and were stopped in their tracks when a shape appeared in front of them. For a moment she thought the demon, the tenebris, had come back, but that was impossible. Though the sun was low on the horizon, Lavinia could sense its presence in the sky, sapping her strength. Demons only walked after sundown.

A closer look revealed that the shape wasn't a demon, at least not any kind that she had ever seen. It looked like a man, but as if seen through a grimy window. There was a blurriness to him, as if he wasn't quite within this world. The man simply floated before them, immobile. His head tilted back, his mouth opening in a wordless scream. Agony crossed his face as if invisible irons tortured him. His mouth closed, and he aimed his absent gaze at Lavinia.

Without any further warning, he lurched forward, feet floating an inch above the concrete floor. Lavinia held her ground, planting her boots firmly on the floor in a defensive stance, sword raised. Still, he came at her, undeterred. As he came within range, she stepped aside, slicing through the figure's waist. The shape muddled, disappeared for a blink of an eye, before reshaping behind her, tendrils of mist folding back together. Before it had had time to fully restitch itself, Octavia lunged, crossing her twin short blades and slashing through his neck, some of the mist wisping away.

The figure floated unmoving, slowly reassembling.

"Shit," Octavia swore.

"We have to find the rogue," Lavinia urged. Unless they

stopped the source of the magic, they might never reach him. He might slip through their fingers, still.

"I'll keep this one busy," Octavia agreed. She hacked again, the figure blinking away and back again. Lavinia turned, coming face-to-face with another one of the strange ghosts, this time a woman, her arm outstretched, a face full of melancholy and regret mouthing at her in complete silence.

"Don't let it touch you!" someone yelled behind Lavinia, and she didn't need to be told twice. She ducked, the sudden movement jostling her hip painfully. She hacked at the woman's legs, dangling above the concrete. Her blade didn't connect, but it arrested her movement.

"What are they?" she shouted back, not taking her eyes off the woman, who was joined by yet another figure. She stabbed this one through the heart, another attack that merely seemed to slow them down rather than do any type of damage.

"Souls," Arran answered, appearing beside Octavia. He carried no visible weapons but clearly needed none. His hands moved in fast, complicated shapes, which produced gusts of wind that tore at the figures, peeling shreds of mist from them. "They're the souls of the victims that the warlock commanded the demons to tear from their flesh."

Lavinia looked at the figures again. That man... Black hair, thinning along the crown. His brown eyes were mournful, pain distorting his features. A white line ran across the side of his neck, which Lavinia had assumed was a scar, but the flesh was still parted. It was the man she had found hidden underneath a pile of garbage in the alley, behind where Lavinia had fought that demon the night she'd saved Michelle. A moment of horror overtook her. This was a *soul*? Their being had somehow been detached from their bodies after a horrifying death, and now the rogue was using them like puppets, forcing them to do his bidding?

There was no time to dwell on the perversity of it. Victim after victim appeared before her, faces of agony and regret compelled by some invisible magic. She rolled out of the grasp of reaching hands, jumping back up to slash at them. One had crept up behind her, and she reacted instinctively. She dodged a hand, jumping onto her right leg, trusting it to bear her weight. The joint wobbled, then held, but the fraction of time it took to regain her balance, a woman Lavinia didn't know—a victim they had never discovered, perhaps—grasped her shoulder, her face full of remorse.

Chapter Twenty-Seven

An agony like she had never felt before burned through her. Every nerve in her body screamed. It was a mindless, searing pain, unmooring Lavinia from reality. It was so intense that her consciousness tried to dissociate from it. Dark spots bloomed in her vision, a blackout beckoning. Without thinking—any rational thought was impossible—Lavinia scrambled backwards, finding herself on the concrete floor. The movement tore her from the woman's grasp, and the sounds and smells around her burst back into her senses. Echoes of pain cascaded through her body still, but she was able to force herself to rise back to her feet and hold off the woman's attempts to touch her again.

"They'll tear out your soul if you let them," Arran warned. Lavinia didn't bother looking at him. Even just moving her eyes hurt. Her soul was staying put, if she had anything to say about it.

"How do we make them stop?" she shouted over the din of battle. Somewhere, a fire was blazing, throwing heat and soot into the air. She hoped that her Sisters were unharmed, whatever horrors they were facing.

"He must be here somewhere, controlling them. He can't be far," Arran grunted. Lavinia chanced a glance towards him. Many of the souls of the victims had surrounded Arran and Octavia.

They stood back-to-back, Octavia dashing forwards and backwards, keeping the crowd at bay. Arran's hands moved, whispered spells tumbling from his lips. In the half-light of the warehouse, she could see the ashen pallor of his skin. Whatever magic he was using, it was taking a toll. Octavia was breathing heavily, beads of sweat running down the side of her face. They were in a stalemate, and Lavinia didn't want to bet on the warlock giving up before Arran or Octavia were depleted of their strength. Who knew the limits of a combined power of vampire and witch, of someone who had collected the power of a dozen souls to do his bidding? If they stayed in a defensive position, they would lose. There was only one way to end this.

Every muscle in her body ached as Lavinia slashed at the souls reaching for her, driving them back momentarily. She didn't wait to see them regain their shape. She turned and ran, trusting that they would react too slowly to grab at her defenceless back. She dashed around the pile of gravel and found herself almost upon Brigh. The young warrior held her battle axe aloft before she brought it down with a splintering crash onto a wooden pallet bearing a large network of interconnected signs and smeared with the telltale bloody handprint of the rogue. Whatever spell the sigils had been driving collapsed. Lavinia didn't stop to find out what it had been. The summoner had to be close. She kept her pace, reorienting herself towards the centre of the building. If none of the Sisters had smoked him out of hiding yet, he had to be somewhere along the north wall.

She launched herself over the top of a pile of leaking sandbags and crashed through a forest. She ignored the trees that sprang up around her, obscuring the cement with their gnarly roots. The smell was all wrong: not the green of sap and the edge of natural decay, but only magic, the scent of magic suffusing everything, lined with the bitter stench of the rogue. Her ears told her that her footsteps were muffled on the forest's earthy floor, but she ignored this, trusting instead on her sense of smell and the reverberations underneath her boots that told her she was still in the London warehouse.

The rogue had employed some kind of magical illusion. Ignoring the intense feeling of wrongness, she barrelled through the forest, not bothering to go around the trees. No branches tore at her arms as she ran forwards blindly. Green flashed before her, and her momentum ground to an acute halt, shifting the earth beneath her feet. The forest had disappeared, and she lay on a pile of broken chairs. Her armour broke her fall, but still she experienced a moment of sharp pain where a nail had pierced the flesh of her palm. She tore it loose, ignoring the sting. The smell of fresh, bitter blood alerted her to another sigil nearby, painted on a piece of cardboard lying on the ground. She pushed herself back up to destroy it with her sword. If her Sisters followed, they wouldn't be blinded by the illusion.

The smell of her blood mingled with the stench of magic thick in the air. A long strip of armour along her left arm had been torn away, the skin underneath scratched. She only briefly took stock of the injury, then dismissed it. It wouldn't kill her. The only one that would die today was the rogue. Shaking off the pain and regaining her breath, she pressed on. She'd ferret the rogue out of whatever hole he'd hidden himself in.

Michelle tried to pass the time by watching some TV, but her mind kept wandering to Lavinia. Twenty minutes had passed since she'd sent her last text, letting Michelle know that they were going to raid the warehouse where they thought the rogue was hiding. It had been a quick, business-like text, and Michelle found herself reading it over and over, wishing for her phone to show a new message, anything to let her know Lavinia was okay.

No message appeared. On the TV, actors cracked jokes on a panel show. Michelle couldn't stomach the laughter of the studio audience and turned the sound off. She glanced back onto the balcony, where Zachary was enjoying his fourth cigarette of the day. Perhaps if she'd picked up smoking, she'd at the very least have something to do with her hands. There wasn't even anything to clean or tidy in this apartment, nothing that could give her the semblance of activity. All she had to do was wait.

Thoughts whirled through her mind, round and round. What if Lavinia got hurt? What if the rogue—this person who had decided to attempt to take Michelle's life for reasons she didn't understand—what if they were too strong? Vampires, witches, and demons were new to Michelle, but it hadn't been difficult to understand the unease that the vampires had shown when they found out that the warlock and the rogue were the same person. Whatever rules there were in the supernatural world, this killer broke them. She trusted completely in Lavinia's skill, her strength, and her speed—but what if there was something about this... abomination that would be too strong even for Lavinia and her Sisters?

There was no way for Michelle to know, and she realised this. Yet there was no stopping her thoughts, her anxious desire to hear something, anything. She was suspended in fear, the not knowing of whether Lavinia was kicking the rogue's ass, or whether she was lying in a puddle of her own blood somewhere. Michelle squeezed her eyes shut, willing that image out of her mind.

She tried to remember Lavinia as she had been this morning, her eyes softened with sleep and satisfaction. Tried to get some comfort out of the memory. But no matter how much she attempted to hold the image in her mind, it kept slipping away from her, fleetingly out of reach.

Michelle stood up, restlessly walking back and forth through the room. The movement helped a little bit. Some of the jitters in her legs stilled—or perhaps they were just less noticeable when she was moving. It had gotten darker in the apartment, the sun disappearing in a bank of clouds. She'd have to turn the lights on, or Zachary would have to sit in a dark room when he was done with his smoke.

Michelle leaned over to turn the switch on the lamp that sat on the side table, when she froze. Her eyes had caught a movement.

"Zachary!" she shouted.

He turned around, cigarette held loosely in his hand, a question in his eyes. Michelle yelled again, gesturing for him to come in, to please get away from the demon that was tearing through reality beside him. Before Zachary could react, one arm cloaked in shadow appeared behind him. It was almost comical, the way he looked at Michelle quizzically, while his death loomed over his shoulder.

This couldn't be happening. It was impossible. Lavinia was with the rogue right now, the Sisters were at his doorstep, and yet somehow he had sent a demon here. In her anxiety and nervousness, Michelle hadn't realised the sun had set. Congealed time moved so strangely. It had snuck up on her, snuck up on both of them. *And the balcony wasn't protected.*

The demon's talons flashed pure darkness, and Zachary screamed. It was a horrible sound, carrying the agony he felt when the talons dug into the flesh of his back. Michelle didn't wait to see what happened next. This time, she would not be a bystander. She wouldn't, couldn't watch as Zachary died, the kind man who had ordered food and made sure she'd eat only an hour ago. She couldn't watch as the demon tore him apart, until he was little more than the dead bodies she'd seen earlier. The Sisters were too far away.

It was just her. And this time, there wouldn't be a gorgeous vampire bursting in at the last moment to save her.

Without thinking, she grabbed the lamp right in front of her and tore its cable from the wall socket. Her hand scrambled on the balcony door handle, Zachary's scream quieting into a low moan. He had collapsed onto his hands and knees. It was only a couple of steps, but in that strange way of nightmares, it seemed like it took minutes for her to reach him. The demon raised its head, the glowing coals that sat in place of its eyes trained on her. Michelle raised the lamp and brought it down onto the creature's head. The lampshade crumpled and burst into flame. Underneath, the light bulb splintered, glass flying.

The demon didn't even flinch. It left Zachary for dead, blood spilling from his shoulder onto the ground. Michelle desperately wanted to check on him, make sure that he was okay. There was no time. The demon came at her, and she warded off his outstretched talons once, twice, wielding the lamp as if it was one of Quintia's training swords. It kept coming, relentless, and her panic rose to a fever pitch. She reached out, trying again to hit the demon. Impatiently, it grasped the metal bar of the lamp stand and tore it away from her, the lamp clattering onto the ground. The railing of the balcony dug into Michelle's back. Somehow, she had gotten turned around. The demon stood between her and the open door to the apartment, the only place where she could be safe.

She was trapped. The demon had no face, consisting only of shifting smoke. Somehow, it seemed to be enjoying itself. It was enjoying Michelle's panic. Savouring the fear that shook her legs. There was no way for her to go.

This was it, Michelle realised with painful clarity. She was going to die. She would never see another sunrise. She would never be able to kiss Lavinia again, tell her how much she wanted to be with her. Tell her she loved her.

The demon lunged and Michelle's world turned black.

Chapter Twenty-Eight

Lavinia had found the rogue. He was crafty, she had to give him that. He had laid trap within trap, spell within spell. Some of them were deadly, others just aimed to delay or confuse. Despite his efforts, the Sisters were closing in, the witches behind them. Lavinia's instinct had been correct: the rogue had hidden himself towards the north wall, as far away from any entry points as could be. The closer she got, the stronger the stench of his blood became, overpowering even the cloying scent of the excess of magic he'd manipulated. As Lavinia slashed through a wall made of a translucent silver web, she saw him flitting behind a pile of upturned desks. Beyond the desks was the wall of the warehouse. There was nowhere for him to run. Even if he somehow blasted through the wall itself—and having seen what he could do, Lavinia didn't doubt for a moment that he was capable of it— Messalina would be on the other side, waiting for him.

It would take only moments for her to get her hands on him.

She renewed her assault on the magical web. Beside her, Brigh let out a wordless battle cry that reverberated in Lavinia's bones. Outside, the sun was setting. A whisper of night brushed up against her, promising power beyond her daytime limits. The muscles in her arms burned, fighting against the strange resilience of the wall of magic. Brigh added the strength of her axe, and two of the witches stood behind them, their eyes closed, an eerie, unnatural light shining from their palms as they did whatever they did to counteract the spell that had summoned the wall.

Sweat poured down Lavinia's forehead, slicked the small of her back underneath her armour. She switched to a two-handed grip, putting all of the strength of her shoulder and back into the thrust. A few strands of the web unravelled. Octavia joined, then Luce. The invisible force that fuelled the Sisterhood rose between them, around them. Together, the witches at their backs, they tore through the wall.

There was no time for celebration. They were like hounds who had caught a scent. Wordlessly, they surrounded the pile of furniture that hid the rogue. A glance was shared between them. Outside, the sun cast its last rays across the city. The stars rose, keening a hunting song.

The Sisters charged. Lavinia vaulted over the desks, her knees and hip protesting as she landed. The moon took over, blanketing her in the power of the night, raising her strength despite her fatigue.

The rogue sat in a circle of blood. By the bitter smell of it, it was his. He bled freely from a cut on the inside of his arm. With one finger, he drew another sigil onto the concrete beside him. At the rush of approaching footsteps he looked up, his bloodshot eyes flashing yellow. He hissed, baring stubby and poorly formed fangs. Then, he smiled, planting his hand onto the floor and whispering a word in a language Lavinia didn't understand.

Reality tore, not just once, but twice, thrice, countless times. The tears birthed shapeless horrors of shadow and fire. Demons.

There was no time to think, no time to breathe. One moment, there had only been one rogue to contend with. Now the Sisters were inundated in demonspawn, tearing, burning, snapping at the Sisters. She had a fleeting thought that she'd hoped the witches had taken cover, as their skins were unprotected. Lavinia spun out of the path of a hellhound, giant fangs snapping shut where she'd stood only a moment before. She stabbed through the heart of a tenebris, its body of shadow curling back into itself with a hiss. The rogue, where had he gone? She scanned the battlefield, ignoring the blood and fire and unholy screeching of the demonspawn. The rogue was at the heart of all of this. He was the one who directed all of them, who controlled them. He had to be stopped—not just now, but forever.

He would never be able to threaten Michelle ever again.

A white-hot rage tore through Lavinia at the thought of Michelle, at how close she had been to death if Lavinia hadn't happened to be at the right place at the right time. Michelle could have been one of these poor souls, trapped in his unnatural grasp. He had to die.

Lavinia kicked a tall, horned demon in its back, the impact causing it to fall onto the blade of Octavia's sword. She slashed at another, tearing its arm from its shoulder, the limb turning to ash before it hit the ground. The stench of sulphur suffocated the air as she fought her way through the throng.

Everywhere demons roared, crawled, slithered, and strode, their burning eyes full of hate. A brief opening formed after Luce pierced a hellhound with her spear. The rogue had turned away from battle, probably to summon yet another abomination. His energy seemed boundless, spells spilling from him one after another. They had to stop him now.

The fire of night in her veins, the thought of Michelle on her mind, Lavinia let go of any further thought beyond the flow of the battle, the feel of the sword, its grip slickened by her chafed and bleeding hands. She paid the minor injury no mind, only used the pain to focus her on her single objective: reaching the rogue. Step by step, she fought through countless demons, pushing or kicking them aside for her Sisters to finish off whatever they could. She knew they were there. She knew they would protect her back. She was the point of the wedge, coming closer and closer to the rogue, bent over another one of his creations, drawing with one bloody finger.

Lavinia broke through. She didn't waste any time, didn't wait for another demon to appear or attack. Within the blink of an eye, she was at the rogue's back. She lifted her sword, but before she could bring it down, the rogue rolled away, hissing and baring his misshapen fangs as he crouched on the ground.

In a way, finally coming face to face with him was a disappointment. Up close, this rogue looked like any other. His skin was waxy and grey. The blood vessels of his eyes had burst, bathing his irises in red. His clothing was torn and soiled, the blood of his victims coating the fabric of a threadbare hoodie. His gaze had that edge of the predator, that animalistic quality common to all rogues. But at the same time, there was a gleam of cunning and self-awareness, an intelligence that had not yet been burned away by bloodlust. Rather than fleeing or mindlessly attacking, the two instinctual options that a rogue would choose between, this one threw some makeshift magic at Lavinia, forcing her to step aside. The rogue used the opportunity this created to draw further lines, completing the intricate design he had shaped onto the floor. His hand was steady, keeping one eye on Lavinia's approach.

Whatever the rogue was doing, it wouldn't be anything good. Lavinia launched a kick at the centre of his body, forcing him off-balance as he tried to avoid most of the momentum of the kick. She followed it up with a swift punch with the pommel of her sword, connecting with a satisfying crack onto the rogue's right shoulder, breaking a bone. The rogue roared with pain and turned his full attention to Lavinia, no longer able to ignore her. He jumped at her, catlike, fingers outstretched like claws.

Lavinia crouched, angled her body, and slammed her shoulder into the rogue's midriff as he sailed through the air. The blow forced the rogue's breath from his lungs and he slumped to the ground, gasping. Lavinia lifted her blade again, but before she could strike, the rogue skittered across the ground on hands and knees in an uncomfortably insectile movement. His fangs bared, he bit into the wound on his arm, refreshing the blood streaming from it. His eyes gleamed red and he smiled a bloody grimace at Lavinia. Then he placed one bloody handprint in the middle of his design.

Nothing happened. No further monster from the depths of hell appeared. No magical wall of flame or shadow. Lavinia didn't wait for anything to show up. She struck, and this time her sword found its target. The blade sank deep into the rogue's bowels, and the vampire screeched. He writhed in agony on the floor for a moment, then subsided, panting through the pain and blood loss. His body had already been weakened by the barrage of magic he had summoned. The blade had severed his spine, piercing vital organs. It was a killing blow.

His bloodshot eyes were filled with a potent combination of agony and hate. "You're too late," he hissed, bubbles of blood forming on his stained lips.

Lavinia's breath caught in her chest. Rogues didn't speak—especially not ones that were so deep into their descent into bloodlust as this one clearly was.

She didn't answer. The rogue laughed, a horrible coughing and wheezing sound, blood spilling from his mouth. "All of the little candles out in the night, their wicks unlit. It was so easy, so incredibly easy to take them for myself. To take the magic that they didn't realise they had." He bared his misshapen teeth again. "You've spoiled my fun, you bitch." Dark blood pooled around the wound in his stomach. Lavinia pulled out the sword, the lethal injury widening. The rogue gritted his teeth, stifling an agonised moan. There was no joy in watching him die. Lavinia merely stood guard, her eyes cold.

"What did you do?" she said.

"I sent one of my friends to visit a little candle I haven't snatched yet. The one you kept away from me. She shines so brightly in the night, surrounded by moths, but none of her little moths are with her now, are they? She has left her little cage and is all alone." He took a shivering breath.

Lavinia's heart stood still in her chest, a spear of icy fear piercing her. *Michelle.* She was unguarded right now, but she was in the apartment. She had to be safe. She knew not to leave, and she wouldn't be reckless. Was the rogue lying?

The hateful mirth on his face wasn't feigned. He had done something, had somehow sent another monster to Michelle.

There was no way she could defend herself against a demon.

Michelle would die, and Lavinia would not be able to save her.

Chapter Twenty-Nine

If there was even the smallest chance that Michelle was still alive, Lavinia had to go to her. Right now. She turned, immediately stopping in her tracks as she found herself facing the forever child. His small, childish body looked incongruous on the battlefield. No dirt or blood marred his tunic and trousers. He glanced around her, seeing the bloody ravage of the rogue's body. He smiled. "I see you have prepared him for us."

"What?" Lavinia said.

"We will take him from here," Balor said, his high childish voice serene. "He has broken our laws. He has taken the powers of others for his own and imprisoned their souls. He will pay."

"Death is justice," Lavinia said, the oft-said phrase tumbling from her lips without thought. She didn't have time for this. Somewhere, Michelle was facing an unfair battle alone. She had to be with her.

The child tilted his head. "Oh no, Lavinia, you don't believe that yourself. There is no justice in death. It would be a release, one that he doesn't deserve. This one here," he nodded towards the rogue, "will enjoy a taste of his own medicine." Without any further words, Balor strolled to the rogue. He bent over the vampire's ruined body, examining him as if he were a particularly interesting bug.

Lavinia didn't wait to see what Balor would do to him. The witches had the rogue now. He'd been incapacitated and secured. That had to be enough.

She sprinted across the battlefield, dodging a couple of straggling demons. Her Sisters were there, sweat dripping from their brows, covered in soot and blood, exhausted and bruised, but still on their feet.

"What's wrong?" Luce called out.

All Lavinia could force out was, "Michelle." It was enough. Luce nodded and continued the dirty work of sending every single demon back to the hell they had crawled from. In the corner of her eye, Lavinia saw Arran and the two other witches surrounding the souls of the victims, guiding them together. Safe, safe, they were all safe. But not Michelle.

Lavinia ran like she had never run before in her life. There were the short dashes in battle, or the leisurely midnight jogs through the hills around Thornblood she so enjoyed. This was nothing like either of those. She sheathed her sword as she skidded out of the building. Her boots thudded against the pavement, her legs pumping. Her lungs burned as they struggled to draw in enough oxygen. A leaden fatigue was spreading through all of her muscles, but she ignored it. The distance between her and her apartment, between her and Michelle, was twelve miles. Such a small distance in daily life. Now the space separating them loomed impossibly large.

The clouds from earlier had drifted aside, the night sky guiding her. The light from the stars and moon bathed her in their power, lending her strength. Though they were difficult to see through the city's light pollution, the stars were ever present, ever watching. They shivered in the sky above as Lavinia ran as fast as her legs could carry her.

She didn't think about being seen by humans. Their petty

concerns weren't important. *Please be alive. Please.*

Stars, don't let me fail. I cannot bear losing her.

Three miles. Two miles. One mile. The familiar streets around the apartment. All was quiet apart from a couple of humans coming home from work. Lavinia paid them no mind. There was the building. There was no time for keys and elevators. She climbed the decorative wrought-iron fence surrounding the building with ease. Somewhere, an alarm started to blare.

No matter. She leapt up against the building, pulling herself up by the balustrade of the first balcony. She climbed, using the building's rough stone exterior as hand guides. Within moments that felt like an eternity, she vaulted over the balustrade of her apartment's balcony.

She was too late.

She took in the scene as if through a series of images, snapshots of horror that flashed before her. Michelle. Michelle on the ground, covered in blood. A demon bent over her, his talons sunk in the flesh of her arm. Zachary, eyes closed, slumped on the far side. His chest rose and fell slightly with his shallow breaths. Oddly, the little lamp from the living room lay between his limp fingers.

It was too late. All of this had been for nothing. Michelle was dead, dead, and nothing made sense anymore.

A rage within her boiled, bathing her vision in red. She roared, a wordless scream tearing from her that could move mountains with their raw grief. Lavinia pulled her daggers from their holsters on her hips and barrelled at the demon, stabbing, tearing, rending whatever she could get within her grasp. The demon tried to resist her but was overpowered by the relentless assault, and when Lavinia planted a dagger directly into one of its infernal eyes, it disappeared.

Lavinia stood panting, her hands covered in the demon's blood. There was nothing left to do. Her knees buckled, and she slumped to the ground, head bent with sorrow.

"Vinia?" a small, shaky voice said, almost masked underneath the ringing of the apartment's alarm system.

Lavinia's head whipped up. She turned to Michelle, saw the small movement of the lips, the rise of her chest. *She's still alive, thank the stars, she's alive, she's alive.* She dragged herself to Michelle, not trusting her legs to carry her.

"You're alive," she whispered over and over. "You're alive." She cradled Michelle's head in her arms, kissing her forehead, her cheeks. The sweet saltiness of Michelle's blood coated her lips.

"Yes," Michelle whispered. "You have to stop saving me."

Lavinia leaned back and gently removed Michelle's hair that had gotten stuck in the blood on her face. "Never." And she kissed her on the lips, the sweetest meeting. It was a small touch, a merest brush: a promise.

"I meant to tell you," Michelle said, wincing as Lavinia shifted her slightly in her arms.

"What's that?"

"I love you," she whispered, a small smile forming.

Lavinia felt as if she could burst with joy. Her body was suffused with pain, the battle taking its toll. But her soul, her soul sang with triumph and bliss until she felt like the stars themselves would shine out with her happiness. "I love you too." Then more words tumbled from her lips, finally flowing free after having been dammed within her. "I think I may have loved you from that very first night, when you told me to keep still so you could take care of the scratch on my stomach." She caressed Michelle's cheek. "I would slay a thousand demons if that was what it took to keep you safe. I would face the most devious rogues or run around London like a woman possessed, all for you. I will do anything."

Michelle smiled and leaned into the touch. She closed her eyes. "Please stay with me." Pain distorted her features for a moment.

"I'm right here," Lavinia said, kissing her forehead. "Right here."

Chapter Thirty

Michelle woke up in her own bed. The familiar weight of her blankets covered her, the scent of her favourite brand of laundry detergent filling her nose. She breathed in deeply. *Home.*

She'd been away from home for a little under a month, but it had felt like years. So much had changed. Michelle nestled deeper into her blankets, revelling in the feeling of not having to get up just yet.

A whole new world had opened up to her, which had brought both unspeakable nightmares as well as wonderful delights. But it wasn't just the supernatural stuff. *She* had changed.

She hadn't realised just how much until she'd returned to her apartment. The sight of her things brought rushing back the thoughts and fears and concerns that had once plagued her every day. Suddenly, those worries seemed so insignificant after having nearly died—twice. It was wonderful to have access to all of her clothes again, and to drink tea from her favourite mug. To look at the familiar view, and to feel like the mistress of her own home instead of a guest. They were small pleasures that she luxuriated in.

But although her belongings were exactly as she left them, she was finding that sliding back into her old life wasn't as easy as she'd expected. It was no longer an easy fit. It had taken six weeks for her to recover sufficiently from the demon's attack to be able to go back to work. The demon's talons had left deep gouges in the muscles of her left arm, and it would take months of physiotherapy to get her full strength back. Still, the litany of bruises had largely faded, and she'd started leaving the house, had worked a couple of shifts at the hospital again, had eased back into the life she'd always known. It was wonderful to be able to go wherever she wanted without needing a guard. Still, she found she struggled to walk home alone at night. She jumped at shadows, fear rising in the pit of her stomach.

On the surface, it was like everything was back to normal.

Well, not *everything*.

Michelle turned, opening her eyes in the soft light of a wintery early afternoon. Lavinia's emerald eyes greeted her, her smile creating tiny wrinkles at the corners of her eyes. God, she loved those eyes. Loved those wrinkles. Loved how they looked at her, ever steady, ever gentle. Waking up together was a decadent pleasure—one Michelle didn't think she would ever tire of.

"Good morning," Lavinia said. Her arm snaked around Michelle's waist underneath the covers and pulled her close. Michelle nestled her head in the crook of Lavinia's shoulder, nuzzling her neck.

"Good morning." She kissed the soft skin she found there.

"Sleep well?"

Michelle hummed her assent and continued the trail of kisses down Lavinia's shoulder. "You?"

"Wonderful," Lavinia said, her voice breaking ever so slightly when Michelle found a particularly tender spot on her neck. Michelle smiled to herself and caught Lavinia's lips in her own. She rolled onto Lavinia, and Lavinia's arms wrapped themselves around her back tightly, drawing her close.

"I've been meaning to ask," Michelle said, tracing the silvery scar bisecting Lavinia's eyebrow. "Where did you get this one?"

Lavinia closed her eyes for a moment, enjoying the sensation of Michelle's touch. "A rogue who'd been hiding in some basement for over a month had a rusty knife. Almost took my eye out."

Michelle traced the scar with tiny kisses, following its path to Lavinia's hairline. "And this one?" she said, pointing out a pink line on the front of Lavinia's bare shoulder.

Lavinia laughed, a delightful sound. "I can thank Quintia for that one. She stabbed me by accident when we were both fighting the same demon a couple of years ago. Didn't realise I was behind it, she said." Michelle made a little sympathetic noise and kissed this scar, too. Lavinia's breath caught as her kisses trailed lower.

"And this one?" she muttered, but Lavinia was no longer capable of answering her questions. For another hour, they lost themselves in the delights of touch and taste, revelling in their closeness.

"What is your schedule like today?" Lavinia asked later, as they sat down for a very, very late breakfast.

"I'm going to pop in and see Mum and Bob. I promised her I'd come and help her pack for their cruise. What about you?"

Lavinia spread some butter on her toast. At first, Michelle had felt self-conscious about having Lavinia over. Lavinia was used to living with luxury: having a housekeeper, living in a fancy apartment or a frigging *mansion*. All Michelle had to offer was a cramped and somewhat damp London one-bedder and pretty average cooking skills. When she'd voiced her insecurity, Lavinia had told her that the only thing that mattered to her was that they spent time together. That she loved toast made by Michelle as much as a whole feast served at Thornblood. That any room or bed would do, if only they could share it. It was all horribly romantic, and Michelle, to her embarrassment, had teared up. Well, it had been an emotional time.

"I have to check in with Octavia in an hour or so. She's keeping watch over a couple of runaway youngsters. Do you have time tonight? There's something I want to show you."

"Sure. What is it?"

The corner of Lavinia's lips quirked upwards. "It's a surprise."

It had been an incredible relief to Michelle that Zachary, too, had survived that night. Both of them got pretty battered, and although the demon hadn't been sent to kill *him*, it hadn't shied away from mauling him. She had no idea how between them they had managed to keep the demon busy enough for Lavinia to be there in time to save them. It turned out that the heavy base of the lamp they'd used to inexpertly clobber the demon with had been made of pure iron. "It leaches their strength," Lavinia had explained. If Michelle had grabbed anything else, they would have both been dead. It was a thought she preferred not to linger on.

The fate of the warlock-rogue was equally disturbing. Lavinia had been somewhat tight-lipped about it while Michelle was still in the hospital that first week. She finally caved and had told her that the witches had taken him.

"So he's not dead?" Michelle had asked.

"Not exactly." Lavinia said that there were rumours that the witches, led by Balor, had torn the rogue's soul from his body. That they had *preserved* it somehow, keeping it imprisoned. For the vampires, it was enough that the rogue had been neutralised. Vampire law made no allowances for punishments of souls, only of bodies. And the rogue would not be coming back, Lavinia was sure of that. Still, it was a disturbing thought, and Michelle was infinitely glad she wasn't a witch herself after all. Unfortunately, this also meant that the Sisterhood wasn't able to find out how a vampire could turn into a witch, or vice versa. The Witch Council had not been willing to share any further information. That was a mystery that remained unsolved, for now.

That evening, when they arrived at Thornblood, the sprawling mansion nestled between the Pennine hills, it seemed like everyone was waiting for her. Five of the Sisters crowded into the entryway to greet them.

"Michelle!" Proserpina exclaimed, bending forwards to hug her. "I'm so glad you're here. It has been so *dull* without you."

"Always glad to hear we bore you, Pina," Vesta said, but there was only laughter in her voice. "Still, we're all happy to see you."

"Thanks," Michelle said, somewhat dazzled by the throng of vampires around her. Luce, with her dark eyes, had smiled, and Brigh had shaken her hand with vigour. Even Quintia, scowling as always, gave her an awkward slap on the shoulder. The vampire somewhat misjudged her strength, and Michelle was glad Lavinia was at her elbow to steady her.

"What's going on?" she said, whispering in Lavinia's ear. She'd never been the centre of attention like this. It was a bit perplexing, to be honest.

"You'll see." Lavinia shooed the other Sisters away and led Michelle up the familiar main staircase. When Michelle had come to Thornblood the first time, she had been overwhelmed by the splendour of the house. Now, familiarity had eased the discomfort, allowing her to enjoy being back here. Lavinia led her into the west wing, towards Lavinia's room. Michelle wasn't sure what she'd been expecting, but it wasn't this.

"You're taking me to your room?"

"Sort of."

What did Lavinia want to show her that had the whole house in a tizzy? It must be something significant, or they wouldn't be making such a big deal out of it. Anticipation mingled with an edge of anxiety as they stopped one door short of Lavinia's bedroom.

"Here we are," Lavinia said, and opened the door.

Michelle stepped inside. It was a spacious room, with windows lining the outer wall. Two doors led away from the room. She looked around, not sure how to respond. It was completely empty, nothing interrupting the expanse of its hardwood floor. "It's... a room."

"It's *your* room. If you want it." Lavinia stepped beside her, wrapping her arm around Michelle's waist. "You're welcome to decorate it however you like. Mrs. Frost can put you in touch with our builders if you wish. There's a bathroom over there." She pointed to one door. "And my bedroom is through the other door. Or, it could be *our* bedroom. If you'd like."

Michelle's thoughts whirled in her mind. "Lavinia, are you asking me to move in with you?"

Lavinia looked at her earnestly. "With me. With all of us." She smiled. "I do have eight housemates. Plus Mrs. Frost, of course."

Vampire housemates. "And they're okay with this?"

"Yes," Lavinia said definitively. "We all voted. It was unanimous. We would love to have you here. *I* would love to have you here." Her voice lowered. "I want you close to me. Always."

"Oh," Michelle said, words struggling to form. She looked around the room again.

"You don't have to decide right now. You can take your time."

"No. I mean, yes." Michelle laughed, nervousness dissipating. "I don't need time to think about it. I would love to live with you." Michelle felt like everything was starting to fall into place. There was just one snag.

"I'll have to think about my job. I really appreciate you guys letting me live with you, but I'm not sure I'd be comfortable... I mean..." It was one thing to be the Sisterhood's guest out of necessity. She didn't want to be a burden, and it was too far to commute. Also, she had nowhere near enough money to afford even the most basic of rents...

Lavinia's eyes sparkled. "I thought you might say that." She paused, as if gathering her thoughts. Michelle looked at her in anticipation. "We seem to have an opening for a doctor. Someone recently alerted us to the fact that it was irresponsible not to have any medical support nearby."

Michelle blushed, then laughed. "But I'm not a doctor. I'm a nurse. For humans, not vampires."

Lavinia shrugged. "We asked Benjamin, and he has agreed to take you on as an apprentice. You impressed him when you took care of Pina." She tucked a stray hair behind Michelle's ear. "Don't feel like you have to. The offer to live here is unconditional. But I think you would be a fantastic doctor."

Michelle took a moment to think it over. Living here, with the Sisters of Twilight. Learning to become a doctor to vampires, under the tutelage of another vampire. It was such a far cry from that boring everyday life she'd known in London. It meant giving up her apartment. It meant giving up her normal human life and stepping into a whole new world.

"Yes," she said. "Yes to everything. To moving here, to being with you, to learning to take care of you all. Lord knows you all need someone with a bit of sense." Lavinia closed her eyes, as if in relief. Michelle realised that Lavinia must have felt nervous too—that she had been braced for a rejection.

"Good. I'm—I'm so glad." And then Lavinia bent down, and they sealed their new life with a kiss.

A Couple of Months Later

The grass outside of Finchley Animal Rescue looked even more forlorn in the deadness of winter. The concrete of the building mirrored the colour of the grey sky. Despite the cheerless environment and typical British winter gloom, Michelle was in excellent spirits. Lavinia walked beside her, her long blonde hair buffeted by the bracing wind. The vampire's usually pale skin had gained the faintest edge of pink in the cold. "Ready?" Lavinia asked, her mouth quirking up at the corners.

"Ready," Michelle agreed.

They walked into the warmth of the rescue's reception. A grey-haired woman sat behind the desk. It was the same person they'd talked to when they were here last time. Nasim—that was her name.

Nasim raised her head at the sound of the door opening. She looked at them for a moment and then smiled. "Paul's girl! And her... housemate!"

Michelle laughed. They'd pretended to be housemates when they'd come here before, trying to find any clues that would bring them closer to the rogue warlock. It felt like a lifetime ago. "Partner, actually." It gave her a little thrill to say those words.

"Of course, partner," Nasim corrected herself with a twinkle in her eyes. "How can I help you ladies today?"

"We wanted to have another look at Dora," Lavinia said.

"I knew it," Nasim said with obvious glee. "The missus has fallen for sweet Dora. I said to my colleague when you left last time, 'those two will be back!' And here you are!" Nasim led them out to the kennel, keeping up a steady stream of chatter. Soon, they reached the part of the kennel they were aiming for. Dora lay on a threadbare towel, her head heavy on her front paws. Her single brown eye looked at the commotion outside the fence with mild interest.

"Let me get the gate for you," Nasim said.

At the opening of the gate, Dora stood up and shook out her thick Shepherd coat. She plodded towards them, sniffing Michelle. Her tail wagged slightly.

Lavinia knelt down. Extended her hand. Dora looked at it with a measure of suspicion. When Michelle had asked Lavinia whether she'd been open to adopting a pet, Lavinia had warned her that not all animals were willing to be around a vampire. Something about a predator recognising another predator. Still, Michelle could not get Dora out of her mind. Somehow, the dog had already wormed its way into her heart, and she'd been keeping an eye on the rescue's website, watching Dora remain unadopted. Now that she had fully moved into Thornblood and had settled into a routine—albeit a very peculiar one in which she slept through most of the day and spent most of her nights with Lavinia—they were ready.

Dora's nose rose in the air, her nostrils flaring. She sniffed Lavinia's fingers. Then sneezed. Her brown eye blinked at them trustingly. She nudged Lavinia's hand with her head.

"She wants you to pet her," Michelle said.

"Oh," Lavinia said in wonder. Her hand stroked Dora's fur. "She's so soft."

"She'll need plenty of brushing," Nasim said matter-offactly. "Plenty of walks, too. She's an older lady but she still has a lot of life in her. Do you have some outdoor space for her to use?" Michelle thought of the huge lawn surrounded by a man-high stone wall at Thornblood. If the wall was good enough to keep vampires out, it was probably sufficient for a dog. Dora would have several acres to explore safely.

"Yes," she said simply.

"And holidays? Have you thought of who will take care of her then?"

"We've got options," Michelle said. "Friends who will look after her." A whole house of vampire friends. A housekeeper, a groundskeeper. There would be many new people in Dora's life. She would have space to run, a warm place to sleep, and as much love as one human and her vampire partner could give a dog.

They watched as Dora closed her eye, leaning her body fully into Lavinia's leg. Lavinia rubbed the dog's flank, fondness shining through every movement. Michelle's heart burst at the sweetness of the image. It was perfect.

"Can we take her home today?" she asked Nasim.

After a number of forms, it was done. The couple walked out of the rescue hand-in-hand, their new canine companion trotting beside them, ready to enjoy the rest of their lives together.

Quintia didn't do feelings...
Did she?

The story of the Sisterhood will continue in *The Gathering Shade*, coming in spring 2026.

To read the first chapter of *The Gathering Shade* for free, join Celia Thorn's newsletter on www.celiathorn.com!

Acknowledgements

The idea for this book has been percolating in my brain for several years, slowly expanding into the book you are reading right now. It has been an absolute pleasure to write about these characters, and I can't wait to tell more stories in the Sisters of Twilight world.

It only takes one person to write a book, but it goes through several hands before it's ready for the public. Ellie gave feedback on the beginning of this novel, giving me the confidence to press on with publication. Blake deserves a huge thank you, as he not only tightened my prose, but also called out many inconsistencies that had snuck into the manuscript. The book also wouldn't be the same without Claudia's stunning artwork on its cover—words can't describe how thrilled I am to see my characters visually represented.

I would also like to thank friends and family for their enthusiastic support during the writing of this book. Having you all to cheer me on has made a world of difference. Finally, my eternal gratitude to Charlie, my first reader, who patiently listened to my midnight thoughts about sword-wielding gay vampires and who has been the sweetest partner any writer could wish for.

About the author

Celia Thorn is an author of paranormal romance novels living among the foothills of the Pennines in the United Kingdom. She has a PhD in English Literature and spends most of her time reading and dreaming up stories. For news about Celia's upcoming books, visit her website (www.celiathorn.com) or subscribe to her newsletter.

www.ingramcontent.com/pod-product-compliance
Lightning Source LLC
Chambersburg PA
CBHW010341170726
48283CB00009B/2912